THE PERFECT MOTHER

Justina bundled Cornelia up in a comforter and moved toward Nurse Cornish's fireside chair. She settled herself into the comfortable chair and asked Mary to bring her a tumbler of the barley water. Cornelia, only half awake, sipped a few drops before snuggling against her aunt and falling into true sleep.

Justina touched the damp curls, gently running her fingers through them. Her hand settled around the small head, and her other arm tightened, holding the child close. She laid her head back, feeling fulfilled and content, and then, exhausted by her labors, she too drifted into sleep.

And that was how Mowbray found them.

His heart leapt at the lovely vision of woman and child. Then it settled on Justina, and the warmth of his newly recognized love filled him to overflowing. . . .

From "Happily Ever After" by Jeanne Savery

BOOK YOUR PLACE ON OUR WEBSITE AND MAKE THE READING CONNECTION!

We've created a customized website just for our very special readers, where you can get the inside scoop on everything that's going on with Zebra, Pinnacle and Kensington books.

When you come online, you'll have the exciting opportunity to:

- View covers of upcoming books
- Read sample chapters
- Learn about our future publishing schedule (listed by publication month *and author*)
- Find out when your favorite authors will be visiting a city near you
- Search for and order backlist books from our online catalog
- Check out author bios and background information
- Send e-mail to your favorite authors
- Meet the Kensington staff online
- Join us in weekly chats with authors, readers and other guests
- Get writing guidelines
- AND MUCH MORE!

Visit our website at
http://www.zebrabooks.com

A KISS FOR MAMA

Jo Ann Ferguson
Valerie King
Jeanne Savery

ZEBRA BOOKS
Kensington Publishing Corp.
http://www.zebrabooks.com

ZEBRA BOOKS are published by

Kensington Publishing Corp.
850 Third Avenue
New York, NY 10022

All Kensington Titles, Imprints, and Distributed Lines are
available at special quantity discounts for bulk purchases for
sales promotions, premiums, fund-raising, educational, or in-
stitutional use.

Special book excerpts or customized printings can also be created to fit specific needs. For details, write or phone the office
of the Kensington special sales manager: Kensington Publishing Corp., 850 Third Avenue, New York, NY 10022, attn: Special Sales Department, Phone: 1-800-221-2647

Zebra and the Z logo Reg. U.S. Pat. & TM Off.

First Printing: April, 2001
10 9 8 7 6 5 4 3 2 1

Printed in the United States of America

CONTENTS

THE DOWAGER'S DILEMMA

Jo Ann Ferguson

One

"The gentleman is here again, my lady."

Camilla Hoxworthy, widow of the late Lord Worthington and mother of the current holder of the baronage's ancient title, turned from the vase of flowers she was trying, without much success, to arrange. Such sedentary pursuits seldom held her attention long, and she had no talent with flowers. She lamented that she had not inherited it from her mother, Lady Flora Keller. Today she could have used that skill to focus her scattered thoughts on something other than her ongoing concerns about her son's simply atrocious behavior.

"Gentleman?" she asked her butler, Palmer. "Which gentleman?"

"The one who called yesterday all in a pelter when you were out enjoying a ride in the Park."

Camilla was tempted to correct the ever-correct Palmer. She had not *enjoyed* her ride in the Park. So much talk about her son Seth and his exploits might appeal to the gabble-grinders of the Polite World, but they were unsavory subjects in his mother's ears. Even her own mother had been so agitated by the latest round of gossip that Lady Flora had requested a quick return to the house on Soho Square.

"Does the gentleman remain in a pelter this afternoon?" Camilla asked.

Palmer shook his head. "I believe he is in a much more

tolerable mood today. However, he is quite insistent on seeing you without delay."

"Then it would be wise not to leave him cooling his heels in the foyer. Show him in, Palmer."

"Yes, my lady."

Camilla reached for the bellpull, then hesitated. A gentleman who was in a grim mood might not be interested in tea and freshly baked cakes and conversation. She sighed. What had Seth done now to cause an uproar?

She loved her son dearly, but he was a trial. This was the third Season that he had participated in as a most eligible bachelor, and he took advantage of every chance to flirt and break young misses' hearts before joining his tie-mates at his club to drink and play cards. She had thought that, by this time, the young misses would have grown the wiser to his *à suivre* flirtations that meant less than the words he spoke. Yet they seemed drawn to him as much for his fast reputation as the sandy blond hair he had inherited from her and the dark brown eyes that were as puppy-dog warm as his father's.

Sitting on the light-blue settee in the middle of her small parlor, her favorite room and her sanctuary in this house on Soho Square, she tried to guess what her son had done now that would so distress a gentleman that the man was calling on her. She shuddered as her imagination supplied too many answers.

Palmer appeared in the open double doors. In his most formal tone, he said, "Lady Worthington, Lord Overbrook wishes to speak with you."

Lord Overbrook! She had not expected *him* to call. Egad, she had assumed Seth would limit his pranks to companions of his own age, not set his sights on irritating an experienced man like Lord Overbrook. Who among the *ton* had not heard of Jeremy Garrison, the earl who once had been as shameless in his search for entertainment as her son? His reputation for loving the flats as much as he loved the ladies who so clearly adored him had made him the source of much scan-mag when Camilla first came to London out of the schoolroom.

Camilla clenched her hands in her lap. Although she must apologize for whatever misdeed Seth had perpetuated at Lord Overbrook's expense, there was some sense of justice in the earl suffering much as he had made others suffer during his reckless youth.

Her thoughts froze when a tall, dark-haired man appeared in the doorway. Instantly she was transported back to a night during the Season before she had met the man she would marry. It had been a rout at the home of some lord whose name she could not recall now. She had been emerging from her carriage when a horse nearly rode her down. Another rider had sped up and lifted her out of the way just before she was trampled. When he had set her back on her feet out of danger's way, the light from the carriage lamps allowed her to see his glistening black hair and compelling green-gray eyes.

The same black hair and compelling green-gray eyes that faced her now. The black hair was tinted silver at his temples, and there were lines etched in his bronzed skin, deepened now by his scowl. She waited for him to speak, for she had never forgotten the rich warmth of his voice when he had asked her that long-ago night if she would be all right. When he had received her answer that she would be fine, he had chased after his thoughtless companion.

"Thank you for receiving me without an invitation, my lady," Lord Overbrook said as he entered the room. He bowed over her hand, giving her a chance to compose herself before he met her eyes.

It *was* the same man. Apparently, even then Lord Overbrook had possessed a sense of decency that others had suggested he did not.

She could find no fault with him today, for his navy coat and the cream waistcoat embroidered with green and blue were as impeccable and stylish as the white cravat that matched his breeches. The hat he handed to Palmer had nary a hint of dust, so she guessed he had come here in a closed carriage. That would explain as well the perfect gleam of the buckles on his shoes.

"I apologize that you needed to call a second time," she replied, hoping he did not note how he had put her to the stare.

"To the contrary, my lady." He regarded her coolly. Did he find some fault with her? She was wearing her favorite yellow gown, and her hair was neatly in place. Unlike her son, she had always prided herself on her exemplary reputation, the very thing that had persuaded Ernest Hoxworthy to fall in love with her.

"I would say that *you* have nothing to apologize for," Lord Overbrook continued, drawing her attention from her uneasy thoughts back to him.

Camilla wanted to groan. His words warned her that he believed someone else in this house did have something to atone for. Surely a man who had been as unthinking in his youth as Seth was now would comprehend the need for forgiveness for misplaced exuberance.

Coming to her feet, she said, "My family takes full responsibility for the actions of any one member, even if those actions might be deemed beyond the canons of the Polite World. However, I do ask that you consider the age of the offender and that sometimes it is possible to misread the intentions of another."

"I had heard that you were plainspoken, my lady, and had hoped that you would be so with me, which is why I sought you out first before another uncomfortable confrontation might lead to problems on the square. Yet, instead of being forthright, you are using the polite, say-nothing words of a politician."

Camilla flinched. He was right, and she knew it. Had this disquieting scenario of her apologizing for Seth been played out so often in this house that her words had become banal?

Was her apology generic, repeated too frequently, so that she knew the words by heart even though they did not come from her heart? Mayhap she had come to depend too much on the fine manners that she had learned from her mother and once believed she had passed along to her son.

"Forgive me, Lord Overbrook."

"Again, allow me to say *you* have done nothing for which to be forgiven." He ran his fingers through his raven hair, but a thick lock fell back toward his eyes.

"I will attempt to be more candid about what you clearly deem as an intolerable situation."

His eyes hardened as fury tightened his lips. "It is beyond intolerable, my lady."

"I understand." How many times had she said *that* in the past three years? "I would like to promise that you would not be so inconvenienced again, but—"

"Inconvenienced?" His voice rose; then he took a deep breath. In more temperate tones, he added, "Forgive me, Lady Worthington. It is not my habit to speak so to the gentler sex. If I were not so agitated, I would be watching my manners more closely."

"You are clearly distressed." She sat on the settee again and motioned toward the chair across from her. "Will you please sit? I can ring for something to make our discussion more convivial, if you wish."

He smiled and sat facing her. She could not keep from noting how his every motion had a sense of grace that reminded her of clouds floating overhead on a perfect summer day. Yet she was not soothed into complacency, for his green-gray eyes still snapped with strong emotions.

"You are very kind when I burst in here uninvited, Lady Worthington. It was not neighborly of me."

"Neighborly?"

His brows lowered, but in puzzlement rather than in anger. "I had assumed that you knew that I recently purchased the house next door to this one."

"No, I did not." She wondered why her mother had said nothing of that. Lady Flora was endlessly fond of sharing every word that was spoken in the Park or during some gathering of her bosom-bows, but on this subject, Mother had been silent. Squaring her shoulders, she said, "Now you do have a reason to let me apologize. I should have called upon you and your family before this."

He chuckled. "You can be excused for not noticing that the house is to be occupied once more, because the wagon carrying our furniture is broken down somewhere between here and Overbrook Manor."

"You must allow me to offer you some furniture from here, so that you are comfortable until your own things arrive."

"That is generous of you, my lady."

"It is what neighbors do for one another." She reached for the bellpull. Tugging on it, she said, "And neighbors also welcome one another with conviviality." When Palmer came to the door, she said, "Please bring tea for Lord Overbrook and me."

The butler nodded.

"I had hoped for something a bit more convivial than tea," Lord Overbrook drawled, the corners of his lips tilting up in a smile.

"I believe Seth did not finish all the brandy," she said, standing. As he set himself on his feet, she asked, "Would you prefer that?"

"It would make the situation more convivial."

Camilla smiled. She could not help herself. No wonder Lord Overbrook had garnered such a reputation for himself. His charm had not diminished, for he possessed a sense of humor that remained even in the wake of whatever trouble Seth's high spirits had created.

Going to the table next to where she had been arranging the flowers, she picked up the crystal decanter. She was pleased to discover there was more brandy within it than she had guessed. Seth and his tie-mates enjoyed playing cards in the larger parlor across the hall, but he had begun recently to put his best brandy here for safekeeping. She had hoped that was a sign of maturity on her son's part. Apparently she had been too optimistic.

She brought the brandy back to where Lord Overbrook waited. A maid came in with a tray at the same time, revealing that Palmer had anticipated—as always—her request. Thanking the maid, Camilla sat and handed Lord Overbrook a goblet. Palmer had also anticipated the earl's request for something more than tea.

She poured a cup for herself. When she looked at her guest, she saw that he had made himself quite at home. He was relaxed against the back of his chair, one leg propped on the opposite knee. Again she did not allow herself to be lulled into thinking he was completely at ease. His eyes remained filled with angry sparks.

"I trust the brandy is to your liking," she said, unsure how to restart the conversation now that it had lagged.

"It is excellent."

"Seth does have a good palate for brandy, I must own."

"Seth? I thought your husband's name was Ernest."

"My late husband." She lowered her cup to her lap.

His eyes narrowed as he said hastily, "It appears it is my turn to ask for your forgiveness, Lady Worthington. I have been away from London for a long time, and I fear that particular *on-dits* did not reach me during my journeys."

"Ernest died nearly fifteen years ago." She forced a smile. "Seth is my son."

"Your son?" He leaned toward her, his smile more genuine than hers. "Are you telling me that that young man I have seen coming and going at your door is your son? If I may be so forward, you do not look of an age to have a son of that age."

Flustered by his unexpected compliment when she had been certain he was about to lay out what concerns had brought him here, Camilla said, "Of course Seth is my son. I do not understand, my lord. I assumed you knew he was my son."

"No, I did not."

"Then why are you here?"

"Excuse me?"

Setting her cup on the tray, she resisted the temptation to ask him straightaway if he found the whole of this—and her—an amusing way to waste an afternoon. She could not have been mistaken about his vexation when he arrived, but now he professed to have no knowledge that she was the mother of the oft-outrageous Lord Worthington.

"Why are you here if not to complain about whatever Seth has done to disturb you?" she asked.

"Seth? My lady, I fear you have mistaken the reason for my call. I am not here to speak with you about the conduct of your son, but of your mother."

Two

"My mother?" Camilla's voice came out in a most uncomely squeak. "My lord, if this is your idea of a jest, it is a very unsavory one."

" 'Tis no jest. I would not joke about something like this."

Camilla stared at Lord Overbrook. His smile had disappeared, and he had his arms folded over the front of his chest, giving him the appearance of a furious parent about to dress down a naughty sprig. He did not give the impression of being in the least amused by this turn of the conversation.

Neither was she. "My lord, I do not appreciate my mother being spoken of in such a tone."

"Then you should make more efforts to restrain her indecorous behavior."

Camilla was about to reply, then noticed the adamant set of his mouth. Lord Overbrook had been gracious . . . until now. He was, without question, distressed, and he seemed to believe most fervently what he had said.

Yet how was that possible? She searched her mind in an effort to determine what her mother could have done to send their neighbor up to the boughs when he had only just moved to the square. Lady Flora Keller was well respected among the Polite World for her kindness and her hospitality. It was true that she enjoyed gossip, but that was no reason for Lord Overbrook to be so vexed.

Picking up her teacup, Camilla steadied it when she saw

how her hands trembled with her own dismay. "Mayhap, if you speak in more specific terms, I would better understand what has brought you here in such a pelter," she said, realizing her voice was as unsteady as her fingers.

"Specific? Is the word *outrageous* specific enough for you?"

"Outrageous?" She pressed one hand over her heart, then drew her fingers away when she saw how his eyes followed her motion. Mayhap he had not outgrown his youthful lack of manners, after all. A gentleman should not stare at a lady's bodice simply because she put her hand there to calm her frantic heartbeat.

Her heart thudded harder when the hint of a twinkle in his eyes stole the hard edge from his frown. He was quite aware that he was discomforting her, and he was not ashamed to have done so. That such a rogue would dare to come here and speak disparagingly of her mother, without explaining why, tested even her sense of hospitality.

Quietly, because she would not grant him the satisfaction of goading her into raising her voice, Camilla said, "I am waiting for an explanation of why you have spoken so."

"The explanation is simple." He finished the brandy in his glass and set it on the tray between them. He did not lean back as his gaze caught hers. "Lady Worthington, this afternoon, not more than an hour past, your mother burst into my house and spirited my uncle out the door on some mad excuse."

"My mother is very friendly. She would see it as her duty to welcome our new neighbors."

"I would say that her actions go beyond friendliness. She abducted my uncle."

"Abducted? That is a strong word, my lord. May I ask you to choose another?"

Jeremy Garrison, Lord Overbrook, took a calming breath. He could not mistake the fury in Lady Worthington's blue eyes, nor did he fault her. His manners had not been beyond reproach. Quite the opposite, for he had called uninvited and had accused her mother of a most heinous crime. None of this was going as he had hoped.

Mayhap it was nothing more than the fact that he found it difficult to concentrate on the problem of her mother persuading his uncle to go off with her when Jeremy would rather have spent his call gazing into Lady Worthington's eyes as he admired her heart-shaped face that was accented so perfectly by her golden curls. Her simple gown did not attempt to draw his attention away from her cheeks where her color was, he guessed, uncommonly high. She had been the pattern-card of decorum while he had acted like a lout.

"You are right. 'Twas a strong word," he replied.

"But one you do not retract, I see." She came to her feet, necessitating him to do the same. He noted how the top of her head was even with his chin, a most pleasant height. "I appreciate your call to share with me your dismay, my lord. However—"

Before she could give him his *congé,* he grasped her hands. She was so startled that she halted her dismissal in mid-word. He should retort while he had the opportunity, but he was as amazed as she was at his precipitous action. Even more, he was astonished at how pleasurable it was to hold her slim hands.

"My lady, I would like to remain until your mother and my uncle return."

"Of course." Her fingers became as rigid as her voice. "You are welcome to wait here."

"Alone?"

Her eyes grew wide again. "My lord, you should consider your own behavior before you chide someone else for theirs. While you are in my house, you are my guest."

Jeremy had to admire her impeccable manners. Years ago, when he had been the age of her son, he would have found such *bon ton* irritating and hypocritical. He had learned that being pretty-spoken was no crime and that gentility had granted him access to those who had once disdained his roguish ways.

That lesson had stood him in good stead . . . until today and Lady Flora's audacious determination that his uncle should go with her to take the air. Her ragged manners did not give him the excuse to be so impolite.

Putting his hands on the back of the chair, he said, "I wish I could say that I would be so gracious if our situations were reversed."

This time when her eyes widened, he could not keep from admiring their sapphire warmth. "The circumstances do not change my duties as your hostess."

"True." This was going nowhere. He had vented his spleen, but had achieved nothing more than vexing this woman whom he needed to be his ally in keeping her mother from doing something absurd. "May we sit?"

"Yes." The answer was reluctant.

Sitting as she did, Jeremy cleared his throat. "Lady Worthington, I did not explain myself well."

"It seemed you made yourself very clear."

"My concern is twofold. One for my uncle and one for my daughter."

Camilla lifted her cup and balanced it in her hands. She did not want her fingers clenching in her lap, for that would have revealed too blatantly how furious she was at Lord Overbrook's accusations. "My mother would never do anything to create a stir for either of them."

"I hope you are correct. However, a father becomes vitally aware of the need for an exemplary reputation when he has just fired off his daughter into the Season."

"Marianne Garrison is your daughter?" Camilla set her cup back on the table because it clattered against its saucer with her trembling fingers. "She is a charming young woman. I had the pleasure of meeting her at a rout a few weeks ago. You should be proud of her, my lord."

"I am. It was at her insistence that I decided to buy a townhouse so we might better enjoy the Season."

"And now you fear my mother's attempts at friendliness will be misconstrued to create a cloud over your daughter." Smiling, Camilla was able to relax for the first time since Lord Overbrook had arrived. "I can assure you, my lord, that my mother is held in the highest regard by the *ton.*"

"The regard of the *ton* is as changeable as spring weather."

That, she had to agree with. She had seen a person be the darling of the Polite World one week and be turned away from doors the next because of a *faux pas*. Before she could answer, she heard a flurry of footsteps on the stairs.

Jeremy came to his feet when another woman paused in the doorway. Lady Flora Keller was still a handsome woman, and a woman, he had already seen, who refused to be ignored. She was not as tall as her daughter, but it was easy to overlook her diminutive stature because no one could miss her determined presence.

Handing her bright crimson cloak to the butler, Lady Flora eyed him up and down. "You wasted no time in coming here, I see, Lord Overbrook. Have you filled Camilla's head with all of your tales of woe?"

"I came to express my dismay only." He bent his head toward her, then took Lady Worthington's left hand and raised it toward his lips. He paused as he noticed that she wore a simple band that must have been her wedding ring. Her husband might have died many years ago, but, in spite of the light colors she wore, she must still be in mourning for Ernest Hoxworthy. That startled him, but not as much as his own reaction of disappointment at the thought. Relinquishing her hand unkissed, although the caress of her soft skin within his hand was delightful, he said, "I bid both you ladies a good afternoon."

As he turned on his heel and left, Camilla sank to the settee. She released the shuddering breath that was thick in her throat.

Her mother chuckled. Picking up a clean cup, she filled it with tea and laughed again. "Oh, Camilla, do not look so woebegone. 'Tis your good fortune that Lord Overbrook has taken his leave."

"Of course it is. Why would you think I would feel differently?"

"Your expression." Lady Flora sat where the earl had been sitting and selected a cake from the tray. "You look very put upon."

"I am unaccustomed to having my family accused of unspeakable crimes."

"Nonsense. Seth gets himself into such predicaments on a regular basis. You simply are familiar with his."

"Mother, whatever gave you the idea of acting so out of hand? Lord Overbrook fairly accused you of kidnapping his uncle. That is unlike you. Your behavior is usually the standard to which the rest of us aspire."

Taking a bite of the cake with its yellow frosting, Lady Keller smiled. "Cook put just the perfect amount of lemon in this one. I shall have to let her know."

"Mother!"

Lady Flora patted Camilla's hand. "Do not fret, my dear. Lord Overbrook has been beastly about his uncle. Never lets the man do a thing without his say-so. I thought it would be fitting to welcome Mr. Winston to Soho Square by taking him for a carriage ride about the area, despite his nephew's objection."

"But persuading him to go without Lord Overbrook's say-so is—"

"Mr. Winston is a man of enough years to know his own mind."

"That is true, but you must understand Lord Overbrook's concern for his daughter when she is in the midst of her first Season."

Lady Flora sat straighter. "His daughter? Did he bring her to call?"

"Of course not. You would have seen her here in the parlor if he had."

"Mayhap. The man keeps such a close eye on his family that one would think he never had done a misdeed in his life." She laughed before taking another bite of cake. "It may be, rather, that he knows all the trouble his daughter could seek out, and he is doubly determined to give her any chance to avoid scandal."

Camilla folded her hands in her lap as her mother had taught. "And it would behoove us, as his neighbors, to comply with his wishes in this matter."

"Do you truly think so?" Her mother rose and patted Camilla's clasped hands. "Ask yourself, Camilla, and answer truthfully. Do you think so?"

"It was what you always taught me. One should judge one's own actions by how others will perceive them."

"Oh, dear! I suppose I did say that once."

"More than once, Mother."

Lady Flora waved aside the words as unimportant. "It is said there is a first time for everything, and it appears that I have proven the rule by being wrong about that." With another wave, she went out the door.

Camilla did not move. She was not sure if she could when she was so shocked. Then she frowned. Her mother was up to something. Camilla recognized that twinkle in her eyes because she had seen it far too often in her son's eyes. Yes, Mother was up to something.

The only question was . . . what?

Three

Camilla's mood upon waking was no better than her mood when she had sought her bed the night before. Sleep had been difficult to find, and she wished she could think of something other than Lord Overbrook. He was overbearing in his assumption that he could scold her for her mother's actions, which, in retrospect, seemed harmless. Mother had been kind enough to take a new neighbor to call upon a mutual friend.

As she dressed in her room with its blue wallpaper, she guessed her ill-temper must be obvious, because her abigail, Marie, did not chatter as she usually did. Or mayhap it was as simple as the whole house knowing of the conversation in the parlor yesterday afternoon. Palmer was an excellent butler, but he had a habit of listening at half-closed doors.

"Mayhap," Camilla murmured to herself as she came down the stairs, "that is why he is so competent. He always knows what we need because he has heard us speaking of it."

"Is something amiss, my lady?" asked Palmer, coming up the stairs toward her.

Although she was tempted to give him a list, she forced a smile. "Good morning, Palmer. I believe a cup of hot chocolate will put me in a far more jovial mood this morning."

She saw his doubts and shared them. This disquiet was not something that could be eased with hot chocolate or a good breakfast. Mayhap a ride in the Park later would help.

Fresh air always gave one a fresh outlook. How many times had she heard her mother say that?

Camilla's uncertainty wavered even further when she came into the cheerful breakfast parlor, where her mother was almost hidden by the morning paper. "Good morning, Mother."

"Do try the apple muffins. They are delicious." Lady Flora did not lower the newspaper.

There was something so comforting about her mother's usual fascination with the gossip columns that Camilla had to smile. Everything was as it should be this morning. Nothing important had changed.

She went to the cherry sideboard and poured herself a cup of the creamy hot chocolate. She went to her chair, not surprised that her mother continued to be mesmerized by the newspaper. At least, Mother did not read the articles aloud as Seth did. Holding the cup close to her face, Camilla let the steam waft over her as it eased the dry fatigue in her eyes.

A whistle came along the hallway. In amazement, she turned to see her son approaching. She smiled as she did each time she saw him. The gangly boy had grown into a strong man who had developed an excellent eye for clothes as well as for the ladies. His golden hair could have used a trim, for it hung over the top of his high collar, but his cravat was perfectly tied, even for breakfast with his mother and grandmother.

"Good morning, Mama," he said, kissing her cheek even as he chuckled.

"What is so amusing?" Camilla asked.

"At the moment, I would say Grandmama."

Lady Flora lowered her newspaper just far enough to peer over it. "And why, pray tell, am I setting you to such a jolly expression?"

"Because I am glad someone else is setting Mama to a boil other than me," Seth said while he bent to give his grandmother a kiss on the cheek as he did on the occasional mornings that he came into the breakfast parlor. If he stayed out for the whole night, which he did so often, he offered his grandmother a buss as soon as he returned home. "Now I have a proper back-answer for Mama the next time she asks me where I learned my wild ways."

His grandmother slapped his arm playfully. "Do not use my indiscretions as an excuse for your own."

"Why not? I think your misdeeds are the perfect justification for mine." He smiled as he turned to face Camilla. "Don't you believe so, Mama?"

"You are cheerful this morning." She knew she should chide him for his words that were aimed at teasing her, but she smiled. "I trust that means you had good fortune last night."

When he chuckled again, she could hear the echo of his father's voice in his. So often lately she had noted that Seth had taken on more and more of his father's ways, save for Ernest's common sense, which seemed to have been denied their son. That might have been the only thing Seth lacked, for he was handsome and witty and seemed genuinely to care about everyone he met. If he only would consider his own reputation as carefully. . . .

"I had the chance to enjoy a conversation with a divine creature who took my thoughts away from anything or anyone else." Seth went to the sideboard to pour himself a cup of coffee. As he sat, he nodded his thanks to the maid who placed a plate of eggs in front of him. Reaching for a muffin, he glanced at Camilla. "You are showing a rare lack of interest in my comment, Mama."

Lady Flora laughed as she turned the page of the newspaper. "That is because, my boy, she is a-twitter with thoughts of her caller yesterday."

"A caller?" Seth leaned toward her. "Mama, you did not say anything about a caller."

"Your grandmother speaks of Lord Overbrook, and from your comments, it is apparent you know quite well why our neighbor was calling."

"Or his excuse for giving you a look-in at any rate." Seth earned a pat on the arm from his grandmother as they both laughed.

Camilla bit back her retort when Lady Flora arched a graying brow toward her. Did her mother believe as well that Lord Overbrook had used the slimmest of excuses to call here? Both her mother and her son would have thought otherwise if they had seen the honest exasperation in Lord Overbrook's eyes.

"Your grandmother gave him all the excuse he needed to call." Camilla smiled. "Now tell me about this divine creature you met."

An hour later, his breakfast barely touched, Seth finally ran out of superlatives to describe "the angel with a devilish smile," as he called his special young woman again and again. Only when he went off to the kitchen to wheedle some freshly cooked eggs and muffins from Cook did Camilla realize that not once had Seth mentioned the miss's name. She smiled when she recalled how he spoke of introducing this paragon to his mother at the first possible opportunity. Looking back as she walked out of the breakfast parlor, she saw her son sitting down with a fresh plate and her mother lowering her paper. Her mother would obtain all the pertinent information in no time, and she would be eager to share it with Camilla in even less time.

This was, Camilla decided, just the thing to persuade her mother to focus on her grandson instead of leading her neighbor into mischief. And, if Camilla knew what was wise, it would be just the thing to keep herself from thinking of Lord Overbrook's intriguing gaze.

Camilla doubted that she could be wise when, as she came down to the walkway, she could not keep from glancing at the steps leading to the house next door. She recognized the young woman standing on them because she had seen Marianne Garrison in the distance at several gatherings during the Season before they had been so briefly introduced. Lady Marianne had inherited her father's height, but on her, it was willowy and feminine. Her black hair had a reddish tint that added fire to it in the sunshine that was chasing the day's early mist back toward the Thames.

"Good day," Camilla said as Marianne Garrison came down the steps of her house.

Opening her parasol that was trimmed with lace that matched the decoration on the sleeves of her blue-sprigged gown, Lady Marianne smiled. "Oh, Lady Worthington, I was so hoping I would have the chance to see you today."

"I suspect we shall see much of each other now that you are living next door."

"I hope so." She hesitated, then said, "I would very much like to invite you for tea on Thursday. Papa has had me instructed in all the skills that are necessary to hold an at-home, but I own to being puzzled about some things. I had hoped that you could help me by explaining them."

"It would be my pleasure."

Lady Marianne beamed. "Thank you. You are as kind-hearted as I have heard."

"And I am sure that she will be kind-hearted with your errors," came a deeper voice from behind Camilla.

Turning, Camilla was not surprised to see Lord Overbrook. She wondered if he had guessed how his well-tailored coat and breeches would invite her to stare. He was a deucedly handsome man, and the pale-green coat only accented the hidden strength that had not lessened from the night he had saved her life.

"Papa!" Lady Marianne greeted him with an embrace.

"I thought you would be gone by now for your ride in Green Park." His green-gray eyes turned toward Camilla.

She held out her hand. "Good day, my lord."

"It is a *very* good day." He took her hand and he bowed over it.

When he raised it slightly, she held her breath. Was he about to kiss her fingers in front of his daughter? There would be nothing untoward about such a commonplace action, save for Camilla's own unsettled thoughts. She hoped he could not guess them as he released her fingers with proper speed.

Lady Marianne laughed. "That is much better, Papa. You owe Lady Worthington an apology if Great-uncle Ronald was not exaggerating. You should have chosen another reason for your first call on her."

Lord Overbrook frowned. "Marianne—"

An open carriage paused in front of the house, and Lady Marianne said, "I must go, Papa. I do not want to delay my bosom-bows from our outing." She rushed to join the two young women sitting in the carriage. As it drove away, she waved.

Camilla took a step toward where her own carriage was stopping in front of the house. She could not leave without saying something to Lord Overbrook . . . but what?

She was saved from having to decide when the earl said, "My daughter and my uncle are partially correct. Storming into your house to express my fury was a poor excuse to call upon you."

"Yes, it was," she said when he paused. If she did not know better, she would accuse him of eavesdropping on her conversation with Mother and Seth earlier.

"I should first have come to introduce myself more properly."

"Which I assume you would have done if Mother had not . . . If she had not—"

Lord Overbrook laughed, his eyes crinkling with good humor. "I believe it would be simpler to avoid the words I chose in anger yesterday."

"It would."

"Even before Marianne chided me in your hearing, my uncle chastised me for what he called an overreaction to a kindness by your mother. Mayhap he is right, but I feared, knowing your son as I do, that . . ." He shook his head. "Forgive me again, my lady. That was not an appropriate remark."

Camilla took another step toward her carriage, then paused once more as he matched it. "You have said nothing that I have not already heard. I doubt if you *can* say anything I have not already heard."

"I am sure you have been regaled with many stories. Some of them might actually have been true."

"I believe most of them are true."

"Then you have not been privy to all the tales I have heard." He smiled and held up his hands. "Do not regard me with a furious expression. I am not about to repeat them, for I learned in my own youth that one would be wise to heed little of what one learns only as gossip."

"An excellent idea."

"And I have another." He gestured toward the carriage. "Must you be somewhere by a certain hour?"

"I was going to Hatchard's to obtain a gift for my mother for her birthday. She is very fond of some of the French poets."

"This may sound overly bold, but I would like the chance to apologize."

"It *is* overly bold."

He smiled. "You speak your mind."

"Yes." That was not completely the truth. If she spoke her mind, he would be shocked. She could not keep herself from thinking about how, when he had taken her hand, the heat of his touch had oozed delightfully through her glove. It brought other thoughts to her mind, thoughts that reminded her of how long it had been since the last time a man had touched more than her fingers.

Camilla almost gasped aloud. Letting her mind wander in that direction was as absurd as the idea of her mother abducting his uncle. She forced a smile while she said, "I must ask you to excuse me, my lord. I have several other errands to run today as well."

She whirled to step into her closed carriage. When a hand appeared in front of her, she faltered. To refuse to let Lord Overbrook hand her into the carriage would be an appalling insult.

Raising her fingers to put on his, she made a huge mistake. She looked up into his eyes. The storm of emotions erupting through them awed her, for she could not discern what all of them were. To stand here on the walkway in front of her house and stare up into his eyes might give her a chance to comprehend what those emotions might be, but she could also discover more than she should.

His fingers closed over hers as he handed her into the carriage. She started to draw her fingers away, but he put one foot on the step and leaned forward to brush his lips against her hand. This gasp she could not silence, for the emotions that had burned in his eyes exploded through her. Her hand was reaching out toward his cheek before she could halt it.

She jerked her hand back. When he chuckled, she was sure her cheeks had captured all the fire that had raced along her. Only now the fire was icy cold with embarrassment.

"This is a very, very, *very* good day," he murmured as he closed the door of the carriage.

In spite of knowing that she should look forward while the carriage rolled along the street beyond the square, she glanced back when she heard a shout. She saw a lad rushing up to Lord Overbrook, but only from the corner of her eye. Once again, her gaze was held by his. The connection between them was broken just before the carriage turned the corner and the lad tugged on the earl's coat. She saw Lord Overbrook bend to speak to the lad.

Camilla sagged back against the seat. During the ride to Picadilly, while shopping for the perfect book for her mother, and as she drove back, she could not ignore the echo of the pleasure that bubbled within her.

When the carriage turned back onto Soho Square, she tried to smother those ripples of sensation. She had her face under control when she emerged from the carriage. Without a glance in either direction, she hurried up the steps and into her house. She was sorry that Palmer held the door open for her, because she would have liked to close it and lean back against it to make sure that she was safe within her home.

"At your earliest convenience, Lord Worthington would like to speak with you, my lady," Palmer said, his face stolid.

"In my parlor?"

"Yes, my lady. He is waiting there with Lady Flora."

Camilla murmured her thanks and went up the stairs. Just now, the familiar problems that usually vexed her seemed somehow comfortable.

Seth came to his feet as she entered the room. "I am glad you have returned," he said.

"Is something amiss?"

"Do not assume the worst." He chuckled. "Even though I have given you cause in the past to assume the worst on many occasions." Seating her in her favorite chair, he continued to smile as he said, "What I am about to say will persuade you that the tales of me being a heartless rake are baseless."

"I never believed that, Seth," Camilla said.

Her mother stretched to pat her hand. "The boy never said you did, child. Give him a chance to explain."

"Explain?" Camilla looked back at Seth. "Explain what?"

"How I have done something that will make you very proud of me, Mama."

"And what is that?"

"I have invited Lord Overbrook and his family to move in here with us."

Four

Camilla came to her feet. "What did you say, Seth?"

"Oh, my dear child, do not pretend to be hard of hearing like your Aunt Mae," replied Lady Flora. "You heard quite well what the boy said." She smiled. "He invited Mr. Winston and his nephew and great-niece to stay here with us until new furniture arrives to replace what was destroyed."

"Destroyed?" Camilla frowned. "I was certain Lord Overbrook said something about the wagon carrying it here suffering some sort of mishap."

"A fire would be defined as a mishap."

"A fire?" asked Seth, his eyes wide. "You did not mention that, Grandmama."

Lady Flora flung her hands into the air. "Whoosh! All gone in a blaze that reached, if one listens to what the servants here have heard from the servants next door, nearly to the top of the trees along the road. I do hope there was nothing irreplaceable on that wagon. I understand Lord Overbrook was more exasperated than dismayed at the news."

Camilla nodded as she recalled how the lad had tried to obtain the earl's attention. She had not been able to see Lord Overbrook's face, but his shoulders had stiffened. "This is horrible."

Seth came to his feet and moved to sit next to Lady Flora. "Mama, I heeded your request that you have repeated so often to make decisions that would make you proud." He flashed a smile at his grandmother. "And, Mama, having them stay here is certain to give countenance to Grandmama's continued conversations with Mr. Winston. You must own that it is an inspired idea."

"Yes, it is." Her voice was rather faint as she tried to guess what about this caused her stomach to knot. Leaving her neighbors without the most basic of furniture was unthinkable. To own the truth, Seth's offer of hospitality made more sense than when Camilla had suggested moving some of the furniture in this house next door. There was plenty of room, for Lord Overbrook's family would not need to bring many servants with them. The household here would tend to their needs, and their own servants were just a wall away. It made perfect sense.

Then why aren't you agreeing posthaste?

The answer to that was simple. Lord Overbrook had disconcerted her with his brazen touch today far more than she had guessed any man could do again. She had scurried into her house like a child seeking a haven under a blanket. Now she would have no sanctuary, even within the walls of her own house.

Camilla set herself on her feet and wiped her oddly perspiring hands against each other. "If we are to have guests for the next fortnight, for I cannot doubt that the earl will have replacement furniture delivered from his country home by that time, I must speak with Palmer and Cook and Mrs. Cashman without delay."

"I already spoke with them." Seth's nose wrinkled. "Mrs. Cashman did wish to wait for your approval."

With a smile, Camilla nodded. Mrs. Cashman still saw Seth as a naughty lad, and the housekeeper would not have acquiesced to such a request easily. "I shall discuss it with her without delay."

"Excellent," replied her mother. "It would be best to have all the details settled before Lord Overbrook and his family arrive for dinner this evening."

Camilla repeated the word *dinner* silently. When she saw both her mother and her son grinning, she wondered what capers they were thinking of now. She suspected that she soon would find out.

Jeremy looked into the mirror, which was hung too low for him, and grimaced. When he bent like this, he could not be certain that his cravat was set properly. He usually would not have given his appearance this much thought, because he had left his dandy-set opinions behind him when he asked Nancy to be his wife. His valet should be back soon with the few things that Jeremy had brought to town with him.

"You look in prime twig, Papa," called Marianne from the doorway of his borrowed bedchamber.

Turning, he smiled. Marianne resembled her late mother more every day, from her sparkling eyes to her teasing tone. Tonight, she was dressed perfectly in a white gown that would be the envy of any miss during the Season. She rushed to him and took his hands.

"Papa, I am so happy that Lady Worthington and her family were generous enough to ask us to stay here. I hated the thought of remaining a moment longer at that inn." She shivered. "The men in the stableyard gave every woman who passed such knowing looks."

"You would not have had to suffer that if I had been less zealous in my determination to have the house decorated in something other than the funereal colors of the past owners."

"But soon we shall be settled in with our own things, and it will be wondrous." She looked around the room. "You might wish to ask Lady Worthington's opinions about our new house, Papa. She has an elegantly light touch with color and decoration."

Jeremy simply smiled as he steered his daughter out of the room. If Marianne suspected that her father had an ulterior reason for accepting Lord Worthington's generous invitation, she would guess it was because Jeremy wished to keep a watchful eye on his uncle and Lady Flora. That was all for the best, because Jeremy wanted no one to know how pleased he was to have this opportunity to continue the truncated conversation he had enjoyed with Lady Worthington this afternoon. As his hostess once more, she would not have the excuse of errands to scurry away before the thoughts in her eyes urged her to give in to folly.

Marianne slipped her hand through his arm as they went into the small parlor where Lady Worthington had received him only yesterday. He sensed his daughter's tension through her fingertips. Putting his hand over hers, he gave her a bolstering smile.

"Ah, here you are!" called Lady Flora from where she was sitting in a chair next to Uncle Ronald, who was looking through a book. Mayhap the very book that Lady Worthington had gone to buy this afternoon. "Do come in and join us. Camilla went to check on our dinner, but she will be returning soon."

"Lady Flora, we appreciate your allowing us to intrude on your family."

She smiled and gestured toward the young man standing by the hearth. "You should thank Seth. The suggestion was his."

Jeremy stepped forward and shook Seth Hoxworthy's hand. "Then my words of appreciation should be to you, Worthington."

"It will be our pleasure to play your hosts for as long as you need to stay."

Hoping no one noticed his flinch at the words that echoed Lady Worthington's, Jeremy listened to the conversation around him. He took a glass of wine from Worthington and sipped it as he watched Lady Flora and his uncle point out their favorite poems in the book. Beside them, Worthington and Marianne were laughing while their elders debated if Byron had written a certain line in a certain poem.

Some sense he could not name drew his attention from them and to the door. Had his ears caught the hushed sound of Lady Worthington's footfalls? Impossible, for the laughter within the room masked them as she entered.

He admired her openly, for she was looking elsewhere. Her golden hair was pinned up so that the curls curved along her ears. A pair of strands draped down her neck, drawing his gaze down that slender column toward the fullness beneath her sedate bodice. His fingers tightened on his glass of wine as he imagined those curves against him when he drew her into his arms.

Her eyes, like twin pieces of lapis lazuli, widened when her gaze turned toward him. Had she taken note of his stare? He could not be the first to look at her so, for she had been married.

Without releasing her gaze, he picked up the glass of wine her son had poured for her and walked toward the door. Her lips parted while her head tilted back. So easily, he could have swept his arm around her, pulled her up against him, and sampled those inviting lips.

He held out the glass, and she took it. Her fingers brushed his in a most commonplace motion, but he would have sworn an oath that he had been struck by a spark snapping off the hearth. When she looked hastily away, he knew he had not alone experienced that incredible pulse.

"Ah, Camilla," called Lady Flora, "come and join us." Her warm laugh filled the room. "I see you are already greeting one of our guests, but I do not believe you have met Mr. Winston."

Camilla went to where Mr. Winston and Seth were coming to their feet. As she welcomed the older man, who was completely bald, she tried to mend her ragged composure. Lord Overbrook had not said a single word, yet he had overmastered her completely.

"Forgive me for being so tardy in greeting you," she said.

"I suspect," Mr. Winston replied as he bowed over her hand, "that we have turned your house topsy-turvy."

"That, unfortunately, is quite true." She warmed to Mr. Winston's kind smile straightaway. "I am afraid dinner will be a bit late."

"Late?" Seth smiled. "If dinner will be late, then we have the perfect excuse to go to the Park and check for ourselves, Grandmama."

"Check what?" Camilla asked.

Her mother's smile was as broad as her son's. "Mr. Winston and I were discussing a poem in this new book about the shadows in Hyde Park. That is an excellent idea, Seth, my boy. Go and have the carriage brought about. We shall see for ourselves without delay."

"I shall tell Cook to delay the meal even longer." Camilla went to the door. When she realized Lord Worthington was still there, she said, "Excuse me, please."

"Do you always cede your will so readily to those within your walls?" he asked.

"No." Her lips quirked in a reluctant smile as she heard the excited voices behind her.

"Ah, now I see the truth. You expect your guests to be on their best behavior, so you deem it only proper that you must as well."

"*All* of us must."

"I hope the rest of our families agree with you." He looked past her to where Lady Flora was talking excitedly with his uncle. Seth and Marianne were listening with broad smiles.

Camilla's own smile wavered. "I hope so, too."

Camilla hoped that her mother and her son shared her determination to make these circumstances gracious and stay within the canons of propriety. When she heard the light-hearted conversation in the open carriage, she tried to relax.

It was not simple when Lord Overbrook sat across from her. With every bump along the street, his knee brushed hers. She tried to draw her legs back, but there was no room.

"Stop here," Lady Flora ordered the driver.

The coachman wore a baffled expression that Camilla guessed mirrored the one on her face. When she saw the same puzzlement in Lord Overbrook's smile, she wanted to ask her mother why she was acting so oddly. Lady Flora had not behaved like herself since Lord Overbrook had taken possession of the house next door. Could her mother have found a *tendre* for Mr. Winston with such speed?

As soon as the carriage rolled to a stop, her mother opened the door beside her. She let the footman help her out, then waited for Mr. Winston to step down. Putting her hand on his arm, she motioned toward a stand of trees near the Serpentine.

"My lady?"

Camilla looked down to see Lord Overbrook's hand held up to her. When had he gotten out of the carriage? In amazement, she saw Lady Marianne alighting with Seth's assistance.

She held her breath and steeled herself as she put her fingers on Lord Overbrook's hand. It was useless. At the moment her skin brushed his, that same warmth spread through her. It was as if she were stepping from the shade into the bright sunshine. She pulled away as soon as her toes touched the road. She started to follow her mother.

Hearing a laugh, she stiffened again. She glanced from the carriage to the twosome walking toward the trees. She could not leave Seth and Lady Marianne here alone. Nor should she let her mother, in spite of her years, walk off with a man who was little more than a stranger. How had she allowed herself to get caught up in this ridiculous quandary?

"I could remain here while you go with Mother and Mr. Winston, Lord Overbrook," she murmured.

"That is one suggestion." His smile became rigid, and she knew he understood what she had not said. He gestured toward Seth and Marianne. "However, I would rather send Lord Worthington to be *their* watchdog."

"You do not trust my son here with your daughter when they are being watched by two servants? What sort of man do you think my son to be?"

"I consider him simply a man. There is a reason why chaperons were invented, my lady, and it was not because a man wished a young woman to share only conversation with her." His expression became wry. "It is with obvious knowledge that I can say this."

Camilla could not argue with such common sense, especially when she shared the earl's concerns. She knew Seth would treat the young lady with respect, but the reputation he had gained from his being in suds with his tie-mates too often could damage Lady Marianne's standing in the Polite World.

Calling to Seth, she asked him to join his grandmother and Mr. Winston. She was pleased when he agreed without any questions. Seeing him look at Lord Overbrook before walking to where the others were lingering by a bush that would be a profusion of bright flowers at midday, she wondered if Seth was determined not to be shown up by their guest's polished manners.

"This is all moving too quickly," Camilla said as she walked with Lord Overbrook along the path parallel to her mother and Mr. Winston.

"Your mother appears to know her mind and follows what it tells her."

"That I can agree with wholeheartedly, my lord."

He paused and faced her. "Would it ruffle your sensibilities if you were to address me as Jeremy and I used your given name?"

"As you are living beneath my roof, I would think such informality would be a good thing."

He smiled, his green eyes brightening with silver twinkles. "You make our arrangement sound as if it borders on sordid."

"I did not!"

"Do not fly up to the boughs at my simple comment." He laughed.

"I fear I am uneasy about all of this. My mother *does* know her mind, and it has kept her out of trouble instead of courting it."

"I doubt if courting *trouble* is what she has in mind." He looked past her. "My uncle is as giddy as a schoolboy suffering from his first case of calf love."

Camilla could agree with that. It was clear that Mr. Winston was enrapt with every word her mother spoke, everything that she did. They must have settled their debate quickly, because they returned to the carriage, laughing, with Seth trailing them like an obedient pet. She was not certain of the outcome of their discussion, but suspected her mother had been wrong. Mother was talking about anything but poetry.

"Allow me to help you, Camilla," Jeremy said as he opened the door to the carriage.

She froze as he spoke her name for the first time. The undeniable warmth of his voice caressing it sent a shiver of an emotion along her that she had thought forgotten. As she sat on the comfortable leather seat of the carriage, she chided herself. She was no longer a young miss who could be overmastered by the attentions of a gentleman with enticing eyes and a teasing smile.

As Mr. Winston handed her mother in, Camilla made certain that her face would not betray her agitated thoughts. She needed to have no worry that anyone else would notice her silence. Seth and Marianne were laughing together over their elders' determination to trace down the truth of the poem as the carriage came to a stop. They continued talking while they went up the steps to the door Palmer had open. Lady Flora and Mr. Winston followed, sounding equally young and carefree.

"Thank you," Camilla said as Jeremy assisted her out.

When she started to walk toward the steps, he put his hand on her arm, but said nothing until the others had gone inside. Palmer kept the door ajar, leaving the street in the deepening twilight awash in the glow from the lamps within the house.

"There is something I would like to say to you without other ears heeding it," Jeremy said softly.

"In my parlor—"

He smiled. "You have a remarkably efficient staff, Camilla. That tells me how closely your servants listen to everything spoken within your walls."

"Palmer has trained them to meet *his* expectations."

"And well." He chuckled as he drew her hand within his arm. "A walk around the square will offer me ample time to say what I wish and leave the curious without a clue about what we say."

Camilla laughed. Palmer would be vexed beyond words to discover that Jeremy had read him so accurately. "We are back sooner than I had guessed we would be, so we have a few minutes before our dinner is ready."

"Excellent." Walking toward the far side of the square, he was quiet for a few minutes.

The sound of the birds warbling their good nights was louder than the distant noise from the streets beyond the square. Lights gleamed in the windows of the houses they passed.

"Is this far enough?" she asked when they were on the opposite side of the square from her house.

Jeremy's smile caught the last of the day's light. "You must think me beyond mad, Camilla."

"As one whose family seems to have been infected with a bit of insanity in the past week, I do not think I am the one to judge."

"Spoken as prettily as I would have expected from you." His smile disappeared. "And spoken as distancing as I would have expected."

"Distancing?" She faced him. "What do you mean?"

"You know exactly how to keep a conversation from at all intimating your true feelings."

"I had no idea that you intended this walk to lead to anything intimate." She knew it was the wrong thing to say as soon as she let her own thoughts betray her into speaking carelessly.

His fingers curled over hers on his arm. Lifting them, he drew off her glove and pressed his lips to the back of her hand. Sweet fire blazed outward from his touch, and a quiver shot through her. His other hand curved along her cheek, and she closed her eyes to savor the sensation of his rough skin against her. She had forgotten how the caress of a man's rugged palm could be so dazzling.

She looked up into his shadowed eyes. Did they burn with the passion that he was reawakening within her with no more than this touch? Or did they twinkle with merriment at her reaction?

She had her answer, for his whisper was low and husky as he said, "I owe you an apology for my accusations yesterday."

"You had every right to be angry, because you did not know either Mother or me." She tried to keep her own voice even while her heart thumped with delight at the undeniable desire in his tone.

"I appreciate the turn of fortune, however appalling I first deemed it to be, that has brought my family as guests to your house."

"It is our pleasure."

His arm slipped around her waist as he drew her closer. "I would like to hear you say that again after . . ."

She watched his mouth descend toward hers. She was sure time had slowed to a crawl, because she had never guessed it would take so long to move that short distance. Her hands were rising toward his shoulders in anticipation of his lips against hers when she heard her name shouted.

"Mother," she whispered as it was called again.

When Jeremy laughed, she stared at him in amazement. She had not thought he would be amused at the interruption.

"She makes it sound as if you are a naughty child who is late for dinner, Camilla." He offered his arm. "We should hurry back before she has the whole square out searching for you."

"Yes, we should."

"But?"

"No but," she answered, although her heart urged her to toss caution aside and throw herself back into his arms. Hurrying around the square to where Palmer held the door, a reproving frown on his face, she did not want to own that she had not guessed that she would compound the problem of her mother's mistake of being so unthinking as to nearly kiss Jeremy Garrison in plain view of everyone on the square. She must not be so witless again.

Five

Jeremy knocked on Camilla's sitting-room door, but did not wait for her reply before he walked into the comfortable room where the chairs were set for quiet reading or conversation. When her abigail rushed forward to halt him from entering, he waved her aside. He did not have time for protocol now. After spending the day arranging for more furniture to be purchased or delivered from his country estate to the house next door, he had expected to spend a quiet evening with the newspaper and a glass of port.

Instead . . .

His exasperation eased when he saw Camilla come to her feet. Her golden hair was loose on the shoulders of her wrapper, which was the pale pink of the sky just before dawn. The color matched the tint of her cheeks, but they grew rosier as his gaze swept along the lace decorating her wrapper and then back to her face.

"I did not expect to be receiving anyone *here*," she said coolly as she motioned for her flustered abigail to wait in the other room.

"I can see that," he replied while her maid rushed to obey, leaving the door open in her wake. "Forgive the intrusion, but I think you will agree with me that our circumstances necessitate this."

"Our circumstances? Simply because you have been staying here for the past two days while you wait for your house to be habitable is no excuse for impropriety."

Jeremy bit back the words that would not be proper to speak in her hearing before saying, " 'Tis not those circumstances I am speaking of. It seems that, once again, your mother is leading my uncle astray."

"Where did they go?" She glanced toward the window overlooking the square.

"I thought you might know."

She shook her head. "I have no idea."

"Your mother has not spoken of any entertainments she has been invited to or some theater production she wished to attend?" He paused as he paced back toward the door. "My uncle is uncommonly fond of the theater."

"My mother is not. She finds it silly and the crowds bothersome when they talk during the performance."

"One would suspect that, as she invited him, they would go where she would like to go. If I had not met you, I would have to ask if all the women of your family are so outrageous." His lips quirked. "Mayhap, having met you, I *should* ask that."

"Do not ask such absurd questions."

"I do not consider it absurd. I consider it a legitimate query. If your mind works in a similar direction to hers, it might enable us to find them before they discover that they have gotten themselves into a difficult situation."

"My mother has been married and widowed twice. I believe she is past the point of needing a *duenna* to accompany her wherever she goes."

"Good."

"Good?" Camilla repeated. Had she misheard him? She was frequently astonished by his reactions.

"If you believe that, there is no reason why you should feel ill at ease in accompanying me on our search for them."

"But, my lord—"

"I thought you were going to call me Jeremy now. As I

doubt our search will be a short one, we may as well enjoy the camaraderie of friends sharing a single pursuit."

She shook her head. "I shall not allow you to bamblusterate me into going with you in this unseemly manner."

"What is unseemly about saving your mother from the gossipmongers?"

"You have a rare skill for being able to twist any argument to defend your own opinion," she retorted, trying not to smile. She knew she had been less than successful when he chuckled.

"It was one that I honed from an early age, when I needed it to avoid the anger of my tutors and then my teachers." He caught her hands in his. "Get dressed, Camilla, so we can find our elders and remind them of their obligations."

"I will be quick."

He did not release her hands. Again his gaze swept over her, and again she was suffused with the luscious warmth. "If my tie-mates of years past had heard what I just said, they would have lambasted me as a fool. To be alone with such a lovely woman and not to take advantage of it . . ." He smiled. "You have every right to slap my face for the thoughts going through my mind."

"I cannot slap your face when you are holding my hands," she said softly.

"An added benefit of this opportunity to caress your fingers."

Again she smiled, despite her misgivings with him and her dismay at her mother's pranks. "You have not lost an ounce of the charm that created so much poker-talk about you, Jeremy."

"I did not realize you had followed my so-called legendary exploits so closely."

"How could one not hear of Jeremy Garrison and his friends, who were so outrageous that one of them, mayhap even Jeremy Garrison himself, had jumped up onto the stage at a Covent Garden theater and kissed the heroine of the play before the actor playing the hero could?"

"Yes, there was that story, which was true." He laughed. "Adams had swallowed a hare that night, and I doubt if he could have known if he kissed the actress or the actor."

"Or what of the time when Jeremy Garrison and his tie-mates held a party at Vauxhall Gardens, where everyone who attended was required to dress like a fish?"

"That story is untrue." His eyes glittered amusement. "Too bad, because that sounds like a delightful idea. I would have rather fancied myself as a shark in those days."

"And now?"

The rattle of a carriage on the street halted his answer. He went to the window. His sigh reached her as he turned to face her, and she knew he had hoped to see Lady Flora and Mr. Winston returning home. "And now, Camilla, you must get ready to accompany me on this search."

Camilla blinked back sudden tears when Jeremy rushed out of the room. His concern for his uncle was exemplary, but was that the only reason the searing tears filled her eyes? She had been hoping—as she had on the square—that he would take the opportunity to kiss her. Not just on the fingers, but on the mouth, a deep, lingering kiss that would allow her to sample the flavors waiting there.

With a curse that had gotten her a fearsome reprimand as a child, she whirled and went to her dressing room. She called for her abigail. Keeping her mind on keeping her mother out of trouble would be the wisest thing she could do. She knew that . . . and it was time she remembered it.

"Not here," said Jeremy as he climbed back into the closed carriage. Sitting, he slapped the side of the carriage. "I had been so sure that Uncle Ronald would want to attend her grace's assembly tonight. Mayhap we would have better luck if we were to find your son. I thought we might try Lord Pryor's rout."

Camilla started to demur, then nodded. "Seth and his grandmother seem lately to share a delight in seeking out mutual escapades that leave me shaking my head."

"Do not judge your son so harshly." He put his arm along the back of the seat.

"I do not."

He shifted so that he faced her. With his arm still behind her on the cushion, his fingers brushed her shoulder through the thin fabric of her paisley shawl. "But you do, Camilla. Your voice changes when you speak of him. It is almost as if you are fearful that he will do something that will ruin him in the eyes of the Polite World forever."

"I do."

"Why?"

She edged away from his arm and folded hers in front of her. "I would be a widgeon to repeat the tales spoken in gossip about my own son."

"So you believe them?"

"Yes."

"All of them?"

"I don't know. I mean . . ."

His fingers curled down along her shoulder, keeping her from edging farther away. "You should not believe all the *on-dits* repeated about anyone." He smiled coolly. "Even me."

"I have heard no gossip about you, Jeremy."

"Recently."

Camilla knew she was blushing because her face was as heated as if she had stood in the garden without a bonnet. "That is what I meant. I am talking about now, not the past. We all made mistakes when we were young."

"That is exactly true." His other hand tipped up her chin. "In making mistakes we learn."

"Yes."

"If we made no mistakes, we would remain foolish children."

"Yes." She could not say anything else as she was captured by his powerful eyes.

"So why do you deny your son the chance to learn from his mistakes?"

She pulled herself away before he could use his facile words to twist her into agreeing with him. Sharply, she retorted, "Why do you deny your uncle the same?"

He laughed.

Camilla stared at him, unsure what to say because she had anticipated a fierce response instead of laughter. Would she ever be able to guess what his reaction would be to her comments?

"Is that what you believe, Camilla?" he asked through his chuckles. "That I am trying to protect my aged uncle from making anew the errors of his youth?"

"Aren't you?"

"No. If my uncle wished to have an *affaire de coeur* with your mother, I would be most eager to offer my blessing on the whole of it. After all, as you said yourself, they are old enough to be quite aware of the pitfalls of any such relationship."

"Then why are you so eager to find them?"

He was abruptly serious. "My father died from a heart illness. My uncle suffers from palpitations unless he takes the powders prescribed by his doctor and remains quiet. Any exciting event could be his last."

"And you fear my mother will create just that?"

"Yes." He grimaced. "And if you think your family is the focus of the gabble-grinders now, imagine how much worse it would be if your mother finds she has a corpse as an escort."

Camilla recoiled. "Do not even say such a thing."

"I must, because it is the truth."

"Why didn't you say anything before this? I would have understood."

"I know you would have, but I did not want to remind you of how you lost your husband."

Once more, hot tears flooded her eyes. Slowly she unfolded her arms and put her hand on his. "That was very kind of you, Jeremy, but that loss is something that will be a part of me forever."

"I did not realize that you loved him still."

"Of course I do." She squeezed his hand gently. "Do you love your wife less because she died? It is not shameful to continue to love those who are gone, you know."

"I never meant to suggest it was." He laced his fingers through hers. Lifting her left hand, he tapped the ring on her finger. "I have seen that you keep his memory close to you."

"It is tradition in the Hoxworthy family for a mother to wear her wedding ring until the heir weds. Then it is given to the woman who will become the next Lady Worthington."

"A lovely tradition."

"But one I fear that will not come to pass for many years at the rate Seth is enjoying his bachelor's fare."

"Mayhap that will change. Marianne revealed to me that she believes your son has found a young woman who may persuade him to set aside his frivolous ways."

"Really?"

"Really." He laughed and looked out the carriage as it slowed on the east side of Grosvenor Square. "Ah, here we are at Lord Pryor's house. If fortune smiles on us, we shall find all the missing members of our respective families here."

Camilla hoped he was correct. When she entered the crowded ballroom on Jeremy's arm, she pretended not to see the stares as the guests bent to whisper. Let the gossipmongers speculate about her and Jeremy. That would keep their attention from Mother and Mr. Winston.

"You look as if you could use this." Jeremy pressed a glass of champagne into her hand.

Taking a sip, she asked, "Do you see them anywhere?"

"Not your mother and my uncle, but I do see our children and another young woman by one of the doors to the garden balcony."

Camilla smiled as she went with Jeremy to where Seth was speaking with Marianne and a miss she had never met. Was this the young woman who had created Seth's smiles lately? She wished she could ask outright.

"Mother," Seth said as they neared, "allow me to introduce Miss Sandra Wright."

Camilla smiled. It was easy to see why Seth's attentions had been captured by this lovely young woman. Miss Wright was a petite brunette with an obvious flair for fashion because her pristine white gown was *à la modality*. She had, Camilla noted, her fingers on Seth's arm, clearly considering him hers. No doubt Miss Wright was familiar with the number of women who had flirted with Seth since the Season began, and she wished to warn away any competition.

"Good evening, Miss Wright," Camilla said. "Do you know Lord Overbrook?"

"Yes, he and my father were schoolmates." Miss Wright flashed him a scintillating smile. "And Marianne is my dear bosom-bow."

When Camilla watched Jeremy bow over the young woman's proffered hand, she was surprised that he turned his head slightly and winked. What was he thinking about now?

She understood when he began to talk with Miss Wright about her father, asking how Mr. Wright fared and what was keeping him busy now that he had sold his factories in the Midlands. Jeremy's clandestine motion must have been seen by Seth as well. Seth stepped away from the young women and offered his arm to Camilla.

"You are showing pretty manners to give Jeremy a chance to catch up on the tidings of an old acquaintance," Camilla said as he led her toward a table where glasses of wine waited.

He took one. "You taught me well, Mama, although I suspect there are times when you doubt that."

"There *are* times."

He chuckled. "And there are times when you despair about Grandmama's determination to enjoy this Season as if it were her first."

"If we do not find where she has gone, this may be the last Season for Jeremy's uncle."

"*Jeremy?* That sounds a bit too cozy, Mama, when you are sharing your house with him. You must take care that the ears of the Polite World do not heed you and misunderstand your intentions."

"My intention is to find your grandmother, so will you heed what I am saying instead of jesting?" She lowered her voice to a near whisper when she saw curious glances cast in their direction.

"I am listening closely." He put his hand on her shoulder. "It is pleasing to hear you speak a gentleman's name with such lightness in your voice. I know how you promised Father that you would remain true to him, but you were too young and too distraught when he died to make such a pledge."

"Who told you that?"

"Grandmama, of course. She would tell me only if I promised never to tell you until you got over your mourning. It seems that you have."

Camilla stared up at her son. Mother! Mother wanted everyone to be happy all the time, so she must have invented this tale so that Seth would not feel guilty that Camilla was remaining at home with him instead of making calls because she was worried about him missing his father. Instead Mother had devised a story about a deathbed promise. To tell Seth the truth now might do Mother irreparable damage in his eyes. Camilla could not do that.

"Where did you meet Miss Wright?" she asked as they walked back toward where Jeremy was still talking with his daughter and Miss Wright.

Seth's relief with the change in subject was clear when he smiled. "Marianne introduced us. They have been friends for many years."

"Many years," seconded Marianne with a hushed laugh. "I do believe we met while still too young to walk."

"At the hunt near Wright's dirty acres, if I recall." Jeremy paused as an orchestra that had been half hidden behind a broad column began to play a waltz. "Would you stand up with me, Camilla?"

"I thought we were going to—"

"While we waltz, we shall have a chance to view all of the room."

Nodding, she put her hand on his and let him lead her to the center of the floor. She looked back, amazed to see Seth leading Marianne after them.

"Do not appear so dumbfounded," Jeremy said with a laugh. "While you were speaking with your son, those two young lasses were plotting to get Seth to dance with my daughter. I suspect she has her eye on someone she does not want to let know she has her eye on. This way, she can see what he is up to without appearing to be spying on him."

Camilla laughed as he drew her closer. When he turned her to the swaying tempo of the dance, she forgot about her mother and his uncle and her son and Jeremy's daughter and Miss Wright . . . and all the world but the yearning that glowed in his gray-green eyes. Her fingers at his nape sifted up through his thick black hair. His slow smile thrilled her.

"This is very nice," he whispered, although no one seemed to be paying them any attention amid the other dancers.

"Yes, very nice."

"It has been a long time since I last danced."

"Since your wife died?"

"Actually long before that. Nancy did not enjoy dancing. She said it made her dizzy to try to watch her feet and those around her."

"Then she would have enjoyed waltzing."

"I think she might have." He paused, then added, "I haven't told anyone else that."

"If you do not want to speak of her—"

He kept her close when she was about to pull away. "No, no, do not look so dismayed. As I realize you do, I savor the memories of the time I had with my departed spouse. It is simply that, until I met you, I did not wish to share those memories with someone else."

Camilla bit her lower lip, not sure how to reply. His words touched her heart in places she had been certain no one would find again. Softly she said, "I see your charm has grown only more potent with the passing years, Jeremy."

"I meant my words sincerely."

"There was no question of that." She hesitated before saying, "So did I."

His hand rose to cup her cheek, but he quickly lowered it as Seth came up to them, both young women in tow. Clearing his throat, Jeremy asked, "What is amiss? Have you seen Lady Flora and my uncle, Worthington?"

"Not a hint of them."

Marianne smiled. "Papa, I do believe I heard Great-uncle say that he would be playing cards this evening with a small group of friends."

"At his club?"

"I do not think he would ask Lady Flora to join him at his club. That might cause a mutiny within it." She laughed.

Camilla put her hand on Jeremy's arm. "Cards are a quiet pastime, Jeremy. Your uncle should not strain himself in that pursuit."

"I hope you are right." His voice grew grim. "I hope you are right."

Six

"It has happened again."

Camilla looked up as she heard the exasperation in Jeremy's voice. Putting down the book she had been reading, she smiled. "If you are speaking of Mother and your uncle, I can tell you exactly where they are. They are acting as chaperons for Seth and Marianne and Miss Wright for an outing this evening."

"Do you know where they are bound?"

"I did not ask. I trust them. You should, too, Jeremy. Then mayhap—"

"Trust?" he roared. Lowering his voice when she gasped, he said, "Camilla, this has nothing to do with trust. I thought you understood, but apparently you do not."

She came to her feet. He was far more disturbed by this than he should be. Lines of worry were etched deeply into his forehead, and his eyes were dim. "Jeremy, it is not like you to take on so. What is wrong?"

"Did you know the doctor called here today while I was next door and you were out on calls with my daughter?"

"The doctor? Here?" Her shoulders sagged. "No, no one told me. But that makes no sense. Palmer would have let me know straightaway on my return."

"Unless he was told not to say anything."

"Mother! You believe that Mother told him to remain silent!"

"Yes. Don't you?"

She went to the door. As she had expected, Palmer was in the hallway, his back to her. He was trying diligently to appear busy, but she knew he had been lurking there to eavesdrop as he so often did.

"Well?" Camilla asked.

The butler turned to face her. "Well, my lady?"

She locked her arms together in front of her. His baffled expression could not bamblusterate her. "Palmer, do not act the innocent with me. I know you know what I want to know."

"If you know that I know what you want to know, my lady, I still do not comprehend your question."

Under other circumstances, she might have smiled, but she was irritated by his back-answer. "You know what I want to know now."

She heard a chuckle behind her. Looking over her shoulder, she savored the enthralling pulse as her gaze met Jeremy's. The sparkle in his eyes divulged that all his thoughts were not focused on his uncle. Shaking aside the image of being in his arms, an image that should not be in her mind now, she focused a scowl on Palmer.

The butler said, "My lady, Lady Flora asked me to inform you if you were to ask—"

"If?" Camilla shook her head, amazed. "You and Mother have become staunch allies. Go ahead, Palmer. I *am* asking."

"Lady Flora asked me to inform you, if you were to ask," he repeated in his most officious tones, "that the doctor called simply to confirm that nothing was amiss."

"That makes no sense," Jeremy said.

"With all due respect, my lady," Palmer answered, "I must be honest and say that there have been many times when Lady Flora's orders made no sense."

Camilla hid her smile. Mother must have insulted the butler by not making him privy to some information he had been eager to know. When she glanced at Jeremy, she lost all desire to smile. She could tell by the rigid line of his shoulders that he had come to the same conclusion. What did Mother want to hide from the voluble Palmer?

Putting her hand on Jeremy's arm, she said, "Palmer, you must know where Mother went this evening."

"She did mention speaking with Mrs. Forbes."

"And Mrs. Forbes will be at Almack's tonight. Palmer, have the carriage brought around."

"Yes, my lady."

Camilla told Jeremy she would meet him by the door. She could not appear at Almack's in the gown she had worn for a quiet evening at home. Calling for her abigail, she went up the stairs at an unseemly speed. She changed as quickly as possible and was hooking her bracelet in place while she came back down to the foyer, where Jeremy was waiting. His smile told her that her elegant white gown would meet the standards that were *de rigueur* for Almack's.

She had to own that he had been wise to don more formal clothes as well. His navy coat and white breeches accented his athletic build. When he offered his arm, she put her fingers on it. He swept her closer as he led her down the steps to the waiting carriage.

Taking a deep breath of the still-warm air, she wished she could be thinking only of enjoying the company of a handsome man on a beautiful spring evening. Suddenly she felt as young as she had when she had embarked on her first Season, as young and as full of anticipation of all the excitement such a night could bring.

When Jeremy handed her into the carriage and sat beside her, he said, "I understand now what folks mean when they say one is glowing, Camilla. You shall challenge the brightness of the rising moon." Before she had a chance to reply, he added, "But you are so quiet."

"I am confused."

"About your mother?" His dark brows rose. *"That* I can understand."

She chuckled. "No, I understand why Mother would want

to spend her evening at Almack's, but it seems so unlikely that Seth would go there. Almack's bored him the few times he visited."

"But now he wishes to impress his lady fair with his *entrée* into the very highest level of the Polite World." He laughed as he relaxed against the seat. "You should know, Camilla, that a man will do almost anything, including feasting on his own words, in an effort to impress a woman."

"Have you always been so cynical?"

"Cynical? No, I don't think I ever have been cynical. However, there were times when I was not as honest as I am now."

She laughed. "Honesty? Is that what you call speaking your mind so bluntly?"

"Wouldn't you?"

"I think, Jeremy, if you wish me to be honest, that I believe you say such preposterous things to keep from speaking what is truly on your mind."

"Do you honestly think so?"

"Yes." She laughed again, but the light sound evaporated as he leaned toward her.

Catching her face between his broad hands, he whispered, "Do you want to know what I am thinking? Honestly?"

"Jeremy—"

His lips coursed along her cheek, leaving breathtaking fire in their wake. When his mouth found hers, she feared she would never be able to breathe again. She feared that if she did, this magical moment would end. Slowly her hands curved around his shoulders as he deepened the kiss until her lips softened beneath his.

With obvious regret in his emotive eyes, he raised his head far enough to whisper, *"That* was what I was thinking. That and so much more."

"What so much more?"

His laugh was a soft caress against her mouth when his mouth slanted across hers. The tip of his tongue outlined her lips, burnishing them with rapture. Knowing she was being too bold when she had known him such a short time, she pressed closer to him. He leaned her back, deepening the kiss until her breath was frayed against his mouth. His hand cradled her head as he explored her mouth, teasing her to throw aside any qualms and be as unabashed as he in discovering each pleasure waiting for them.

As her fingers combed through his hair, she heard an odd sound. A laugh, she realized. Jeremy's? No, impossible, because his mouth was busy against hers. Looking past him, she saw her son leaning his arms on the carriage window and peering through. She had not noticed that the carriage had stopped.

Seth grinned at her, and she wondered how a single mistake on her part could even out all the ones her son had made. She could no longer chide him for a lack of common sense when he had discovered her in Jeremy's arms in the street in front of Almack's.

"Jeremy," she whispered, turning her face so she could speak.

"Sweetheart, you should—"

"We are at Almack's."

When his gaze followed hers, she could not keep from laughing as she saw his astonishment. He sat and drew her up. "It is easy to lose track of time when enjoying oneself so much." His hand tilted her face toward him. With his lips so close to hers that she could sense their heat, he murmured, "I would like to lose track of much more time with you."

Camilla smiled with a shyness she had not experienced in years. Was her face scarlet while Jeremy stepped out of the carriage, giving her time to brush her hair back into place? She tried to keep her smile in place as he handed her to the walkway.

"Good evening, Mama," Seth said, bending to kiss her cheek as he did his grandmother's each morning. "May I say that the color here is most becoming?"

"You should not." Dash it! She must be blushing like a schoolgirl.

"Has it become ungentlemanly to compliment a lady?" Seth looked at Jeremy and chuckled. "I appeal to you, Overbrook. What is one to do with a mother who teaches a son to be most laudatory to the ladies, then changes her mind when a son speaks so to her?"

"In my opinion, a son must make his own decisions when he reaches the age when others acknowledge him as a man," Jeremy replied, earning a frown from Camilla. "If you will not be complimented, Camilla, may I say that is a most unbecoming expression?"

As Miss Wright, who was standing next to Marianne, giggled, Camilla sighed and shook her head. She wagged her finger at her son and at Jeremy. "You two are seeking any excuse you can devise for your untoward behavior."

"No truer words have ever been uttered in my hearing," Seth said. He motioned toward the door. "Shall we? Grandmama and Mr. Winston are waiting for us inside."

Miss Wright giggled again, this time in nervous anticipation. When Marianne bent and whispered something to her, she nodded, wide-eyed.

Camilla wondered if Miss Wright's parents had been able to prepare her for this moment that every young woman recognized as important above any other in her Season. An invitation to Almack's and a first appearance must be made without a blemish.

She could not keep from comparing the two young women. Miss Wright was pretty but so childish in many ways. Although Lady Marianne was also taking part in her first Season, she seemed much the more mature of the two. Had Seth noticed the difference as well? Mayhap he was so captivated by Miss Wright that he had not, or her lack of polish did not concern him.

Linking her arm through Miss Wright's, Camilla said, "Smile. A smile will take you far tonight."

Miss Wright tugged at her lacy gloves nervously. "But I heard that conversation is of utmost importance here."

"It is." Leaning her head toward Miss Wright, Camilla murmured, "I have learned that one is considered a brilliant conversationalist when one listens to others and nods at the appropriate times."

"Lady Worthington is correct," Marianne said, chuckling. "Why, just the other day, Lord Worthington was telling me how he enjoyed speaking with me the first time we were introduced. Odd, for I recall saying not a word."

Giggling again, Miss Wright went with Seth and Marianne into Almack's.

"If she heeds you," Jeremy said, bringing Camilla's hand within his arm, where it seemed to fit so perfectly, "she should succeed."

"You heard what I said?"

He laughed. "How could I when you were buzzing together with Miss Wright and my daughter like a collection of honeybees in a freshly blooming garden? However, I know your advice to her would be sage, for you survived your own Season intact."

"Barely."

"Was it so rough?"

Camilla hesitated; then, knowing she could not let the chance connection in their past remain unspoken, she said, "It was smooth, save for when I was nearly run down one night by a rider on Grosvenor Square."

"That was not what I meant. If . . ." The amusement vanished from his eyes as he frowned. Drawing her to one side so they did not block the door, he waved aside her protests that they should not linger there when they were needed to chaperon Seth and Miss Wright. "Not only is Marianne with them, but my uncle and your mother must be nearby. Even if our families do not watch over your son and Miss Wright, they will have dozens of eyes upon them, so you need not fear any misdeed. We need to talk, for you have stirred a half-forgotten memory in my mind of a pretty young girl who was nearly trampled by a horse ridden by one of my tie-mates."

"I have never forgotten," she said softly. "Not the incident or what you did." *Or how your eyes glistened with kindness.* His eyes were what she had not been able to forget, even when the temptation in them had urged her to forget herself in his arms.

"Why have you said nothing of this before now?" he asked with a puzzled expression.

She smiled. "What would you have had me say when we met again, Jeremy? That I am glad you saved my life? That I never had the chance to thank you for risking your life as you did?"

"That night seems to belong to another life now." He gave her a warm grin. "Shall we see what this night brings?"

"Yes."

"You look startled, Camilla," he said as he put his hand over hers on his arm. "Did you think I would want to reminisce about the misspent nights of my youth?"

"I did hope that you would consider saving my life not time misspent."

He chuckled. "You would not have been endangered if we had not been riding neck-or-nothing through the square. It seems odd that you are so forgiving for my distant past, yet you cannot forgive your son his recent one."

"Mayhap I could if you were to forgive Mother these past few days."

"Ah, there is the rub, isn't it? It is much easier to be generous about mistakes of the past than those of the present."

Camilla had no chance to reply as they were swept into the conversations swirling through Almack's. The room was filled nearly to overflowing, and all attempts by an orchestra to provide music were lost amid the conversation. She scanned the crowd and relaxed when she saw Seth standing between Miss Wright and Marianne as they spoke with some other young people.

When he leaned toward Marianne to whisper something, Camilla frowned.

"That is a frightful expression. Here," Jeremy said as he handed her a glass of the tepid lemonade. "If you wish to look as if you have bitten into a lemon . . ."

She could not keep from laughing. "I did not realize I was wearing another frightful face."

"Oh, no, you misunderstand. Your face is always lovely." He brushed her cheek with a single finger. "Even more lovely now than I remember it from that encounter on Grosvenor Square."

Putting up her hand, she pressed his finger to her. She delighted in the warm roughness of his skin and the male aroma of it. How could she have forgotten the very thing she once had delighted in—the scent of a man that combined both strength and vulnerability when he let a woman close to him?

"There are times," she whispered, "when not being completely honest can be a very kind thing."

He gripped her shoulders and brought her to face him, ignoring the eddies of people surrounding them. "Is that what you think, Camilla? That I was being kind? Look around here at the young misses and tell me if you see even one with more liveliness in her steps or more flirtatious designs in her eyes than yours." His hand brushed a strand of hair back from her face. "I was a young fool once, and I thought as a young fool does. Now I am older and hopefully possess more wisdom. Your face, which reveals the memory of past laughter and past regrets, delights me more than any young miss's."

For once, Camilla was completely speechless. She did not want to speak and ruin this so-perfect moment as she gazed up at him while she imagined his mouth on hers in a feverish kiss like the ones they had shared in the carriage.

"Ah, here you are!" An arm around her shoulders spun her away from Jeremy and almost off her feet.

Camilla fought for her footing and her composure as she faced her mother. Her eyes narrowed, for her mother's face looked oddly flushed. Mayhap it was nothing more than the crowded room that was making it too hot.

"Mother, Seth told me you were here. I am surprised to see both of you paying a call on the Polite World at Almack's tonight."

Lady Flora tapped Camilla's arm with her fan. "I thought to be certain the rest of my family did not get into trouble without me."

Seth laughed as he came to stand beside his grandmother and a broadly smiling Mr. Winston. "Grandmama, you know that we would want to include you. Isn't that true, Mama?"

"Of course," she replied automatically. Unable to keep from staring at her mother's flushed face, she added, "I think we should go outside where it is a bit cooler."

"Nonsense!" Her mother waved her hands. "The children wish to enjoy the *bon mots* and conviviality here."

Camilla glanced from Jeremy to her son. Both must have understood because they began both talking at once, suggesting a return to the house on Soho Square for an evening of cards.

"An excellent idea," Mr. Winston said, and Camilla was not sure if he was truly interested in cards or shared her concern about her mother's high color. "There are a few lessons with the cards that I have been wishing to teach this fine young fellow." He slapped Seth on the back hard enough to make him stumble forward a half step.

Far more quickly than Camilla would have guessed possible, they were in the carriages returning to Soho Square. She was not surprised that her mother had managed to get into the carriage with Seth and the young women. Mr. Winston grumbled something under his breath before stepping into the carriage with his nephew and Camilla.

Jeremy was silent.

Camilla kept glancing at him during the ride and when they arrived at the house. If he sensed her curiosity and concern, he did not acknowledge it as he helped her from the carriage or while they went inside to arrange for the games of whist that Mr. Winston believed would be a delightful way to pass the evening.

After Camilla had given Palmer her request for tables and refreshments, she realized that the others had left the foyer. She heard voices from the back of the house. Walking in that direction, she saw Jeremy come out of the small study that Seth had made his own.

"There you are!" Her attempt to make her voice sound bright fell flat when she saw how hard his face was. Something had distressed him, but what? She was not about to let whatever it was fester. Not when she wanted to share more of the pleasure of his kisses. "I do not know what is bothering you, Jeremy, but please do not be angry."

"I am not angry . . . at you." He stared past her. "This has gone on too long. I turn my back, and she vanishes with my uncle, who should be resting after the trip to Almack's and back."

Camilla turned and groaned as she saw her mother and Mr. Winston coming in from the garden. They were arm in arm and chatting like two youngsters. "Jeremy, think before you say anything you may regret."

"The only thing I can imagine regretting at this point is that I have not said what I should have long ago. She must show some sense before something horrible happens." He strode toward where her mother was laughing at something Mr. Winston said.

Camilla followed, but froze in midstep when suddenly her mother gasped and pressed her hand to her chest. With a soft moan, Lady Flora collapsed to the floor.

Seven

Camilla pushed past Mr. Winston, who was as paralyzed with shock as she had been. Jeremy was squatting beside Lady Flora, chafing her wrist. When he shouted for a doctor and *sal volatile,* Camilla knelt by her mother. Who would have guessed this adventure would end like this? Tears flowed from her eyes, but she ignored them. She gently picked up her mother's other hand.

Palmer rushed forward with the small bottle. "I have sent for the doctor, my lady."

Taking the bottle, Camilla struggled to pull the tiny cork. Jeremy plucked it from her shaking hands and opened it. He squeezed her fingers as he gave it back to her. She wished she could feel the comfort he was offering. She was numb with terror.

Her mother had always been so strong, such an undeniable force within these walls. Her opinions were heard by all and respected by most. The self-deprecatory sense of humor that delighted her grandson entertained others as well.

Grandson! Where was Seth?

Camilla looked around the hallway. She could not see him as servants rushed around them. Someone should send for him, too. How had he failed to hear the commotion? He would want to be beside his beloved grandmother when . . . if . . . She could not bear the thought of losing her mother.

"Camilla?" Jeremy's voice was gentle, but insistent. "The *sal volatile?*"

Nodding, she leaned forward to hold it under her mother's nose to revive her from her swoon. It must be just a swoon. It could not be more than that. It must not be.

Lady Flora coughed and raised a feeble hand to brush the bottle away.

"Mother! Mother, can you hear me?"

"Not only can I hear you, but I can see you, Camilla," her mother said, her voice oddly weak. "That is a grim expression you are wearing."

"I am feeling quite grim."

"You must smile, Camilla. You would not want your face to end up staying like that. No man is going to give you a second look if you wear such a dreary frown all the time."

Jeremy put his hand on Camilla's shoulder. "I would like to think that the only man giving her second looks from this point forward, Lady Flora, is me."

Camilla tore her gaze from her mother's gray face to look at Jeremy. Had she mistaken his words? She hoped not.

"An excellent comment," Lady Flora said. Her eyes closed.

Camilla's stomach twisted. Then she saw that her mother was still breathing, for the steady rise and fall of her chest suggested that she was sleeping.

When Jeremy put his hands on her shoulders and drew her to her feet, Camilla leaned her cheek against his chest. She watched as several of the footmen carefully lifted her mother. She started to follow as they carried her up the stairs to her bedchamber. Jeremy held her back.

"Do not crowd them on the stairs, sweetheart," he said softly.

"But—"

"And I need your help with Uncle Ronald."

Looking at where Jeremy's uncle was staring after the servants, his face colorless, Camilla went to him and put her hand on his arm. "Come with me, Mr. Winston."

"I never meant—I did not know—" His voice broke.

"Come with me," she repeated. "The doctor does not live far from here. By the time we get upstairs, he should be here."

"Upstairs?" Mr. Winston's eyes grew saucer-wide. "You mean . . . Do you think it is proper . . . ?"

"To own the truth," she replied, "just now I do not care what is or is not proper."

"Come along, Uncle," Jeremy said, taking his uncle by the arm. "You can chide Camilla for her lack of good sense on our way up the stairs."

Jeremy offered her a reassuring smile as he led his uncle to the staircase. Camilla held the memory of that expression close to her in the hours that followed. When Dr. Beck arrived and went to examine her mother, Camilla clung to the hope that Jeremy had been smiling because he believed her mother would be fine.

She waited in the outer room of her mother's pale yellow bedchamber. She paced from the window to the door and back so often that she feared she would wear the carpet straight through to the floorboards.

The inner door opened, and she whirled. Rushing to Dr. Beck, she whispered, "How is she?"

Dr. Beck pushed his spectacles back up on his nose and shook his head. "If she had heeded me this afternoon, she would have known that her heart was racing far too fast to set out on an evening's entertainment tonight."

"You came to see my mother this afternoon?" she gasped.

"Of course. Who else?" He frowned. "Seth is not ill, is he?"

"No." She wanted to add that she wished she knew where her son was, but this was not the time to clutter the conversation with other issues. "Will she live?"

"Most likely long beyond all her peers." He closed his bag and pressed packets of powder in her hand. "If she feels her heartbeat is too fast, give her some of this ground lilyof-the-valley in some water. It will ease the pace of her heart and let her rest more easily."

"Thank you," she whispered.

"I will be back in the morning. She is sleeping now, and I doubt if she will wake before dawn."

Jeremy came to stand beside Camilla as the doctor left. He drew her down to sit beside him on the white chaise longue. "How are you doing?" he asked.

"Better."

"Dr. Beck would not give you false hopes. That is not his way."

Camilla's head jerked up at the grief in his voice. "Was he the doctor when your wife died?"

"Yes." Rubbing his hands together, he said, "Dr. Beck was unfailingly honest with me about her condition and how little he could do to stop her from wasting away with consumption. If he says Lady Flora will be doing better by the morrow, you can believe him."

She put her hand over his as she rested her head on his shoulder. "Thank you, Jeremy."

"Thank you?" He laughed tersely. "I would rather think you would want to ring a regular peal over me for dragging your mother from Almack's to here, especially when I was ready to give her a wigging for luring my uncle into mischief."

"Thank you for being here. If you had not been . . ."

"You would have managed quite well all on your own. You are a strong woman, Camilla Hoxworthy, and you would not allow even the palpitations of your mother's heart to defeat you—or her."

She started to reply, then heard a snore from behind her. She smiled as Jeremy went to wake his uncle, who was stretched out between two overstuffed chairs. When Mr. Winston grumbled something at him and turned to face the door to her mother's room, Camilla took a blanket from a cupboard in the corner. She carried it to where Jeremy stood.

"He insists on remaining here," Jeremy said.

"I suspected as much." She handed him the blanket. "Tuck this around him, so he will be comfortable. He needs to rest."

"And you look as if you could use something to bring color back to your cheeks." He draped the blanket over his uncle, then took her arm and led her back out into the hallway where Palmer was pacing. He gave her no chance to calm her butler, who had been with the family since before Camilla married. Steering her into her small parlor, he sat her on the settee, then went to the sideboard and poured two glasses of wine. He handed one to her and took the other back out into the hall to the butler.

Camilla stared down at her glass. The deep rumble of Jeremy's and Palmer's voices eased as Jeremy came back into the room.

"It will not help you if you don't drink it," Jeremy said with a smile.

She set the glass on the table, flung her arms around him, and wept. He drew her close, holding her while she gave way to her fear. Sitting beside her on the settee, he did not release her as her sobs faded into sleep.

"Camilla?"

She opened her eyes, then winced as the first light of dawn burned them. Dry and scratchy, her eyes refused to focus.

"Camilla?"

The voice came from so close that its rumble brushed against her cheek.

"Are you awake, sweetheart?"

Camilla came fully awake to discover Jeremy's face close to hers. When his lips brushed hers, she moaned with the longing that came directly from her dreams. She wanted to wake slowly as his kisses led her from a dream into a reality of love.

When he lifted his mouth away, she reached for him. He caught her hands and folded them between his. "Sweetheart, Dr. Beck just arrived."

Dr. Beck!

Camilla jumped to her feet, paying no attention to her hair, which was lathered to her face with the salty remnants of her tears. Rushing up the stairs, she paused when she heard Jeremy right behind her. She held out her hand to him. With a smile that reached right inside her to ease the pain around her icy heart, he took it and went with her to Lady Flora's rooms.

Mr. Winston was pacing as Camilla had last night. He started to speak, but paused when Dr. Beck emerged with a smile.

"She wishes to see all of you," the doctor said. "I suggested one at a time, but I believe her impatience is more dangerous to her than a visit from all of you at once. However, I caution you. Do not over-excite her."

Camilla nodded and went to the door. She pushed it open to see her mother sitting up in bed, her favorite wrapper matching the lace along the coverlet. Camilla's best intentions vanished when she rushed to her mother's bed and bent to kiss Lady Flora's cheek, which held a hint of its normal color.

"You gave us a scare last night," Camilla said.

"I know." Her mother smiled broadly. "But I daresay it has been worth it."

"Worth it? Risking your health? Risking your very life so thoughtlessly? If you had told me that Dr. Beck had called here to see you earlier, I would have—"

"Camilla, there is nothing less attractive than a child scolding her mother. I heeded Dr. Beck's caution, or as he told me, I would not be here to listen to your admonishments. And, to own the truth, if my time on this earth is short, I do not wish to spend it hearing you lecture me on having good sense."

"I am sorry."

"And you are right." Lady Flora reached across the bed and patted her daughter's hand. Then she lifted it and placed it in Jeremy's. "I can assure you both that everything that has happened is all for the very best."

"She is making no sense," Camilla whispered to Jeremy. "It must be the powders the doctor left."

"I can hear you," her mother said with a return of her testy tone, "and 'tis not the powders. 'Tis the fact that Ronald and I have managed to bamblusterate the two of you completely."

Jeremy frowned. "I must agree with your daughter, my lady. You seem confused."

"No," Mr. Winston said, putting his hand on Lady Flora's shoulder. "You, my boy, are the one who is confused. Lady Flora and I succeeded in our scheme beyond our greatest expectations."

"Scheme?" Camilla's eyes narrowed as her mother chuckled. "What are you talking about?"

"A very simple plan," Lady Flora explained, "although I did not guess at its beginning that my heart would be a conspirator in our plan as well. Ronald and I were determined to keep the two of you occupied with what you believed were a most troublesome mother and a most gullible uncle." Lady Flora smiled up at the older man, who winked at her. "Seth came to me, several weeks ago, concerned that his reputation might haunt him when he had found the young woman of his dreams. He doubted if her father would be willing to consider him as a suitor."

Jeremy nodded. "Wright is very provincial. He—"

Lady Flora laughed as Mr. Winston clapped his hands and roared with amusement. Wagging a finger, Mr. Winston said, "Not Wright, my boy. You!"

"Me? If Worthington ever decides to set his cap on someone other than Miss Wright, all he needs to do is talk to me about calling on my daughter, and we will discuss it as two rational men. There was no need for you to risk your well-being." He looked out into the hallway. "Where is he? I haven't seen him since we arrived back here last night."

"By this time, I would guess the youngsters are well on their way to Scotland."

"Scotland?" gasped Camilla. "Do you mean that Seth and Marianne are eloping?"

"It would seem the most likely thing for two young people in love to go to Scotland for," her mother replied as she tapped the ring on Camilla's left hand. "Dear me! Seth forgot to get the ring from you before he left. You can give it to Marianne when they return. After all, you won't be needing it any longer."

Camilla drew her hand away from her mother's. She wondered if she was still asleep and dreaming. This made no sense. "But Seth was escorting Miss Wright!"

Mr. Winston laughed again. "I had not thought they would baffle both of you so completely. Miss Wright offered, as Marianne's bosom-bow, to feign a *tendre* for young Worthington."

Camilla recalled how Seth had danced as often with Marianne as with Miss Wright. Mayhap more often. Looking back, Camilla thought of how he had shared little asides with Marianne more frequently than with Miss Wright.

Lady Flora chuckled, sounding much more like her customary self. "You might say, Camilla, that Miss Wright was not *right* for your son."

As Camilla grimaced, Mr. Winston added, "Worthington and Marianne are determined to be married before you two own to the truth that you love each other, too. It is so much easier for the children to marry before the parents do. If they had waited until after you two did the obvious thing and made a match, there are all those legal issues to be considered."

"Love?" Camilla whispered, glancing at Jeremy. He was smiling, clearly amused.

"Oh, do not try to deny it," her mother said, waving them away from her bed. "My lord, you will find the rug in the antechamber thick enough to support your knee when you get down on it to ask Camilla to marry you." She paused, then said, "Do leave the door open, so we may hear. After all this hard work to make these matches, I do not want to be deprived of witnessing at least one of the results."

Jeremy leaned over and kissed Lady Flora's cheek. "I will take that as your blessing on our marriage."

"Why are you kissing me instead of your bride-to-be?" she returned, but a flush of happiness scoured away her sickly coloring.

"He hasn't asked me yet, Mother," Camilla replied.

With a laugh, Jeremy spun her into his arms. "After all that these people have been through to arrange for us to be happy, how can we not acquiesce to the truth that they are right? I love you. Will you heed your mother's excellent advice and marry me?"

"Yes," she whispered as she tilted her mouth beneath his.

A
MOTHER'S
DEVOTION

Valerie King

One

Bath, England, 1818

"Sophy, there is a very fine gentleman descending a coach and four in front of our house."

Miss Sophy Deverill did not turn to look at her youngest half brother, but kept her head bent over the household ledgers. "How very nice, dearest. I hope you are not staring at him, for that would be very rude."

"He is coming to the door," Edward said. He was all of five and fascinated by everything.

"Mmm," she responded absently. She had been trying to balance the quarter's income and expenditures for three hours. Her head ached slightly as did her shoulders and portions of her back. She always suffered in this manner at the approach of quarter-day. The allowance upon which she supported herself and her four half-siblings was never sufficient, particularly when the children all insisted upon outgrowing their clothes and shoes!

Therein lay the answer, she thought, laughing somewhat hysterically. Somehow she must find a way to make the children stop growing!

When the knocker sounded at the front door, Edward drew close. "The fine gentleman is here. May I let him in?"

"Where is Mrs. White?" The household had one servant,

a wonderful woman who served as cook, housemaid, and at times abigail and footman.

"She is gone to fetch the fish from Mrs. Bulford."

"Yes, then of course you may let the gentleman in." She was certain it was Mr. Minerty, the banker, who in his great kindness since her mother's death five years past had personally delivered the quarterly portion of her annuity. She frowned slightly and leaned back in her chair to take a sip of tea which she soon discovered had grown cold. Mr. Minerty was five days early. She wondered if something was amiss.

Sophy closed the ledgers and rose to her feet. She heard murmurings from the entrance hall beyond and every once in a while could discern Edward's voice. "Sophy is at home," he chirped. "Do you wish to speak with her? She has the care of us."

These were odd things for Edward to be saying to Mr. Minerty, but then, he was quite young.

More murmurings and then footsteps.

A moment more and Edward appeared in the doorway. "He said his name was Sherry-something." The gentleman stepped into view.

"How do you do, ma'am. I know . . . this must seem . . . good God! Sophy?"

Sophy felt she was staring at a ghost. "John?" she queried. "I feel as though I might swoon. Whatever are you . . . oh, I must sit down!"

She fell back into the chair before her desk and nearly overset her teacup. She scrambled to keep it from falling over. Fortunately, the tea did little more than slosh onto its saucer. She turned and looked at him. "Whatever are you doing here? Why, it must be eight years at least since I last saw you!"

"Nine, I believe," he murmured.

"However did you find me?"

"I wasn't looking for you," he answered cryptically. He

glanced down at a card held in his hand. He shook his head, apparently bemused. "I was told at the White Hart that the parents of Agnes Chenlow resided at this address, that Miss Chenlow resides here."

"She does. Indeed, she does. She is my half sister."

"But this is too fantastic! Agnes Chenlow is your sister? I admit, for a moment I wondered, since I remember little Agnes so well. However, it seemed impossible."

"What do you want with Agnes?" she asked, bewildered. "Oh, but please, forgive me for my manners, Mr. Barrows. Will you not come in and tell me what is going forward?"

"Thank you."

"I will take your hat if you like, sir," Edward said. "We do not have a proper butler, and Mrs. White has gone to fetch the fish for our dinner."

"There's a good fellow," Mr. Barrows said, handing his glossy beaver hat to young Edward.

The little boy waited.

"Was there something more?" he asked.

"Your gloves, sir? I have been told a gentleman always leaves his gloves with his hat."

"You are very right. What is your name?"

"Edward, sir. Master Edward Chenlow."

"Agnes is your sister, then?"

"Yes, but she is quite birdwitted and Sophy tells me I am not!"

Mr. Barrows drew off his gloves and dropped them into the well of his hat, which Edward still very politely held out for him.

Sophy smiled softly at her brother. "Agnes is not birdwitted, Edward."

"George says she is."

"George should not say such things about his sister, nor should you. You may now take Mr. Barrows's hat to the table by the front door."

Edward smiled happily and disappeared in the direction of the entrance hall.

Her guest turned toward her. "I should tell you, I am known as Sheriston now."

"I see. I am sorry, then, for this would mean you have suffered an unfortunate loss in recent years. I know you were very fond of your father." She rose from her chair, and even though her limbs were trembling, she gestured for him to take a seat on the sofa by the window. She joined him, her gaze rarely straying from his face. She could not credit he was here, in her drawing room, the man to whom she had been betrothed so many years ago.

"And how are your many brothers and sisters?" she asked, sitting down. "All faring well, I hope? Each married happily with a score of children?"

He smiled at that, taking up a seat next to her. "Perhaps not a score as yet. But yes, they are all married and I am able to boast of six nieces and nephews—nearly seven, for Arabella is increasing."

"How wonderful for you. I always thought you enjoyed being part of a large family."

"Indeed, you are right," he responded, smiling.

She had not seen the Honorable John Barrows, now Lord Sheriston, in nearly nine years. He had scarcely changed and was as handsome as she remembered. His hair was a rich dark brown and his eyes a matching warm color that had always had the ability to rend her soul in two. His features were noble and strong, his jaw firm and stubborn at times, his nose aquiline, his brow intelligent. His expression of the moment, however, seemed quite strained, even through his smiles, for there was a pinched look about his eyes.

"And is Lady Sheriston with you?" she asked. Had he married? Was he now the father of a hopeful brood himself? Was he happy? In her daydreams about him, this was how she always envisioned his life, a loving spouse and an abundance of children.

He frowned. "Lady Sheriston? You mean, my mother? No, she remained in Wiltshire. She thought it best I come to Bath alone."

"I—I was referring to your wife—the present Lady Sheriston. I would suppose you are long since married. Contentedly, I hope."

"No," he responded with an odd frown. "I am as yet unwed."

"John—that is, Sheriston, you cannot still be angry with me? Tell me you are not. I could not bear it if I thought you held even the smallest grievance toward me."

"No, I do not, I assure you. If I appear perplexed, it is because I do not understand what force has brought me to your door after all these years."

Sophy glanced down at the card still held in his hand. "Why are you in search of Agnes, or more particularly, her parents?"

He cocked his head, obviously bemused. "Is your sister here, then?" he asked.

"I believe so." When Edward reentered the drawing room at that moment, she said, "Dearest, would you please fetch Agnes for me? I believe Lord Sheriston wishes to speak with her on a matter of some urgency."

Edward's eyes got very big. "Are you really a lord? Which rank?"

"Edward," Sophy called out sharply. "These are very impertinent questions."

"I beg your pardon," he said, bowing by way of apology to Lord Sheriston.

"I am a lowly viscount," Sheriston responded kindly.

Edward beamed, then raced from the room. His quick footsteps could be heard on the stairs beyond.

Sheriston glanced at her. "You once told me your mother was quite ill."

"Yes, at the time she was not expected to survive the summer, but she recovered sufficiently to move about her home tolerably well. Her health was never wonderful, however, and five years later—nearly six now—she died in childbed with Edward."

"Poor Sophy," he murmured with so much sympathy that she was nearly undone by it.

"Do not pity me, Sheriston," she said. "He is the dearest boy and has enriched my life beyond words. He is clever and good-natured, both of which you must have already observed."

"I have," he responded, sincerely. "You are a mother to him, then?"

"Yes, very much so, as I am to all my half-siblings."

He stared at her hard for a moment. "You have not changed at all. You are as tender-hearted and as beautiful as I remember you, perhaps even more so. The years have treasured you."

She met his gaze and found that his words were beginning to work strongly in her. She was remembering why she had loved him so dearly. In a sudden, intense wave, the old feelings returned to her, of adoration and love so profound that for a moment she could hardly breathe. "You have not changed either, John. You are as I remember you."

He searched her eyes intently. "You never wed?" he asked.

She shook her head. "I have been much engaged here." She gestured into the room.

He nodded, his expression sobering. "Caring for them all."

"Yes, and my mother as well, until she passed away."

"What of Mr. Chenlow?"

"I believe he still resides in London."

"Does he ever see the children?"

"No. I will not permit it."

His jaw grew stiff. He was remembering now, she thought. How angry he had been when she had asked him to put off the wedding for a year because she could not abandon her mother and her half-siblings.

The argument had raged for days, unresolved. He insisted

she leave her mother and siblings, that her stepfather should have the care of his family, which was only proper. She had tried to explain how incompetent Mr. Chenlow was, how indifferent he was to her mother's health and happiness, how coarsely he treated his own children, all in an attempt to persuade him that no amount of pressure would make Mr. Chenlow either a good father or a loving husband. Sheriston remained unmoved by her arguments.

"I am essential to my family right now," she had said. "I might even say, critical." How she had wanted to tell him the vile extent of Mr. Chenlow's cruelties, but at the time, she had been wholly unable to speak the words. Who would believe her? She had continued, "But I am sincerely hoping that one day mother's health will improve and then we can be married, I promise you."

He had been obstinate in his position, however. She would be his wife. She would concern herself with him exclusively. She would set aside the needs of her mother in order to begin life anew with him. Her devotion was to be to him and, to a lesser degree, the family they would create together.

She had tried to explain that the younger ones depended on her, but he refused to understand her devotion to the care of her family, and most particularly to the care of her brothers and sisters. She had asked for a year. He had refused her. She had had only one recourse, to end the betrothal.

The pain she had endured in leaving Sheriston Hall that summer to return to her former life in the Chenlow household resulted in a form of despair she hoped never to experience again. That she was feeling some of that despair even now hurt her deeply. With the sole purpose of intending to avert a spiraling into those sad feelings once more, she gave the subject a hard turn.

"Only tell me, what is your business with my sister?"

At that, Sheriston said, "I fear you will not find her in her bedchamber." He handed the card to her.

She took it. It was a calling card for a gentleman by the

name of Geoffrey Rodbourne. She frowned slightly. "I recall the name. I met this young man at the Pump Room several weeks past. But what does he have to do with Agnes?"

"Turn the card over."

She read the two brief sentences aloud. " 'Sheriston—I have taken Agnes to Gretna. You shan't stop us now.' "

Sophy felt her complexion pale. She glanced up at Sheriston. "Are you saying she has eloped with Mr. Rodbourne?"

"I can only suppose she has."

"But this is impossible. How could I have known nothing of this? When did they leave?"

"Early this morning."

"Why did you not pursue them?"

"I only learned of the elopement a half hour past. I packed my bags and hurried here to discover if perchance Agnes— Miss Chenlow—had somehow been prevented from pursuing this ridiculous course."

Edward came rushing down the stairs. "Sophy! I could not find Agnes anywhere, nor George nor Felicity. I looked in all the rooms. I even ran up to Mrs. White's chamber in the attic. All I found was a letter on Agnes's pillow."

Sophy took the missive from Edward and broke the seal quickly. She scanned the contents and with enormous surprise found that what Sheriston had told her was true. She read the letter aloud.

Dear Sophy, do not be concerned. By now you will be suspecting the truth, so I will put your mind at ease. I have eloped with Mr. Rodbourne. I love him very much. I wish I could have included you in my happiness, but from the first I knew you would object to my even seeing dear Geoffrey, so I told a great many whiskers and met him at the Pump Room, at the Orange Grove, in the shops along Pulteney Bridge, several times at Cassie Knowles's home, and a dozen other places. I am sorry for not having been open and truthful with you. I feel

*my marriage is for the best since we are so poor and
Mr. Rodbourne so very wealthy. His guardian will not
like the match either, so we are hurrying to Gretna. By
the time you read this, undoubtedly I will already be a
married woman.*

Sophy laughed, disbelieving. "She cannot know how far
Scotland is if she thinks she will be married by now."

Sheriston's expression was quite grave. "She as much as
admitted she married him for his wealth."

At that, Sophy protested. "No, not Agnes. She would never
marry for such a reason. She may not be the brightest of
young ladies, but her heart is good. I believe what she meant
to say was that she would no longer be a burden to me, but
I never wanted her to see herself as such. Oh, I blame myself.
I pinch at them all about economizing and taking care with
their clothes and shoes and trying to make the smelly fish
we receive from Mrs. Bulford taste palatable." She dropped
her head in her hands. Somehow, all the years of watching
every tuppence she spent with the eye of a kestrel became
a wave of pain so great that tears shot into her eyes. "Agnes
could bear it no longer," she said, lifting her head suddenly.
"But she is making the worst of mistakes! Sheriston, we
must stop them! She cannot marry Mr. Rodbourne, nor any
man, for such a reason!"

"Of course we shall stop them. The whole thing is utterly
absurd."

"What power do you hold over Mr. Rodbourne? Can you
prevent the marriage once we find them?"

"Yes, for I am his guardian. He cannot marry without my
consent, at least not until he has achieved his majority."

"And when will that be?" She felt panicky. What if his
birthday was tomorrow? She tried to recall just how old she
thought Mr. Rodbourne might be, but her recollection of him
was vague since she had met him only once. He seemed
very polite with a sweetness of temper not unlike Felicity's.

"Four years."

Sophy started. "Four years!" she cried. "Why, he is nearly as young as Agnes! Oh, whatever could these two children be thinking?"

"That they are in love," he said rather coldly. She met his gaze and saw his accusing stare. "I will give your sister that much, she at least was willing to go with him. A wife ought to at least be willing to follow her husband."

"How unkind of you to say that to me, Sheriston." Tears once more brimmed in her eyes. "Do you think I did not desire more than anything to follow you to the ends of the earth? Do you think for even a moment that I preferred to be here, with the weight of all this responsibility, rather than by your side?"

"Sophy," he said, reaching a hand out to her. "I am sorry. I did not mean to overset you."

"Then you have not forgiven me, have you?"

"Sophy," Edward said, moving to stand by her, his small face crumpled with concern. "Why has Lord Sherry made you cry?"

Sophy wiped her eyes. "He did not make me cry. I was having some very sad thoughts, but now they are gone and I do not mean to shed any more tears. What we must do now, however, is to climb aboard Lord Sheriston's coach and follow after your sister."

"Why?"

"Because she is to be married, and we are to attend her wedding."

Edward eyed her in a disbelieving manner.

Sophy hurried on. "Will you fetch Felicity and George for me? They are visiting next door. Mrs. Newton's cat had her kittens."

"She did?" Edward cried excitedly. "Why did you not tell me?"

"I forgot, dearest. I am sorry. I have been busy with the ledgers this morning. But do fetch your brother and sister and tell them that we are to go on a journey and that we will be leaving shortly."

When Edward left the room, Sheriston rose to his feet. "I did not want to say anything in front of your brother, but I do not think it in the least wise for you to come with me. For one thing, you know how poorly you travel."

"There is that," Sophy murmured. "But I must go. I promise you, it will be necessary once we catch Mr. Rodbourne and Agnes."

"Stay here in Bath, and be comfortable."

For a brief moment, Sophy seriously considered his suggestion. "You do not know my sister," she said at last. "She will not come home with you. Whatever deficiencies she was given in intelligence, she more than makes up for it in strength of will. She will set up a caterwaul and you will be accused of kidnapping her were you to try to force her into your carriage."

A moment more and Edward came running back into the drawing room with George and Felicity behind him. "They were just returning," he explained. "I met them on the front steps."

"What is it, Sophy?" Felicity asked. She was just fourteen and as pretty as a picture with her long blond hair caught up by a blue ribbon. Both Agnes and George were also very blond, while Sophy herself had very black, curly hair which she had inherited from her father. Her eyes, however, were the same cornflower blue as all the Chenlow children's. Felicity continued, "Edward said something about our taking a drive in a very fine carriage."

Sophy introduced both Felicity and George to Lord Sheriston, each of whom offered the viscount a polite bow. She then explained that Agnes was to be married to Lord Sheriston's young friend and that they were to attend the nuptials together.

George stepped forward. He was a powerful young man of fifteen with a physique to rival Atlas. "I knew it!" he cried. "She has eloped to Gretna. I heard her talking about it with that chap she kept meeting at the Orange Grove."

Felicity smiled. "Has she eloped, indeed! How very shocking except that Mr. Rodbourne is so very handsome, quite intelligent, and as sweet as can be. She will be very happy."

Edward piped up. "What does it mean to elope?"

Sophy sighed. "To be married . . . er . . . while traveling."

For the first time, Sheriston actually smiled, then laughed. "Yes, Edward, that is it precisely. To be married while traveling."

"When do we leave?" Felicity inquired.

"I have been attempting to persuade your sister to remain here," Sheriston said tactfully.

George, however, was awake on all suits and addressed the heart of the matter. "My lord," he began most seriously, "if you will forgive me, you do not know my sister if you think you will keep her from marrying Mr. Rodbourne. At the first sound of her shrieks, you will give in, I promise you. We ought to go, all of us, if it is your intention to prevent the elopement. Agnes will not be able to resist the pressure of her entire family!"

"I fear he is right," Felicity said, donning her most earnest face. "You will not want to be around Agnes without her family nearby to protect you."

Sheriston turned toward Sophy. "Is she addled, your sister?"

"Only when her will is crossed."

Sheriston glanced at each of them in turn and finally said, "Very well, then, if this is the consensus. I daresay the journey will require five days, perhaps six. You might each wish to pack a few clothes, but do be quick about it."

Mrs. White was suddenly in the doorway, holding a package away from her. "I have the fish, miss."

The children groaned.

"Why will not Mrs. Bulford send for you sooner?" Sophy cried, exasperated.

"She does not have much sense."

"Well, do what you will with it. As it happens, we are leaving for several days with Lord Sheriston."

"I beg yer pardon, miss?"

"Agnes is gone—eloped, actually."

"Ah, with that Mr. Rodbourne who was always in my kitchen?"

"In your kitchen! Yet you said nothing?"

"To my way of thinking," Mrs. White said, her lips set grimly, "it were a good match, for both of them, and not less so for you, miss. I kept my peace and I would suggest that you remain here and let Miss Agnes be married."

Sophy was stunned. "I fear Agnes is not fit to be any man's bride."

"Aye, that much is true, but I would that yer own burdens were not so heavy."

Sophy sighed. "And I wish that you had told me what was going forward. I cannot allow the marriage. Mr. Rodbourne is not yet eighteen and he is Sheriston's ward."

"Oh, I say, that is a bit young," Mrs. White said. "I thought he were older. Ah, well, then ye must go. However, if ye don't mind, miss, I intend to dispose of the fish. I don't think even Mrs. Newton's cat would touch it."

With that, she ambled down the hall. Sophy led her siblings up the stairs, recommending that they pack lightly. Felicity, however, was not of a similar mind. "Sophy, I have been thinking. What if by the time we reach Scotland, they are already married? Where will they go? If this does, indeed, happen, may I suggest that we journey to Aunt Gwen's house and have a wedding celebration for them, to make it right before the world? In which case, we ought to take at least one very fine gown."

Sophy tilted her head at her youngest sister. "What you say makes a great deal of sense. Very well, take one ball dress and perhaps two or three traveling gowns. I will do the same, although I must confess I am a little surprised at your foresight. I am most impressed."

Felicity smiled. "Well, I have been under your tutelage for years, but beyond that, I do listen, rather intently, to everything that is said in the Pump Room. And I recall rather distinctly Cassie Knowles saying that when her cousin eloped, they gave her a lavish ball by way of announcing that the happy couple had been wed only that morning by Special License. Of course, it was all a hum, but still, no one was the wiser!" With that she flounced in the direction of her bedchamber.

Sophy decided she had rather be prepared for the worst than not, and carefully stowed her best ball gown as well as two walking dresses in her smallest portmanteau. Within less than fifteen minutes she was descending the stairs along with Felicity and her brothers.

Sheriston saw to the the loading of the bags, which gave Sophy sufficient time to put her ledgers away. She had not budgeted for such an expense as traveling to Scotland. Even if Sheriston paid the posting bills, she would still be obligated to pay for the costs of staying the night at an inn as well as feeding herself and her three half-siblings.

There was only one thing she could do. She had an emergency fund laid by these past five years which, if she was very careful and the meals were restricted to the most basic fare, would permit them to travel for five, even six days, including the return trip to Bath. She gathered up the coins and pound notes and stowed them carefully into the purse at the bottom of her reticule. After saying good-bye to Mrs. White, she was ready to leave.

When she approached the coach, she saw that George, Felicity, and Edward were already situated within. One of the grooms was presently checking the wheeler's front hooves. Sophy realized she was not at all anxious to be climbing aboard the vehicle and remained, therefore, standing on the pavement with Sheriston beside her.

"I like Mr. Rodbourne," Edward said, leaning out the open doorway. "He helped me fly a kite once. Felicity likes him, too, but she just told me you do not want Agnes to marry him."

Sophy smiled at him. "Actually, I do not know whether I wish for her to marry Mr. Rodbourne or not, since I am not at all acquainted with him. We are following after them because I do not wish Agnes to marry Mr. Rodbourne—er, *while traveling*. My intention is to bring her home so that we might plan her wedding together, as a family."

Edward seemed satisfied with this explanation.

Sheriston scanned the interior of the coach. "I do not know if this is at all wise," he murmured. "The quarters will be cramped and we shall be traveling the greater part of the night."

For a moment, Sophy feared that Sheriston would change his mind and not allow the family to travel together. She quaked at the thought of leaving any of the children behind, for which of them would not be severely disappointed?

Edward, in his innocence, called out, "But you have a very fine coach, m'lord. We shall deal famously, see if we do not! Besides, I hardly take up any room at all!"

Sheriston chuckled. "I can see that you are determined to go, all of you. Very well, but I warn you, I shall bear no complaints."

The children, one and all, proclaimed that they would be cheerful and agreeable the entire journey.

"It is Sophy you must worry about," Edward added ingenuously. "She is the one who casts up her accounts when she travels."

"Edward!" Sophy cried.

"Well, it's true," he muttered, scowling a little and shrinking against Felicity, beside whom he was sitting.

"Even if it is true," Sheriston said kindly. "I believe you owe your sister an apology."

"I am sorry, Sophy, but I remember the day. It was storming fiercely, and—"

"Edward, that will do," Sophy said, laughing. "Besides, Lord Sheriston already knows of my difficulty."

Sheriston, who was standing very near her, said, "Are you certain you will manage?"

Sophy glanced at the coach, which suddenly rocked ominously as the coachman descended to assist the groom in examining the horse's hooves.

"I will manage," she stated, her stomach already queasy at the mere sight of the rocking coach.

She straightened her shoulders, gathered her courage, and took up her place forward with Felicity and Edward.

Two

Sheriston spoke with the coachman briefly before taking up his place beside George. A moment more and the coach was bowling out of Laura Place.

George sat directly opposite Sophy, which placed Lord Sheriston as far from her as the narrow confines of the traveling coach would allow. She was glad of it, for even as it was, she could scarcely keep her gaze from his face, for he was unutterably handsome. His dark-brown hair was cropped quite attractively *à la Brutus,* and he was as athletically fit as she remembered him. He was, after all, an excellent horseman besides excelling in the usual manly sports of fencing, boxing, shooting, riding, hunting and even swimming, the latter of which he was a particularly strong advocate. He was, in every respect, an acknowledged Corinthian.

More than once, she turned to look out the window not so much to enjoy the delights of the scenery as the coach moved out of Bath, but because she simply could not keep from staring at Sheriston otherwise. He was a ghost from her past, one she had loved deeply and whom she had never forgotten in all these years. How strange that Fate had brought him to her door once more, but to what purpose? To torment her? To show her all she had lost during the past nine years?

The coach stopped frequently, so that Sheriston could inquire after the eloping pair. Fortunately, Geoffrey and Agnes were proving rather easy to follow, for it would seem the pair had decided to quarrel their way to Gretna.

George crossed his arms over his chest. "I am not surprised. Agnes has the temper of a Fury. I only wonder that he has not turned the coach around and taken her home!"

To this remark, Sheriston merely lifted a brow, but civilly reserved his comments.

Sophy thought Agnes's conduct all of a piece. She was an impulsive, willful child of sixteen, as unfit to take on the responsibilities of hearth and home as a girl half her age! Whatever had she been thinking to elope with Mr. Rodbourne?

She did not give herself to such useless cogitations for very long, however. With each creeping mile, the queasiness in her stomach took strong hold of her until every unexpected lurch of the coach forced her to close her eyes and will the nausea away.

"Sophy, are you going to cast up your accounts?" Edward asked.

"No, dearest," she assured him, taking his hand and patting it firmly.

"But your face is very white and you keep sighing."

"I am only a little sick, but as soon as we stop for the night I shall be well enough. You'll see."

Felicity intervened. "Edward, why do we not play cards? You have been wanting me to teach you how to play casino and now would be an excellent time, I think."

Edward admitted his enthusiasm to the idea and before long, Felicity had him fully engaged in the basic concepts of the game. Sophy cast her a grateful smile. Felicity nodded sympathetically and attended kindly to her brother.

Sophy glanced now and then out the window, occasionally listened to George's conversation with Sheriston, and responded appropriately when Edward proclaimed to her that he had just won another hand. Another hour passed, and Edward grew fatigued. He turned to her and begged to be allowed to put his head on her lap. Despite her misery, she acquiesced, gently stroking his hair and singing softly to him. Before long, he was asleep.

More than once during this time, Sheriston met her gaze and smiled warmly upon her. When they stopped to dine in Tewkesbury, he held her back as the children entered the inn. "You have been a good mother to them," he said. "You should be very proud. They are one and all delightfully well-behaved and happy children."

"Save for Agnes's jaunt to Gretna Green," she said ruefully.

"Well, there is that," he said, laughing. "I can only presume you have had the raising of your siblings?"

"I have," she said.

"Edward certainly seems utterly devoted to you."

"Dear Edward," she said, smiling.

"But come, do you feel like partaking of any food at all?"

"A little toast and tea, thank you, but nothing more, though I daresay the children are starved."

"The fare at this inn is some of the finest. They will not remain hungry for long."

She should have warned him of her restricted budget, but she felt so poorly she did not have the strength to address the subject with him.

The meal was, indeed, quite enjoyable, and by the time George had finished his last bite of roast beef, all the while proclaiming that he had not had so famous a meal in ages, Sophy was feeling quite comfortable. She was always amazed at how quickly the carriage sickness passed once she was seated in a chair that did not move about.

Before she left the parlor, she held Sheriston back. "Will you please let me know my portion of the bill?" she asked quietly. "I wish to discharge it at once." She opened her reticule and began searching for her purse.

"On no account," he stated firmly. "I am perfectly able to pay for your family's meals during this journey. Otherwise I would have said something at the outset."

She found her purse and opened it. "Do not be nonsensical," she said. "I had no intention of foisting the entire cost of the journey on your shoulders."

He looked down at her small purse and overlaid her hand and the purse with his own. "Please allow me to do this for you, Sophy. I am not unaware that you are presently sporting the same pelisse you wore nine years ago. You have sacrificed for them all, have you not?"

"Yes," she whispered. She looked into his kind brown eyes, and felt lost for a very long moment. She had not expected this from him, so much understanding and concern. She realized she ought to have felt mortified, yet she did not.

"Come. The bill is already settled."

"Very well. I will permit you this one kindness. However, in future . . ."

"Yes, yes. Well, the future will see to itself. For now, let us see if we can catch up with our miscreants."

When he offered his arm, she took it gratefully, allowing him to escort her to the coach. She had forgotten how pleasant it was to walk beside him with her arm wrapped about his. Memories of former times flooded her mind, of walking in Hyde Park beside him, of accompanying him to the Opera, of taking a turn about Carlton House exclusively in his company.

She might have continued in such happy reminiscences, but the first sight to greet her eyes upon leaving the inn was that of the coach rocking once more as the coachman clambered briskly up to his seat. In that moment, her stomach simply flipped over.

Once on the road, her symptoms returned in full force, worse than before. Sheriston, seeing her distress, insisted upon changing places with her since the forward seat might be adding to her queasiness. She accepted his sacrifice gratefully and found that a little of her sickness abated, but not sufficiently for her to feel at all well.

The hours advanced. The coach stopped and started at every other village in order that Sheriston might inquire after

Agnes and Mr. Rodbourne. The summer sun set in the west and a full moon rose to set the beautiful Shropshire landscape in a glow. One by one the children fell asleep. Sheriston had since taken up a place between Edward and Felicity, so that Edward slept with his coat as a pillow on the viscount's lap, and Felicity fell into her slumbers against his strong shoulder.

George snored quietly against the squabs, his mouth agape. The hours advanced a little more.

"I wonder what time it is?" Sophy asked quietly. She was feeling violently ill. Her head had begun to ache, and only with great difficulty was she keeping her stomach at all settled.

Sheriston kept his deep-timbred voice low as he responded, "At the last village, it was just a little past midnight."

"How far away from Agnes and Mr. Rodbourne were we at that time, do you suppose?"

"Three hours."

"I expect they will travel through."

"I fear it is so. What would you have me do?" he asked. "We can stop at the next inn and sleep for a few hours or we can continue on."

Sophy did not want to stop but she feared for her own health in this moment. If she did not allow her equilibrium to right itself, by experience she knew her headache would worsen and she would no longer be able to keep from, as Edward liked to say, *casting up her accounts*. For these reasons, she said, "I would that I were able to go on. But I must rest for a time. I shall be useless otherwise."

"I had hoped we would catch them by now," he mused.

"I know. This is very bad." Tears started to her eyes and she gently dabbed at them with her kerchief.

"Sophy," he called to her on a whisper. "Please do not fret. If they must marry, then they will marry. I have seen enough today in these children here to convince me that Geoffrey, with all his rather glaring flaws, will benefit very much from marrying your sister."

Sophy met his understanding gaze, aware in this moment

why she had loved Sheriston so much—he had one of the kindest hearts she had ever encountered. "Thank you for saying as much." His gaze held and it seemed, in that moment, that the years peeled away and they were not strangers of nine years, but once more a gentleman and lady deeply in love. She experienced a sudden, powerful desire to nestle herself in his arms and surrender to at least a thousand kisses.

A smile and a chuckle parted his lips. He shook his head ruefully. "You were always able to do that to me, you know."

"Do what?" she ventured, also smiling.

"Slay me with that particular expression of yours. Do you know how your eyes are glittering?"

"I was about to say the same thing of you."

He searched her gaze for a moment, his features sobering. He glanced away from her, and she had the strongest impression he was remembering, or perhaps forcing himself to remember, why she had broken off the betrothal. Indeed, how could he not be reminded, when two of the reasons were sprawled over his person and sound asleep?

She also looked out the window, her heart taking on a leaden quality that seemed somehow perfectly matched to the persistent nausea she was experiencing.

A half hour later, the coach drew before a coaching inn somewhere in the middle of Shropshire. Sophy breathed a sigh of relief so profound that Sheriston glanced sharply at her.

"Allow me to make all the arrangements," he said. "I promise you, we shall not go another mile if I can possibly help it."

"Thank you," she murmured.

He awoke Felicity gently, after which he placed Edward in her arms.

"Have we found them?" Felicity asked, blinking her eyes at Sophy.

"No. We are resting here for the night."

"Oh," she murmured. "Then—?"

"I fear there must be a marriage now."

"You must be disappointed," Felicity said.

"A little. My only wish is that Agnes find happiness in her marriage."

After a few minutes, Sheriston returned and shook George's shoulder. He awoke with a loud snort. "I say, have we caught them at last?" he asked loudly.

"No. We are staying the night here. Be a good fellow and carry Edward, will you?"

At that, George yawned and moved to the edge of his seat. "Felicity, I'll jump down and you can hand him to me."

Brother and sister soon had Edward out the door and slung over George's powerful shoulder. Felicity followed behind.

Sheriston remained to extend his hand to Sophy. "Feeling better yet?" he inquired.

She shook her head. "Not yet, but presently, I'm sure."

"You are nearly as pale as a sheet."

She smiled archly. "Thank you for saying as much." She was, however, feeling quite dizzy. She took his hand and allowed him to support her as she descended the steps. "Oh, Sheriston, I . . . I am so dizzy." The next moment, she was falling forward.

He caught her easily and lifted her into his arms. She would have protested, but she knew quite well that for the moment she was entirely unable to stand, certainly not to walk. She leaned against his shoulder and took very deep breaths.

"Poor Sophy," Felicity said, when Sheriston brought her into the foyer.

Sheriston carried her to a chair into which she sank gratefully. The landlord, in his nightcap and robe, poured her a small glass of brandy. "Drink this, my lady. Ye'll feel better in a trice."

She took the glass, meaning to correct him, but Sheriston performed the office. "The lady is not my wife," he said in a low voice. "We are in search of my ward and her sister."

The landlord lifted a hand and crackled with laughter. "Say no more. They were here a few hours past, brangling like cat and dog. Eloping, were they?"

"I fear so. But I would appreciate your discretion, my good man."

"I will be as silent as the grave," he responded in a hushed voice.

The brandy eased through Sophy's veins and the solidity of the chair beneath her served to settle her stomach in wonderfully quick succession. Within fifteen minutes, she was able to stand without feeling the least dizzy.

When the landlord offered to guide them upstairs, Sheriston gestured for Felicity and George to see Edward to his bed. "I will bring Sophy up in just a few minutes, when she is feeling better."

Her siblings had just disappeared up the stairs when Sheriston drew very close to her and whispered, "Do you wish me to carry you to your room? I should be happy to do so."

Sophy would have answered him, but she made the mistake of looking into his eyes. She was bereft of words suddenly. There was such a crooked smile on his lips that she was put forcibly in mind of a truly wonderful memory. She recalled most vividly a time when he had looked at her in much the same manner the summer of their betrothal so many years past. She and her mother had been guests in his father's home. At the time, her younger half-siblings had been staying with Aunt Gwen Yatesbury in Cumbria. Sheriston had been eager to be alone with her and she had been happy to oblige him.

She had allowed him to escort her into the home wood, where he stopped her scarcely a fraction of a mile down the path but sufficiently out of view of the party enjoying a picnic on the lawn. He had smiled crookedly upon her and afterward quickly enveloped her in his arms, his purpose made quite evident. How passionately he had kissed her, so deeply, that she had become utterly mesmerized. Time dissipated and in its stead was a wonderland of sensation, desire, and magic. She had slipped her arms about his neck and he had dragged her tightly against him, so that she felt joined to him. His voice had been husky. "I would that the wedding were today," he had whispered. "How I long to have you to myself."

"You have me to yourself, right now."

He had laughed against her lips. "That is not what I meant," he had said scandalously.

She had looked at him then, seeing her future with him so clearly. Her heart had expanded to at least twice its size. "I do love you, Sheriston. You cannot imagine how very much!"

"If you love me even a tithe of how much I adore you, then I can comprehend your feelings in this moment."

She blinked, and the taproom returned sharply into view once more. Sheriston was leaning toward her. "Sophy," he whispered. She realized he was intending to kiss her.

"Oh," she murmured softly, as she lifted a hand to his chest. "No, you mustn't. I mean, Sheriston, I do not want you to think I was inviting your attentions."

"But the way you looked at me just now," he said, covering the hand on his chest with his own.

"I know how it must have seemed, but I was remembering, you see." She hoped he would not press her for the details.

A smile touched his lips. *"What* were you remembering?"

Sophy rolled her eyes slightly. "Do not ask me," she countered.

"I can guess at it," he said softly. "That day in the woods."

She nodded. "It was such a magical time."

"My father was so angry."

She chuckled. "Indeed he was, with good reason. We had been gone an hour. An hour!"

"It seemed but a handful of minutes."

"How well I know. I could have stayed there forever."

What next he would have said, she did not know, for Felicity appeared at the top of the stairs. "Sophy. Edward has awakened and is crying. George thinks he had a bad dream. Will you come?"

"Of course," she answered readily.

She started to move past Sheriston, but he caught her arm gently. "Surely Felicity can tend to him. Stay with me for a while."

She felt tense suddenly, old beasts rearing their heads. "He is very young and in a strange place. He will have great need of me in this moment. Pray, let me comfort him until he is once more asleep, and if you wish it, I'll return."

His eyes narrowed slightly, but he nodded in acquiescence.

She moved swiftly past him and began mounting the stairs. When she had progressed halfway up the steps, he called to her, "Sophy. Never mind. We can speak on the morrow. You are very tired, and I daresay you are wishing for your bed."

At these words, and particularly because of the wary light in his eye, she turned toward him fully. "I am not so fatigued that I cannot return to you. I desire it more than anything."

He did not answer for a moment. Finally, he drew a deep breath, "The moment has passed, *long* passed. Anything more, tonight, would be foolishness."

"I see," she murmured. So, this was how it was to be? He would not even permit her to comfort Edward without believing she was once more choosing her family over him? Was there to be no compromise in him, even after so many years? "Of course you are right. You were always right about everything!" she retorted unreasonably.

"You needn't come the crab!" he cried. "I am not the one always called away by obligations belonging to others."

"You never could see from my viewpoint. But never mind! It is clear to me than any discussion is useless."

She turned and headed back up the stairs.

"Sophy!" he called after her. "I did not mean—"

But she was beyond desiring to hear anything more he might wish to say to her. By the time she reached the end of the hall where Felicity awaited her, she found it necessary to swipe at her cheeks. Odd tears had somehow escaped her eyes, even though sadness was not at all what she was feeling at the moment.

Felicity, whose heart was quite tender, watched her carefully. "Are you all right?"

"Yes, of course. Please, pay no heed to me just now."

"You still love him," she stated gently.

Sophy's hand was on the knob as she nodded in quick succession, a lump forming in her throat. "I do, very much, but he was incapable of understanding my devotion to mother, to you and your brothers and your sister."

"Perhaps you have been too devoted," she suggested softly.

Sophy released the handle and snapped her gaze back to Felicity. "Whatever do you mean?"

"I have often thought that you sacrificed a great deal too much for us, particularly when Aunt Gwen has offered to care for us, at least for the summers. And now you have grown into a spinster."

Sophy was shocked by the whole of Felicity's remark, but mostly by the latter. "I am no such thing," she cried.

Felicity lifted a brow. "You are seven-and-twenty and unwed. How else would you define 'spinster'?"

Sophy's mouth dropped open. Where had so many years gone that she was suddenly closer to thirty than twenty? Good heavens! Felicity was right. She had grown into a confirmed ape-leader without being even remotely aware of it.

When she heard Edward call her name, she bade Felicity seek her bed and quickly entered the bedchamber, happy to be diverted from her present distress.

She sang to Edward for a time, lulling him back to sleep in the bed he shared with George, who was already fast asleep and snoring contentedly.

She shared a bed with Felicity, who was also sound asleep by the time Sophy changed her clothes and climbed between the sheets. She ought to have fallen asleep immediately, as tired as she was, but the previous exchange with Sheriston had served to sharpen her nerves. His accusations rang loudly in her head for a very long time. She was deeply frustrated that after all these years, he had not changed even a whit in his attitude toward her responsibilities.

Worse, however, was Felicity's accusation that she was too devoted to her half-siblings. What nonsense was this? Of course it was true that their aunt, presently residing in Grasmere, had offered numerous times to help share in the care of the Chenlow children, but Aunt Gwendolyn was quite old, nearly sixty by now, besides being infirm. Though she was not confined to a Bath chair, she was known to suffer a rheumatic complaint and walked with a cane. How could such a lady have cared for Edward, much less all four children?

No, she had done the right thing all these years. She had kept the children together, she had given Edward a deep sense of security from the time of his birth, and even if she had become that most wretched of creatures—a spinster!— she could at least be at ease in her mind that she had done what was right and true and good. Only, why did she not feel so content as she ought to with such ruminations?

On the following morning, Sheriston sat alone in the dining parlor awaiting Sophy and her siblings. He had reviewed at least a hundred times the latter part of his conversation with Sophy last night and had concluded that he could not regret speaking the truth to her. She had always set her obligations to her sisters and brothers above her obligations to him and so she always would. She was clearly an unselfish individual, but she had no sense of what respect was owed to a husband.

He had observed this flaw in any number of women, even his own mother. His father had had several mistresses and had lived more often than not apart from his wife, and all because his mother had placed the care of her eight children above her duty to her husband. He thought it terribly unfortunate that Sophy was so completely unaware of how wrong she was.

He ought to have felt comfortable in such musings. However, only a rather miserable despondency seemed to have resulted from his numerous self-congratulations. Though he was clearly right in how he viewed the situation, in the end he was bereft of that which he desired most—to hold Sophy Deverill in his arms.

He might have continued in his unhappiness, had not Edward come racing down the stairs in that moment. "Lord Sherry!" he called out.

Sheriston arose from his chair and ventured into the hallway adjacent to the parlor. "Here, young man!" he returned, catching sight of Edward on the bottom step.

Edward was a beautiful child, something from a Renaissance painting. His light-brown hair, tinged with a little red, was layered in natural curls over his head. His complexion was angelically pale and his large blue eyes, so reminiscent of Sophy's, held a great deal of natural inquisitiveness.

"Sophy said I might come down but that I was to ask you if this was all right."

"Of course it is. Come in. You may begin your breakfast, if you wish for it."

"Do I!" he cried enthusiastically. He ran to the sideboard and examined the victuals filling each of several bowls. "Eggs, kippers, potatos, bacon, toast, even strawberry jam!"

"You do not have these things very often at home?"

"Porridge every morning, but I do not mean to complain."

"Of course not." Sheriston handed him a plate and offered to fill it for him. Edward agreed heartily. When the plate grew heavier and heavier, and the food piled higher and higher, Sheriston chuckled and asked, "And you are certain you do not suffer with carriage sickness as your sister does?"

"Not a bit!" was his enthusiastic answer.

"Very well, Master Edward. You may now take your plate to the table."

George arrived at the entrance to the parlor, and immediately his eyes opened wide. "A real breakfast," he cried, then colored up. "That is, how do you go on this morning, Lord Sheriston? Did you sleep well?"

"Yes, thank you. Do take a plate and help yourself." When George dabbed out minuscule portions and ventured to the table, Sheriston said, "The landlord will be refilling all the bowls shortly, so I hope you do not mean to offend his cook by eating so sparingly. I have it on good authority, she is quite proud of her culinary skills."

George, who turned to eye the bowls greedily, said, "Well, I would not offend her for the world."

"Then I suggest you fill your plate at least as full as Edward's."

When George caught sight of Edward's stuffed cheeks and still laden plate, he most properly revisited the sideboard.

Sheriston smiled to himself. His own plate was marginally full. He had never fancied a large breakfast and was content with black coffee, an egg or two, and a slice of toast. He had just poured himself a second cup of coffee when Felicity arrived on the threshold, her cheeks rather pink. At the very same moment, Sheriston heard Sophy's elevated voice coming from the taproom.

He glanced at Felicity. "What is it? What is going forward?"

Felicity bit her lip. "I fear Sophy is arguing with the landlord about the bill."

"Good God," he murmured, laughing as he rose to his feet. "Please, enjoy your breakfast. I shall see to your sister."

"Thank you," she said, obviously embarrassed.

When he moved into the hall, he immediately caught sight of his former betrothed haggling with the landlord over the bill. Sheriston had not only already discharged the bill but had told the landlord not to allow Miss Deverill even to see it. Apparently, she had been more persuasive than he could have wished for.

He moved down the hall swiftly, into the foyer, and fairly plucked the bill from Sophy's hands. When she went to reach for it, he held it aloft. Being much taller than she, it was impossible for her to retrieve it from him. He dismissed the landlord, who wore a slightly harrassed expression. "Never fear," he said to that good fellow. "I shall settle the matter myself with Miss Deverill."

"Very good, m'lord," the man said.

"Oh, and would you see to refilling the bowls in the parlor. We have a large family with several powerful appetites."

"Yes, indeed, sir, I was about to attend to it when miss—er, asked to see the bill."

When the landlord disappeared into the parlor, and Sheriston was alone with Sophy, he could see that she was positively thunderous. He wisely gave her back the bill.

"Thank you," she stated hotly. "I mean to discharge our portion of it. I certainly never expected you to pay for our lodgings."

"Of course not," he said.

She seemed slightly taken aback that he had acquiesced so readily. She waved the bill at him. "These rates are exorbitant, and I certainly mean to argue the point with the landlord."

He grimaced slightly. "I fear it will be of little use to do so because I have already settled the bill. You will need to pay me instead."

"I see. Well, I suppose I shall have to do just that, only I am certain I could have lowered the cost of our rooms. Really, Sheriston, you should have let me settle the matter on my own."

"Why do you not pay me what you think is fair, and I shall absorb the rest? Indeed, if I thought you would allow it, I should offer to pay for your lodgings for last night and for the rest of the journey."

"Of course I cannot allow it."

"Why not?" he pressed her. "We are old friends, I am as rich as Croesus, and you are not."

"That is a bit of plain-speaking!"

"And you are far too proud, Sophy. Will you not allow anyone to help you? Good God, if you mean to continue in this fashion, I shall soon feel I ought to demand you pay half the tolls as well as half the posting fees."

He saw her lip quiver and felt chagrined. "Sophy, I am sorry. I did not mean to make you cry."

"Will you not at least allow me a little of my pride?"

He stared at her, at the worry in her beautiful face. "I wish instead that you would allow me to help you a little on this journey. I can stand the blunt. After all, if my ward had not behaved in an entirely improper manner, courting Agnes when he should not have, you would not be in this predicament in the first place. I have not always known how to guide Geoffrey. If there is a fault, let it be laid at my door. Besides, if you will not consider yourself in this situation, then at least consider Felicity's feelings. She was completely mortified by your haggling with the landlord over a few shillings."

Her expression became thoughtful. "Was she, indeed? I never meant to embarrass her or you. Sheriston, you cannot know how much I dislike being beholden to you in this manner."

"Is it because of last night?"

"No . . . yes . . . oh, I do not know. Perhaps a little. We simply see things so very differently."

"Yes, we do," he agreed, "which is why we were perhaps beyond fortunate not to have married. I daresay neither of us would have been very happy."

"Of course you are right," she said. She met his gaze at that and he saw the question in her eyes.

Sheriston became lost for a long moment in the depths of her blue eyes. He had forgotten what a beauty she was. Her black hair had the richest texture, always full of curls. He loved to touch it and for some reason was only barely able to restrain himself even now.

Was he right that they were fortunate not have married? He truly did not know, not when this powerful feeling had begun growing in his chest from the moment he stood on the threshold of her drawing room.

"Will you then permit me to discharge the costs of this journey? Please, Sophy. I do feel responsible in this situation because of Geoffrey's conduct."

Sophy nodded. "Very well."

"Come," he said at last. "I know you will not want a very large meal, but the bread is excellent and the coffee among the best."

"I should like that."

He gestured in the direction of the parlor, and she walked before him. When she reached the doorway, she called out, "Edward! Good heavens! What is that all over your mouth?"

Sheriston drew up beside Sophy and laughed outright. Since Edward's mouth was full, he answered for him. "I believe it is strawberry jam."

Three

When Sophy tried to take up one of the forward seats, Sheriston would have none of it.

"I observed you carefully last night, and you did much better when we exchanged seats. Besides, Felicity and I mean to play several rounds of casino this morning so the cards would be easier to manage between us, I think."

Sophy let herself be persuaded. She had partaken of a cup of coffee and a thin slice of bread with a little of the jam Edward had so thoroughly enjoyed. However, the sight of the coach was enough to set her stomach rocking anew, as though she had only a few minutes earlier descended the coach, instead of having spent the entire night in a comfortable bed.

The remainder of the morning was whiled away in a convivial manner. Sheriston played at cards for hours with all three children, and through the whole of it told a great number of riddles, to which George and Felicity had to guess at the solutions. Many of their guesses were so ridiculous as to set the entire party laughing boisterously. Even Sophy found she was able to giggle on occasion, forgetting for brief moments her own suffering.

Stopping for nuncheon at an inn on the border of Shropshire and Cheshire, Sheriston discovered that the errant couple had spent the night there, in separate rooms, apparently arguing in a manner that seemed more sibling-like in nature than the tiffs of a pair intent on the joys of matrimony. He also discovered, much to his bemusement, that a third person had apparently joined the wedding party, an older woman who spent the night with Agnes in her room, evidently as a chaperon.

If this was an elopement, it was a very odd one.

When he mentioned the circumstance to Sophy, she shook her head in bewilderment. "Why would Agnes have hired a companion to see her to Gretna Green?"

"I haven't the smallest notion. However, I am now given some hope that the marriage might be averted."

"Do you think so?" she asked hopefully.

"What scandal can there be, if the couple slept in separate rooms while a chaperon shared Miss Chenlow's bed?"

"None at all," Sophy remarked.

After a very fine chicken was enjoyed, along with potatoes, broccoli, apple pie, and lemonade, Sophy once more took up her seat. For herself, she had limited her meal to a cup of tea and a few bites of potato. On such a restricted diet, she was becoming quickly famished and asked Sheriston if it would be possible that evening to end the journey earlier in order that she might have a meal before bed. "For I find I am beginning to feel faint."

"Of course," he said. "I was going to suggest the very thing since you are looking rather drawn and pale, a quite unusual aspect for you."

She thanked him, to which he proferred a kind, "You are most welcome," then took up the cribbage board intending to teach Edward how to play.

Sophy watched him and found herself withholding a very deep sigh. They had scarcely been in company more than a day and she had already quarreled with him. Of course, Sheriston had been impossible last night. She would have returned to him, most happily, but he would not allow her even a few minutes to comfort Edward. Instead, he saw her devotion to her family as a threat, something she simply could not comprehend.

But was it possible that Felicity was right? Was she *too devoted* to her family? She simply did not know.

On the other hand, there was something she knew so well that she could never be mistaken in it—she was still very much in love with Sheriston. Perhaps this was why she had dwindled into—oh, dear!—a spinster!

She could only smile ruefully to herself, for so she had. Sophy Deverill—a spinster! Never in a hundred years would she have believed she would be the age she was and yet unmarried and childless. Not that she had lacked other offers since her betrothal to Sheriston, not by half. Her life with her half sisters and brothers in Laura Place, though relatively impoverished, was not without a great deal of societal connection and involvement. She attended the assemblies quite frequently during the Bath Season, accompanied the children almost daily to the Pump Room merely for the diversion of meeting friends and exchanging gossip, and even took Agnes and Felicity to the Royal Theatre on occasion.

She had therefore been courted by several eligible gentlemen, three of whom had actually begged for her hand in marriage. Unfortunately, her heart had never been touched by these men, something she now felt certain had a great deal to do with the man presently moving his pegs on the cribbage board.

She had but to look at Sheriston and her heart fairly danced. His dark-brown hair was as yet untouched by even the slightest show of silver, his features seemed to have matured and, in the way of men, he appeared to even greater advantage because of it. If only he had been able to accept her duties to her family.

As the afternoon progressed, the three Chenlow children fell into a doze. This time, Sophy held Edward cradled in her arms with his legs sprawled on George's lap. George was leaning his head against the soft interior of the coach wall and snoring lightly, as was his habit. Sheriston had had the foresight to purchase a feather pillow from the inn before departing so that Felicity was fast in her slumbers on the pillow, which was settled on his lap.

With the children asleep, Sophy glanced at Sheriston and realized that she could hardly escape conversing with him. She was about to ask after his mother, when he inquired if she was happy residing in Bath.

Sophy told him of their life in the famous city, of George's gift for mathematics and how a local cleric, residing not far outside Bath, had been guiding his studies all these years and would very soon take on Edward as well. "I, of course, have served as governess to both Agnes and Felicity."

"You have suffered," he said quietly.

She shook her head. "I beg you will not think anything of the kind," she responded, keeping her voice low. "From every quarter I have experienced exceeding generosity. Even our house in Laura Place is let to us at an extraordinarily low rate by a gentlemen of a philanthropic turn who had once known, and I believe loved, my mother. Mrs. Bulford, as you already know, provides us with fish several times a week—"

"But not always of the freshest variety."

Sophy chuckled, trying not to think overly much on just how Mrs. Bulford's fish tended to smell. She was queasy enough as it was. "I fear she has so little sense that more often than not she sends for Mrs. White a day later than she should. I must say, however, that if this is the very worst we must endure then we are beyond fortunate, indeed. Having lived in Bath for so many years now, and having enjoyed a regular attendance at the Pump Room, I have witnessed every manner of ailment possible, from the very young to the very old. The sick arrive from all parts of the kingdom, even from the Continent, seeking Bath's healing waters. So, truly, I do not repine, nor will I allow you to pity us."

"You do seem very happy," he said.

"I am, and part of that happiness comes from believing that I have done what is right. Should I have preferred immeasurably to have married you and left my mother and her children to their own devices? A thousand times, yes. However, as I said before, Mr. Chenlow was a cruel individual."

Sheriston watched her closely, and a certain suspicion suddenly dawned in his mind. "Did he ever strike you?" he asked.

"Only once. I set up such a fierce caterwaul that he never dared do so again. But the others were not so fortunate, particularly when I was not in the house."

"Good God."

"Indeed."

"Was your mother spared?"

She shook her head. She felt tears dart to her eyes. She had never spoken of this before and found the experience unsettling.

"Sophy, I wish you had told me of this before."

"At the time, I couldn't speak of it. It was too horrible, too unbelievable. I was eighteen and he was my stepfather, a very charming man, I might add. Who would have credited such reports had I spoken of the true nature of his conduct? My mother, unfortunately, did not have the strength of will to set herself against him."

"I see," he said. This threw an entirely new light on the circumstance of Sophy's request that their betrothal be extended a year. "You were truly protecting them all."

"I was."

"You could have told me. I wish more than anything you had."

"I would have, in time, I am certain of it. I might even eventually have asked for your assistance."

"I would have given it gladly. Sophy, why must you bear everything by yourself?"

A lump formed so swiftly in her throat that she did not at first answer him. She was not even certain she knew what to say. "I do not know," she responded, never having considered the matter before. "I was ten when my father died. He was an excellent man and I loved him dearly. Mother was inconsolable. Within a year, however, she had remarried Mr. Chenlow and later Agnes was born. I was the oldest and, particularly since my mother was never a very strong woman, the burdens of the family seemed to fall on my shoulders. I bore them as best I could. I truly never gave it a second thought. At the same time, there was never anyone else I could turn to. Even my mother's sister, Aunt Gwen, has lived all these years in Cumberland, so she was not easily accessible."

"You are still bearing your family's burdens," he said.

"Yes."

At that moment, George snorted loudly and woke himself up. "I say," he whispered. "I was dreaming about falling into a lake but I couldn't swim. Only I *can* swim. It was very odd, very frightening." He shuddered.

Since a few moments later the coach drew into the courtyard of another posting inn and all three children awakened, the conversation was let drop. Sheriston immediately went into the taproom to inquire after Agnes and Geoffrey and a possible chaperon in attendance. He returned with the same news. It would seem Geoffrey had most sensibly hired a companion for his bride-to-be and they were gaining on them, but not so swiftly as Sheriston would have liked. "Particularly if we are to stop for the night at an early hour."

Sophy considered this. "Then we should press on until we overtake them."

Sheriston was silent apace. "On no account," he said at last. "I promised you a meal this evening, and so you shall have one. Besides, it would seem Geoffrey has shown a great deal of excellent sense in hiring a companion for your sister. My mind is considerably at ease."

At eight o'clock that evening, in the middle of the county of Lancashire near the coast, the coach drew into the yard of the day's final destination. Sheriston made arrangements first before allowing the family to descend the carriage and returned with the happy news that a parlor was being prepared for them even now and that three bedchambers were available.

Everyone breathed a sigh of relief, Sophy not less so. Traveling fatigue had taken its toll on everyone, and the unmovable cobbles of the inn yard appeared beyond inviting.

Sophy was the last to leave the confines of the coach, but as before, Sheriston was quickly beside her. Only this time he did not wait for her to stumble but simply picked her up in his arms once more.

She was infinitely grateful. "I am so dizzy."

"You will feel better once you have eaten," he said, carrying her across the threshold and asking the landlord for a snifter of brandy for Miss Deverill.

"At once, m'lord," he said, bowing briskly and serving up the aged wine with dispatch.

Sheriston carried her to a chair in the parlor, but instead of settling her in the chair, he sat down, cradling her on his lap.

Sophy was scarcely aware that he had done so. From a distance she could hear his voice rippling toward her like a soft, bubbling brook, murmuring encouragements. "Drink this," she heard him say. She felt the pressure of a smooth glass against her lips. She parted her lips and a moment later her mouth filled with a fiery liquid which she swallowed uneasily, wincing as she did so.

The brandy burned all the way down her throat, but not in a bad way.

"A little more," he said.

She took another sip and very soon began to feel a wonderful warmth in her veins. She settled more deeply into the crook of his arm, her eyes closed. She didn't want to move. Her stomach wasn't nearly so queasy, and the persistent ache in her head was growing dull. She found herself drifting off again.

"Sophy!" Sheriston called sharply to her.

She opened her eyes for a brief second, then closed them again. His voice, however, had awakened her sufficiently to sip more of the brandy. After a time she was able to ease her eyes open. Looking up at him, she smiled. "I have been a ridiculous amount of trouble on this journey, haven't I?"

"Yes, you have," he retorted, also smiling.

She chuckled. "Why, how ungentlemanly of you." She reached up and touched his cheek with her hand. "You are very handsome, you know. I have missed you ever so much."

He cleared his throat. "The children are worried sick about you in this moment."

Sophy realized that George, Felicity, and Edward were in the same room. She sat up slowly. "I—I am not at all myself," she said. She felt a blush creeping up her cheeks. She pressed a hand to her forehead and stared at the three faces watching her. They were blurred together.

"Sophy!" young Edward cried. "Are you going to die like Mama?"

She blinked several times and his face came into focus. "No, darling," she cried. "I am merely fatigued from the traveling sickness and I desperately need to eat something."

Sheriston intervened. "Felicity, will you please have the landlord bring in a little bread for your sister."

Felicity hurried away.

Sophy leaned against Sheriston once more, his arm still surrounding her about the waist. She was conscious suddenly of the fact that she was sitting on his lap and that he was holding her very close, closer than he needed to. "I think I can take the snifter in my own hands now," she said.

With great care she took it from him. Her hands trembled only a little as she lifted the glass to her lips and took another sip. She was feeling better, but what was it she had said to him? Oh, yes, that he was quite handsome and that she had missed him. "Sheriston, I—I should not have spoken to you just now as I did. I believe the brandy was affecting me rather peculiarly."

His hand gently rubbed her back in long, soft strokes. Would that he would continue doing that forever!

George and Edward had moved to the window and were presently staring out at the coaches coming and going.

"George," she said after a moment. "Why don't you take Edward to the stables. In such a large establishment as this, I would imagine there must be at least forty horses kept ready for use."

"Could we, Sophy?" Edward cried.

"Of course."

"An excellent notion," George said. He took Edward's hand, and within a few seconds they were gone.

The moment they disappeared through the doorway, Sheriston took the snifter from her, turned her in his arms, and kissed her quite fiercely. She responded in kind, wondering how it was that she had gone so swiftly from feeling terribly ill to needing Sheriston's embraces more than anything in the entire world.

"Sophy," he murmured against her lips. "I have been wanting to kiss you from the moment I paused on the threshold of your drawing room."

"I wished for it as well," she said. She did not hesitate, but kissed him very hard in return, slinging her arms about his neck.

"You taste of brandy," he said, smiling.

"Oh, Sheriston, where have you been all these years? I have missed you dreadfully, and I vow a day has not gone by that I have not thought of you, and said my prayers on your behalf, and tried to guess at what sort of lady you might have married and how many children you had."

He stroked her cheek with the back of his hand. "I could have married a dozen times over," he said. "But you were always this specter in my life, disapproving of each of the hopeful ladies who came my way, one for laughing too

loudly, another for not laughing enough, a third for not dancing so beautifully as you were used to dance, and a fourth
for not smiling so sweetly as you smile."

"You always knew how to make the prettiest love to me."

He kissed her again quite passionately, his tongue brushing
against her lips. How familiar it all was to her as she parted
her lips and felt his tongue enter her in a manner that was
as intimate as it was sensual. He tightened his hold on her,
and she gathered her arms more fully about his neck until
she could scarcely breathe. He moaned against her mouth.
"Perhaps we should be the ones traveling to Gretna. Let's
forget about your sister and my ward. George is old enough
to see to Felicity and Edward. I'll harness another pair—no
two pair!—to the coach, eight in all, and we shall fly to the
border tonight!"

She chuckled against his mouth and kissed him again. "I
should like nothing more," she said.

"Sophy?" Felicity's voice intruded.

Good heavens! She had forgotten all about her sister.

She drew back and slid from Sheriston's lap, standing up
abruptly. What she saw made her laugh, for Felicity was
standing in the doorway, a tray of bread in one hand and
her eyes covered with the other.

"Dearest," she exclaimed, moving forward swiftly, to put
her arm about her shoulder. "I have embarrassed you terribly.
I am sorry."

Felicity peeked from between her fingers. "Where are
George and Edward?"

"Gone to the stables," Sheriston said. "Felicity, I am sorry."

"Are you to be married?" she asked. "I do not understand."

Sophy exchanged an uncomfortable glance with Sheriston.
His brow was puckered in a frown, and she could see that
he did not know what to say. They had not precisely been
discussing a renewal of their betrothal just now. Sophy said,
"We were betrothed a long time ago and each of us still
holds the other in a great deal of affection. We should not

have kissed just now, and for that I do apologize to you, since nothing has been settled between us."

Felicity lowered her hand and glanced from one to the other. "You love each other?"

Sophy nodded, as did Sheriston.

"Then why are you not engaged?"

Sheriston took the bread from her and carried it to the waiting table. "Because years ago we disagreed quite badly about something of extreme import."

"Are you still in disagreement?" she asked.

"That is uncertain," he said. "However, your sister and I must now begin to discuss the matter, very carefully."

"Sophy can be very stubborn," Felicity offered by way of warning.

Sophy was startled, and her mouth dropped agape. "Is that how you see me?" she asked.

"Of course, but I do not mean it as a criticism precisely. After all, how else could you have accomplished the raising of four children, not your own, unless you were quite stubborn? Such a quality must by its nature, however, be double-edged." She said nothing more but begged to know if she might have a slice of the bread, for she was quite famished and the landlord had just informed her that their meal would not be ready for at least a half hour.

"Yes, of course," Sophy said.

Sophy watched her wonderingly again. When had young Felicity, just fourteen years of age, become so very wise?

Sheriston turned to her and touched her arm gently. "Stubborn? Is that what I battled all those years ago?"

"Perhaps you did," she murmured. His gaze held hers tightly. Familiar feelings rushed at her in a sudden wave of desire and longing. It was as though the past nine years had simply never existed, as though only yesterday they had begun quarreling about the future which they could not resolve.

"Sheriston," she said after a long moment. "We should discuss all of this, do you not think so?"

"Yes," he responded. "I do, very much. But not now. Perhaps when our journey is come to an end."

"Yes," she agreed, smiling.

Sophy enjoyed the evening meal prodigiously. Knowing that she would not resume traveling until the morrow, she partook freely of the freshest summer peas, thin slices of a tender Yorkshire ham, a salad, fried sole, pigeon pie, and fine apricot tarts. A claret was served throughout.

Afterward, she sat by the fireplace, sipping a cup of tea when Felicity said she and George intended to put Edward to bed for her.

"Will you come up and sing to me, Sophy?" Edward asked sweetly.

"Of course I will. Send George when you are ready."

Once the children had disappeared into the hallway beyond, Sophy addressed Sheriston, who was sitting in a chair nearby. "I ate far too much."

"Perfectly understandable since you had not eaten for nearly two days." He was enjoying a brandy, swirling the dark, golden wine in a round snifter. "Are you certain you would not wish to exchange your tea for a little brandy?"

She smiled at that. "Besides having eaten too much, I also had too much claret at dinner."

He chuckled softly, then extended his hand toward her. She placed hers within his grasp. "I cannot credit that I am sitting next to you. How did this happen?"

"Fate, I suppose," she responded. "I can explain it in no other manner. But you really had no notion that Agnes was my sister and that you would find me within the townhouse when you knocked at our door?"

"No, not the smallest hint. There could be any number of Miss Chenlows and there had not been even a small mention of a Sophy Deverill on Geoffrey's card."

"Of course there would not have been," she responded. She shook her head. "Really, it is incredible that we are here together."

He gave her fingers a squeeze, then released her hand that she might take up her teacup once more.

She looked at him and smiled. "You must tell me everything. What interesting twists and turns has your life taken since we were last together? Did you finally travel on the Continent as you had hoped, once the war ended?"

"No, my father had recently passed away and I was quite suddenly beseiged with my new responsibilities. What a mere Mr. Barrows might do, Lord Sheriston will not be permitted to do for a long time. Each spring I am in London sitting in the House of Lords."

"Does this occupation please you?"

"More than I thought it would. There is much to be done in our country at present. I do not account myself a radical, but I am working steadily for reform, for a more equitable representation in Parliament."

She watched him carefully, assessing how well his new responsibilities suited him. As he continued to speak of his present obligations, she saw his enthusiasm increase the more he elaborated on his broadening London acquaintance. "Wellington is become seriously involved in politics. I don't doubt that one day he will be Prime Minister."

"Indeed," she murmured, taking another sip of tea. He was happy, she realized, happier than she had known him so many years ago. His rank suited him, as did his new role in London. She wondered absently whether she would be happy in such an environment. The answer that returned to her was a resounding *yes*.

The Season she had spent in London, when she had first met Sheriston, or rather a mere John Barrows, was the happiest of her existence. She had not known that such delights existed as that which a spring in London could provide. The balls, fetes, musicales, masquerades, card parties, at-homes, the theatre, the ballet, Vauxhall, the daily excursions to Hyde Park, and of course Almack's had been a heady wonderland after the quiet and strained life in Somerset in Mr. Chenlow's home.

Her betrothal and subsequent invitation to Wiltshire, to Lord and Lady Sheriston's home, had been the final, extraordinary blessing to a Season that had been utterly phenomenal. The dissolution of that engagement by the end of the summer because of the terrible events occuring in her absence to her half-siblings, had been as painful as the Season had been exhilarating.

"We were happy in London, were we not, Sophy?"

"Exceedingly."

She could have remained the rest of the night talking in so tender a manner had not Felicity returned to the parlor. "Edward is asking for you, Sophy. Would you prefer that I sing him to sleep?"

"On no account," she stated, rising from her chair.

"Sophy," Sheriston called back to her. "If Felicity will tend to him, won't you stay a little longer with me?"

She turned back to face him. The question was a challenge, a very important one. She felt panicky inside. "I have always been there for him, whenever he needed me. I have put him to bed every night of his life, without exception."

"Every night?" he queried. "You mean not even once did someone else have the caring of him? Even when you were ill?"

"I have enjoyed excellent health these past several years. I might have had a mild cold now and then, but nothing that prevented me from singing a lullaby or two."

"Somehow I cannot imagine that this is entirely healthy for the boy. Surely Felicity can see to him tonight?"

The panicky sensation crowded all other thoughts away. "No," she stated. "Though you may have a point, we are in a strange inn and I have already told him I would come to him. I try very hard always to keep my word to him."

Sheriston held her gaze firmly. "If there is to be more for us, Sophy, this will not do."

Sophy felt angry suddenly. How dared he return to her life from nowhere and make such quick judgments? Where had he been all those years when she could have used his support while dealing with the sufferings of her mother and siblings?

"You do not know what it was like," she said quietly. "You were not there." She then turned on her heel and left the room.

Four

Sheriston did not sleep well, even though the inn's bed was one of the more comfortable he had known in his travels over the years. No, his inability to give himself to sleep was a result of having attempted to force Sophy's hand. He knew he was right, but he could not seem to rest in this belief. He should have been able to, but he couldn't. After all, he knew from past experience that if he asked her to choose between her love for him and her devotion to her family, she would choose the latter all over again, no matter what righteous arguments he might place before her.

She was stubborn. Felicity had been right about that, but to what purpose? What was it about her situation that kept her locked up so tightly in this rigid course she had settled upon so many years ago?

There was only one point in the whole difficulty which was clear to him—he loved Sophy passionately. No woman had equalled her since her first, and only, Season so many years ago. She had never been far from his thoughts and he had spoken truly when he said he compared every lady who ventured near him to her. Somewhere betwixt this thought and the hope that he could help Sophy see in what way she erred, he fell asleep.

On the following morning, while he awaited Sophy and the Chenlow children in the parlor, he once more reviewed the unhappiness between them and realized he could draw no conclusion except that once this ridiculous situation between Geoffrey and Agnes was resolved, he should have a long discussion with Sophy. Perhaps the result might be the same, and afterward they would again part, but at least a conversation might ease some of the distress in leaving her again.

Sophy arrived after a few minutes, and he could see by the way she carried herself that she had no interest at all in resuming their former involvement. Felicity accompanied her and immediately glanced from one to the other.

"Have you quarreled again?" she asked.

Sophy glanced sharply at her.

Sheriston cleared his throat. "How is it you can assess a situation so accurately when you are so young?"

Felicity smiled faintly. "I am not in any way exceptional; rather, your expression is quite stony this morning, m'lord. And as for Sophy, she is strangely quiet, which is her way when her sensibilities have been wounded."

At that, Sheriston glanced at Sophy. Had her sensibilities been wounded? She met his gaze and he realized Felicity was right. This was no simple matter of arguing angrily; Sophy was hurt.

She addressed her sister. "Whatever might be amiss, Felicity, I hope we know how to be civil to one another."

"Who gives a fig for that!" Felicity cried with surprising vehemence, "when it is love which hangs in the balance? I begin to wonder how many couples lose what is most precious to them by obeying the proprieties. If Agnes and Mr. Rodbourne have truly eloped because they love one another, then I applaud them."

"You cannot mean that!" Sophy cried.

"Yes, I do, particularly when I look at the pair of you. I have never witnessed two people more in love, yet you do not seem able to cherish what you have between you. I begin to think you have both played fast and loose with something more precious than gold." With these strictures completed,

We'd Like to Invite You to Subscribe to Zebra's Regency Romance Book Club and Give You a Gift of 4 Free Books as Your Introduction! (Worth $19.96!)

If you're a Regency lover, imagine the joy of getting 4 FREE Zebra Regency Romances and then the chance to have these lovely stories delivered to your home each month at the lowest price available! Well, that's our offer to you and here's how you benefit by becoming a Regency Romance subscriber:

- 4 FREE Introductory Regency Romances are delivered to your doorstep

- 4 BRAND NEW Regencies are then delivered each month (usually before they're available in bookstores)

- Subscribers save almost $4.00 every month

- Home delivery is always FREE

- You also receive a FREE monthly newsletter, which features author profiles, discounts, subscriber benefits, book previews and more

- No risks or obligations...in other words, you can cancel whenever you wish with no questions asked

Join the thousands of readers who enjoy the savings and convenience offered to Regency Romance subscribers. After your initial introductory shipment, you receive 4 brand-new Zebra Regency Romances each month to examine for 10 days. Then, if you decide to keep the books, you'll pay the preferred subscriber's price of just $4.00 per title. That's only $16.00 for all 4 books and there's never an extra charge for shipping and handling.

It's a no-lose proposition, so return the FREE BOOK CERTIFICATE today!

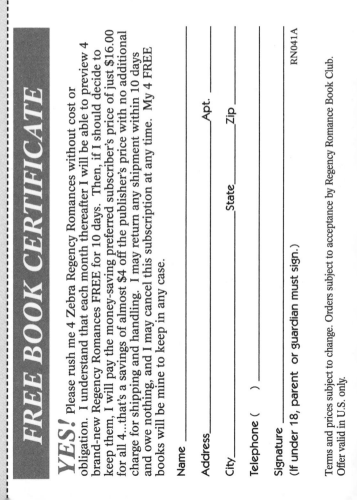

she moved to the sideboard and began loading her plate with a variety of victuals.

Sheriston watched Sophy stare at the floor. Her color became very high, and he realized she was close to tears. He rose from his chair and called her name softly, but the moment he did so, she turned and ran from the room.

He felt frozen, immobilized by the sure knowledge that nothing good could come of following after her, even though his heart ached to comfort her.

Felicity was suddenly beside him. He had not even been aware of her approach. "For heaven's sake, Lord Sheriston, do not be a fool. You must go after her. There is no finer lady in all of England than dear Sophy."

"You are right," he whispered. "Of course you are right."

She tugged on his arm, drawing him in the direction of the doorway. His feet gained momentum, and the next moment he was running, his boots loud on the wood floors of the hallway and the taproom. He met the landlord, George, and Edward on the way.

"Where is Sophy?" he cried.

All three pointed toward the inn yard. He saw her at once through the window. He ran outside and called to her. She turned and swiped at her cheeks.

Felicity watched Lord Sheriston cross the inn yard and suddenly sweep Sophy into his arms. She pressed a hand to her bosom and cooed against the drapes which hid her from the scene before her. Her plan was working quite well, better than she had hoped. It had all begun with a letter she had discovered secreted deeply in Sophy's glove drawer. She had gone to the bedchamber to fetch a pair of gloves for her sister for the theatre some few months past.

Of course, she should have never unfolded the missive, but something prompted her to do so. Once committed to this entirely ignoble course, she had read the letter not once

but at least a dozen times. She had never encountered so
much love in the written word in all her life, and she was
a great reader of poetry. The passionate style of the letter
put even Byron to shame! In that moment, she had come to
understand Sophy's womanly heart as well as the extent of
her sacrifices.

She had begun a correspondence with her Aunt Gwen and
later with Lady Sheriston. Reading the letter had initiated a
long train of events which had to this point culminated in
Sheriston kissing Sophy quite scandalously in the inn yard.

Sophy had turned to find Sheriston walking briskly toward
her. She had had only enough time to wipe several straggling
tears from her cheeks when he gathered her up in his arms
and began a profession of his love for her which was sweeter
than the finest honey she had ever tasted.

"Oh, John," she murmured against his lips. "Whatever
have we done, all these years!"

"We have wasted them," he said, placing kisses all over
her face. "I know we disagree, but Sophy, we shall find
some means of coming to terms with our difficulty."

"Yes, we shall," she returned. He found her lips once more
and deepened the kiss so that she felt it to her toes which,
were presently standing in a shallow puddle from an early
morning shower. She did not care.

"I love you, Sophy, so very dearly. You have lived in my
dreams nigh on ten years now. Yet, how much I want the
person instead of the dream."

"You shall have me, Sheriston."

Since at that moment the distant sounding of a horn her-
alded the arrival of the mail coach, Sheriston drew her back
toward the door. In what seemed but a few seconds, the
Royal Mail came barreling swiftly into the yard. The hostler,
quite used to the speed and efficiency of the kingdom's mail

service, was already bringing forward a pair of horses with a stableboy following swiftly behind with yet another pair.

Sheriston guided her back into the inn, where George and Edward were seen, their noses pressed to the window.

Sophy felt a blush on her cheeks. "Have you been there all this time?"

Edward said, "Yes, Sophy, for the landlord said the mail coach would be arriving any moment! And look! Here it is!"

"I should like to handle the ribbons some day," George cried, his gaze mesmerized by the sight of the many-caped coachman directing the hostler in sharp tones. There were any number of passengers, several sitting atop the coach and several within. All remained in their seats while the horses were exchanged. It was, indeed, a marvelous sight to behold.

"Do not wait too long to have your breakfast. We must be leaving very soon."

"We won't!" George cried, his eyes wide and fascinated by the bustling activity in the inn yard. "The horses are nearly harnessed already!"

With that, Sophy allowed Sheriston to guide her into the parlor, where tea and toast awaited her yet again. She saw the spare viands and could not repress a sigh. "What a poor creature I am," she remarked as she sat before her pauper's meal.

For the first time in the journey, Sophy sat beside Lord Sheriston, and it was not long before she found herself caught up in conversation with him. The squabble of the night before was long forgotten, and in its stead was a warmth and good will that set her heart to bubbling happily, even if her stomach was experiencing its usual discontent. She felt that the difficulties which existed between them were not in the least insuperable, that somehow they would be able to overcome the disagreement that had separated them for so many years.

For the present, however, the subject did not cross her lips, nor did Sheriston bring it forward. She asked him to tell her more about his ancestral home in Wiltshire, which she knew to be very dear to his heart. His father had left him an estate perfectly maintained, so that his own interest in Sheriston Hall involved looking into the future and discerning ways to prepare the land and the family for whatever might come England's way over the next fifty years.

Already, he had familiarized himself with many of the agricultural improvements of the past three decades, and he was intrigued by the recent manufacturing advances. "I believe that in this century, our generation will see changes unimaginable by our grandfathers. Have you seen the mechanized looms in Derbyshire and some of the other northern counties?"

"Unfortunately, I have been in Bath almost exclusively, but I have witnessed some of the less happy results of these inventions. Many of our laboring families have had to leave for the new factories. The ancient wool industry in the western counties is suffering badly."

"There will be a certain amount of displacement."

"Of course, with any improvement. I have begun to wonder what will happen to our carriages and horses. I have heard that a steam engine has been shown to be highly effective on rails and has even reached speeds exceeding our fastest coaches."

George piped up. "Nothing will ever supplant the mail coaches!" he cried. "They travel on the established roads. How could an engine, dependent on rails, ever replace that?"

Sheriston smiled. "I know it seems impossible, but many of the experts with whom I have conferred over the past several years indicate that railways are the way of the future."

The conversation continued in just such a manner as the coach continued following Geoffrey and Agnes's route along the coast of Lancashire. At nuncheon, Sheriston returned from speaking with the landlord. "They were here not two hours past," he said.

Felicity settled her linen on her lap. "I think it awfully

curious that Agnes and Mr. Rodbourne have not chosen a more interior route by now. Surely they are losing a great deal of time by hugging the coastline. I vow they could reach Scotland tonight if they would leave the coast. Why, as it is, we are only a few hours from Aunt Gwen's home."

Sophy blinked and wondered how it had come about that she had not realized the truth of Felicity's observation. "How right you are!" she cried, nibbling on her toast. "Do you suppose—?"

"Suppose what?" George queried, forking a hefty portion of apple pie.

"Well, I know this might seem odd, but I am beginning to wonder if our hapless pair has not perhaps decided against getting married after all."

"Do you think they might have gone to Aunt Gwendolyn's house?" Felicity asked.

"I am beginning to think it probable. What do you think, Sheriston? Our Aunt Gwen resides in Grasmere, which is not all that far from here."

"We could be there by nightfall," he said. "I, for one, hope they have changed their minds. Traveling can have its charms, but not when one has to inquire after a pair of runaways at every stop. I have scandalized the entire west of England with all my questions."

Felicity laughed. "You could never scandalize anyone, Lord Sheriston. You are a remarkably tactful gentleman. I noticed it in particular when you drew the last landlord away from two rather inquisitive serving maids."

"You are very kind, Miss Felicity, but if I have not scandalized the countryside, then I have certainly given several people a severe shock with queries about two such young individuals eloping to Scotland."

George, whose attention was fixed out the window, exclaimed, "Look at that high flyer! Was there anything more beautiful?"

"I do not think I should be at all comfortable riding in something so far from the ground," Felicity said.

Edward added his mite to the conversation. "Do you have a high-perch phaeton, Lord Sherry?"

Sheriston shook his head. "I am afraid not. Only a very modest curricle. But come! If you and George are finished eating, why do we not take a look at the stables at this inn?"

The boys whooped their agreement. Sheriston informed the ladies that he would be bringing round his traveling coach shortly.

Sophy sipped her tea and began to prepare herself for another segment of the journey in a swaying vehicle. She had just stood up and shrugged into her pelisse when Felicity cried, "Sophy! Do come look at George!"

Sophy moved readily to the windows by which her sister was standing. "Well!" she exclaimed. "How very kind of Sheriston to allow him to drive his coach, even if for a few hundred feet." George was smiling from ear to ear. He sat beside the coachman, handling the ribbons with great enjoyment if not remarkable skill.

The ladies ran outside and George called from his lofty perch. "Sophy! Felicity! Look! Sheriston said I might! Is this not the most famous thing!"

"Famous, indeed," Sophy called back happily.

A few minutes later, George reluctantly gave up the reins and jumped happily to the ground. The party then reassembled within the confines of the coach and after a handful of minutes was bowling farther north up the coast of Lancashire.

As the day progressed, the object of Agnes and Geoffrey's journey became more and more apparent. Perhaps there had been a change in plans along the way; perhaps the couple had panicked and decided against marrying. Whatever the case, by late afternoon, it was evident that Scotland was not the object of their journey at all, but rather Aunt Gwen's house in Grasmere.

Because of this shift in destination, the children grew excited about visiting their aunt, who had always been a great favorite. As for Sophy, she was infinitely relieved that the terrible object of Gretna Green had been set aside. She found she could breathe a little easier.

The mountainous terrain of the Lake District, however, had a worsening effect upon her traveling sickness. The lanes grew more curved, besides dipping and rising in great swells. She soon came to feel she was on a sailing vessel. "I forgot how difficult this part of the journey always is for me," she murmured.

Sheriston, fortunately, took to cradling her against his shoulder, which seemed to ease her sufferings. Felicity kept George and Edward occupied with round after round of casino. Sophy drew into her own mind. She was unable to listen or to speak. She could only stay as calm as possible as she strove to keep from casting up her accounts.

Oddly enough, with Sheriston holding her fast, she fell sound asleep. When she awoke, he was speaking her name.

"Sophy, we have arrived. Sophy? Your aunt is here, asking for you."

She awoke feeling better than she had in ages. "Are we arrived at Grasmere?"

"Yes, you are, Sophy, my dear," Aunt Gwen said. She clicked her tongue. "I forgot how ill you become when you travel."

"I feel wonderful now," she said, sitting upright. "And not in the least dizzy. I must have fallen asleep in Sheriston's arms. Oh, have you met?"

"Yes," Aunt Gwen murmured, nodding. "But come! The children have already gone inside, and I daresay you will be anxious to speak with Agnes and Mr. Rodbourne."

Sophy reached out a hand to her. "Only tell me Agnes is as yet unwed and I shall be satisfied."

"She is not married."

"Thank God," Sophy murmured, descending the narrow

coach steps. "Is the companion she hired along the way still with her?"

At that, Aunt Gwen appeared rather flustered. "Er—yes, she is. You will also want to speak with her. As it happens, she is already known to Sheriston."

"Indeed?" Sheriston cried. "How is this? How could I possibly be known to a lady Miss Chenlow hired during her travels?"

"You will have to see for yourself, but do come. Agnes has been sorely distressed by her misadventure and wishes to be assured that both of you will forgive her. Of course, Mr. Rodbourne feels equally regretful."

"Just as he should," Sheriston said sternly.

Aunt Gwen went before them, plying her cane carefully on the gravel, which afforded Sheriston the opportunity of holding Sophy back a little. "I have never seen you so well after traveling for so many hours," he said, holding her arm tightly.

"I cannot explain it," she responded quietly. "This has never happened to me before! However did I fall asleep in your arms?"

Sheriston smiled down at her. "I should like you to spend the rest of your life falling asleep in my arms."

Sophy's heart swelled. "And I should like nothing more," she murmured.

Upon entering the house, Sophy finally released Sheriston's arm. Aunt Gwen's cottage was a large, elegant structure, settled quite near the lake's shore. A wood composed primarily of fur trees formed a northern boundary, her stables were situated to the northwest, and a large cutting garden bloomed to the east.

When she arrived on the threshold of the drawing room, the delightful fragrance of potpourri filled the air. The principal receiving room was a small, cozy chamber whose windows were flanked by lively, yellow chintz draperies. A view beyond encompassed a great part of the lake. Sophy nodded to Agnes and then to Mr. Rodbourne. Her gaze drifted to the hired companion, whom she recognized at once. "Good heavens!" she cried out.

"Mother?" Sheriston exclaimed. "Whatever are you doing here?"

Lady Sheriston, who had been sitting near the windows, rose to her feet. "Why, I had to accompany Agnes and Geoffrey, of course."

"You had to accompany them?" he said. "I do not understand. How did you happen to be in Shropshire?"

"By design, of course."

Sophy glanced from one face to the next. Everyone was watching either her or Sheriston, waiting, it would seem, for comprehension to dawn on one or the other of them.

"Felicity has given us a satisfactory report," Lady Sheriston said, addressing her son. "Is everything settled between you and Miss Deverill as it ought to have been nine years ago?"

Sophy drew in a sharp breath. "We—we were lured here?" she asked, stunned. "But how did you manage it? I mean, forgive me, my lady, but how could you have known we were in Bath?"

"From Felicity. She began to correspond with me and with your aunt some five months past, almost six now."

Sophy glanced at her youngest sister. "How could you have known? I have scarcely spoken of Sheriston all these years."

Felicity bit her lip. "I am reluctant to say, Sophy, for I fear you will be angry with me. Indeed, you would have every right to be overset. You had asked me to retrieve a pair of gloves for you some few months past, and in searching for them I came across a letter. Yes, I know I should not have read it, for it was from Sheriston—at the time, John Barrows. I was caught by how much he loved you and, if you'll recall, I did ask you about him and learned that you had indeed loved him very much as well. I could not rest with such knowledge. I desired to know more and began corresponding with Aunt Gwen and later with Lady Sheriston. The rest you know, because here we all are."

"Then there never was an elopement?" Sophy queried, glancing from Agnes to Mr. Rodbourne. The pair eyed one another with great hostility.

"Never!" Agnes cried vehemently.

"Only my desire to be of service to my guardian," Mr. Rodbourne said coldly.

Sheriston queried, "What letter?"

Sophy turned to him and smiled. "Do you recall the very last missive you gave me, before we ended our betrothal?"

He narrowed his eyes, struggling to remember. "Yes," he answered abruptly. "Good God, you still have that letter?"

Sophy slipped her arm through his. "Of course. I read it every once in a while. You have never been far from my thoughts."

Sheriston smiled at her and squeezed her hand. "Dear Sophy," he murmured.

Felicity addressed Agnes. "I told you it would work."

Agnes scowled. "I can see that it has, and for that I am grateful. However, I wish you had been the one to have had to travel with Mr. Rodbourne! I was never unhappier in my entire existence."

"Nor was I!" Mr. Rodbourne retorted frostily.

Sophy glanced from one enflamed countenance to the other. "And to think, Agnes," she said, disrupting the hostility in the air, "how worried I was that you were actually eloping. I wish I had known how much you tended to brangle with Mr. Rodbourne; then I could have been at ease these past three days."

At that, Agnes moved forward and embraced Sophy. "I hope you were not too distressed," she said. "I was opposed to Felicity's scheme for that reason. I feared you would be greatly overset when you were told I had eloped with Mr. Rodbourne."

"I was, for you are very young. Just promise me you will never consider doing so in the future."

"On no account," she stated with some finality. "I intend to have a very large attendance at my wedding. I think nothing could be sillier than an elopement to Scotland!"

Relieved on that score, Sophy introduced Sheriston to her sister. She then spent the rest of the evening becoming reacquainted with Lady Sheriston.

The next few days were some of the happiest of Sophy's existence. She saw a return of the halcyon days of that summer nine years ago when she had been so deeply in love with Sheriston, and he with her. She did not bring forward the subject of their disagreement, hoping perhaps that something would occur to resolve their difficulties as a matter of course.

For the present, she delighted in being at Grasmere. The temperature was idyllic and the lake a wonderful place for boating and fishing. In addition, Sheriston discovered that several good friends of his had taken up residence nearby for the summer. The evenings were frequently employed traveling to one home or another for a night of whist, music and excellent conversation.

An old and quite excellent friend of Sheriston's, a Mrs. Hawthorne, approached Sophy on the fifth evening after their arrival in Lakeland and asked quietly, "Is it true your sister and Sheriston's ward actually feigned an elopement, under the dowager Lady Sheriston's auspices, in order to lure you both to Grasmere?"

Sophy felt a blush on her cheeks. "Yes, it is all too true. Sheriston and I were to be married several years ago, but my obligations to my family prevented it. My youngest sister, Felicity, hoped to help rekindle our previous mutual affection. You may imagine my surprise when Sheriston arrived in my drawing room in search of Felicity's older sister."

"How very romantic—and Sheriston is still unwed, but of course you knew that."

"Not at the time," she responded. "Now that I do know, however, I cannot imagine how he escaped tying the connubial knot all these years."

"Perhaps he has been waiting for you," Mrs. Hawthorne suggested kindly.

Sophy smiled. "Perhaps he is merely more particular than any man has a right to be."

Mrs. Hawthorne laughed heartily. "You will do, my dear. You will do very well, indeed." She then asked, "Do you mean to attend Mrs. Keynes's ball? I have been given to understand there will be at least thirty guests present, which is a fine complement for the Lake District."

"I have not been to a ball in a very long time. So, to answer your question, I would not miss it for the world."

At that moment, Mr. Chilmark approached. "How do you go on, Miss Deverill?" he asked politely.

"Very well, thank you," she responded.

Mr. Chilmark was an attractive man who was also quite sought after on the Marriage Mart. He was known to have ten thousand a year, rode to hounds in such a manner as to have won the admiration of the gentlemen of his acquaintance, and was a delight in a drawing room for he never refused to sing a duet when called upon and never lacked for an amusing anecdote.

When Mrs. Hawthorne moved away, he engaged Sophy in conversation until she was laughing at one word out of two. He was certainly an engaging gentleman. He had sparkling blue eyes and was as blond as Sheriston was dark. He was always dressed to perfection, even when he went out on the lake, for it was a fortuitous circumstance that Sophy frequently met him there, whether she was boating with Sheriston or with one of the children. Sometimes he had Sir Everett with him, another time the widow, Mrs. Keynes, and once both Mr. and Mrs. Hawthorne.

Presently, he was telling her of having overheard the most amusing conversation between the Prince Regent and Beau Brummell. " 'How do you like my coat, Brummell?' the Prince inquired. Brummell, as sophisticated as you please, lifted his quizzing glass and inquired very quietly, 'Is that a coat?' "

"Oh, dear," Sophy murmured, chuckling.

"Quite put the Prince out of countenance, but then, that was Brummell's way. He lives on the continent, now, poor fellow. Lost his fortune gaming."

"So I have heard, but he is not alone in that company."

"I fear you are right, Miss Deverill. Too many fortunes have been lost in the East End hells, and sometimes even at White's or Boodle's, to be at all comprehensible."

"You are a man of some sense," she responded with a smile.

He smiled in return and took a very small step toward her. "I am very glad you have come to Grasmere, Miss Deverill. Ah, but Mrs. Keynes means to grace us with a song. May I escort you to a seat?"

"Thank you, Mr. Chilmark. I take it very kindly in you."

She sensed his growing interest in her and wondered if she ought to tell him that she was on the verge of renewing her betrothal to Lord Sheriston. However, as she glanced across the room at Sheriston, she began to wonder why it was he had not opened the subject with her. She thought it odd. She sensed he was still having some doubts as to whether they ought to be married at all. Though she could not say precisely what had led her to this conclusion, she knew somehow it was true.

Five

The following day, Sophy was just leaving her aunt's rose garden with a basketful of cuttings, when a scream sounded from the direction of the lake. She heard George crying out, "Edward! Edward!"

Sophy could not mistake the panic in his voice. She dropped the basket and raced along the gravel drive toward the lake. Not twenty yards from shore, the boat drifted aimlessly with neither boy aboard. George's head bobbed up near the boat quite suddenly. He drew in a strangled breath and dove back into the water. Instinctively, Sophy began wading swiftly into the lake, oblivious to how cold it was, or that she was wearing only a thin muslin gown. Frantically she moved deeper until she was swimming toward the boat.

George dove a third time, finally bringing Edward to the surface.

The child gasped for air, drew in a huge breath, then burst into tears. George took him to the boat and with some difficulty cast him in, afterward dragging himself over the side.

By then, Sophy had reached the boat. Edward caught sight of her and held out his arms to her, sobbing. There was nothing she could do, however, since she was entirely unable to get into the boat herself. "We'll get you to shore, darling," she said. "But I must swim."

George immediately began rowing toward the dock.

Sophy swam beside the boat, all the while talking to Edward

who continued to whimper and cry. When she reached the shore, Edward was shivering at the end of the dock. Dripping, she gathered him up into her arms and carried him to the house. Her legs were trembling with fatigue by the time she reached his bedchamber.

"Sophy! Edward! Good God, what happened?" Aunt Gwen cried from the doorway, having followed after them.

George was not far behind and explained. "I told him not to stand up, but he would not listen to me. The next thing I knew, he had tumbled into the water. Thank God he had enough sense to take a breath."

Sophy wrapped Edward in a blanket and cuddled him for a very long time, until he stopped crying. Only then did she attempt to ask him in what way he had erred today. "I should have obeyed George," he said, his lower lip trembling.

"Yes, you should have."

"Sophy, you will stay with me tonight, won't you?"

"Of course I will, my pet. Nothing would prevent me from doing so."

"Not even your ball? Felicity said you were to go to a ball tonight with Lord Sherry."

"I was going, but not now. I mean to stay with you."

He smiled and hugged her, cradling his head against her shoulder.

She then told him he must put on some dry clothes.

Some two hours later, when Sheriston returned from his ride, he met Sophy in the hall outside Edward's room. "George told me what happened."

"Edward is sleeping now," she said quietly.

"You must have been very frightened."

"I was, but George saved him and dear Edward did not even swallow any water. He held his breath the whole time."

"He is a tough little fellow. You ought to be very proud of him."

"I am."

He led her to the drawing room, where she was able to

give a satisfactory report to her family and to Lady Sheriston and Mr. Rodbourne. Everyone expressed a great deal of sympathy as well as relief, for which Sophy was much gratified. When Mr. Rodbourne asked if she cared to play a game of chess with him, she agreed readily.

At six o'clock, Sheriston drew near the game board and addressed Sophy quietly. "We should be preparing for the ball now," he said.

Sophy realized that in all the excitement she had failed to tell Sheriston that she would not be attending Mrs. Keynes's fete after all. She looked up at him and said, "I am not going. I realize I should have told you sooner, but I completely forgot. You see, I promised Edward I would remain here tonight. He was terribly overset, as you may well imagine."

Sheriston frowned slightly. "I do not understand," he said.

She turned more fully toward him and explained, "Edward was in a dreadful state after the accident. He asked me not to go, and I told him of course I would be staying with him. I promised him, Sheriston—you can understand that? I gave him my word."

Sophy became suddenly aware that a hush had fallen over the drawing room. She glanced around and saw that Lady Sheriston had paused in her knitting, her hands and needles suspended in midair; Aunt Gwen held a cup of tea to her lips; Felicity and Agnes, winding a ball of yarn together, held both in mid-wrap; and even George was turning the page of a book and the page was standing straight up, held there by two fingers.

"What is it?" she asked, startled. She wondered if she had said something improper. Even Mr. Rodbourne held his knight above an empty space. "What have I said?"

"Will you come with me for a moment?" Sheriston queried.

"Of course," Sophy responded. She felt very strange, as though she were caught in the middle of a dream.

When she rose to her feet, he offered his arm, which she

took. He then led her out of doors to the large, beautiful rose garden. He seemed almost grim.

"Sophy, I cannot permit you to do this," he said at last, his booted feet crunching along the gravel path.

"Do what?" she queried, entirely bemused.

"You do not even know, do you?"

She turned toward him and bade him stop. "No, I do not," she admitted. "What is amiss?"

"You are too devoted to the boy. He suffered an accident, but he survived. You are crippling him with your attentions, besides the fact that you have entirely overlooked my sentiments in this situation. We were to attend a ball together. Mrs. Keynes is expecting us. To some degree, she is counting on my presence in her home. Without wanting to sound arrogant or prideful, I will probably be the only nobleman present, a circumstance of which I am acutely aware whenever I accept an invitation."

"Surely you are making too much of your importance," she suggested.

"Nonetheless, Mrs. Keynes is expecting me, and I have come to understand how important it is to a hostess, particularly one without rank, and in her case without a husband, to at least make an appearance. Why do we not go for just a brief time? That way I can fulfill my obligations, and you can keep your word to Edward."

Sophy drew back. "I will not go to the ball tonight, especially not for such a reason. I gave my word to Edward, and I do not mean to go back on it." With that, she turned back to the house.

"You will not compromise with me then?" he called after her.

"Not in this instance. However, I do wish you would have a little more compassion for the difficulty of the situation. Although I feel certain that had you seen how overset Edward was, you would not be questioning my decision."

He took several hasty strides and was beside her instantly.

"Sophy, this was precisely why we did not marry nine years ago. You are being unreasonably stubborn—"

"And you are not considering my circumstances," she returned hotly. "Nor my duty to that orphaned boy!"

Sophy stared at his uncompromising jaw and realized how hopeless things were between them. "We should not marry, should we, John?" she said, a lump forming in her throat.

"No, Sophy, I do not think we should. Though it pains me to say this, you have not changed in all these years, and my situation, more than ever, requires that my wife have more understanding of my position in society and what is required of me because of it. So, if you will excuse me, I have a ball I must attend out of respect to Mrs. Keynes."

Sophy watched him pass into the house and tried to comprehend precisely what had just happened. Was it possible that any hope for a renewal of their betrothal had just ended?

Sophy returned to the drawing room where she sat straight-backed in a chair and read from a volume of poetry until Sheriston, dressed immaculately in black and white, quit the house with only a very formal good-bye to her. Once he was gone, she found that tears were biting the backs of her eyes. She rose to her feet, intending to leave the drawing room with the profession of a headache as well as the need for her bed, but Aunt Gwen called to her quite sharply. "Sit down, Sophy. I must speak with you."

Her tone was so peremptory that Sophy obeyed immediately, dropping down into the chair she had just vacated.

Another command from Aunt Gwen and the remainder of her half-siblings, along with Mr. Rodbourne, were sent flying to their bedchambers. Only Lady Sheriston, apparently by prior agreement, kept her seat on a chair opposite Sophy.

"Whatever is the matter?" Sophy queried, stunned.

"You know very well!" Aunt Gwen cried. "Why on earth are you not at the ball with Sheriston? You have mystified me completely, besides oversetting all our plans. I suppose

Sheriston told you he no longer felt you would make him a suitable wife."

"He did," Sophy responded quietly. "He simply did not understand my need to be here tonight for Edward!"

"Pooh and nonsense, child!" Aunt Gwen called to her. "There are five, no six of us including George, who could manage the boy should he awaken in the night, not least of whom is Lady Sheriston."

At that, Sophy glanced at the dowager and frowned slightly.

Her ladyship immediately said, "I have grown quite fond of Edward over these past few days, and if you will remember I raised several children of my own. You do us all a disservice, Miss Deverill, by not allowing us the pleasure of comforting Edward in his distress."

"I never meant it so. I . . . I have merely been used to managing by myself. It is become a habit with me."

"Well, if you are to marry my son, then you will have to share your duties a little. When you have children, I promise you, I intend to be a rather devoted grandmother, make no mistake."

There was such a playful light in her eye that Sophy's attention was truly caught. "Our children?" she queried. "You forget, Sheriston thinks me entirely unsuitable."

"I agree with your aunt—pooh and nonsense. Now, do what is right and change into your ball gown."

Sophy glanced at her aunt.

"Yes, do go, Sophy. You were right to have cared for your half-siblings when they were so very young, but you must learn to relinquish a little of your motherly devotion now. It is not good for Edward to be dependent solely on you, particularly when there are so many others about willing to love him."

Sophy did not know how it happened, but she rose suddenly to her feet. "If this is how both of you truly feel"—here more tears started to her eyes—"I vow I do not feel so hopeless. However, I did promise Edward I would be with him throughout the night."

"Leave him to us, child," Lady Sheriston responded. "He is of an age that we can tell him the gist of what has happened, that his dear sister had an obligation to fulfill this evening to—er, Lord Sherry, and that she will be home before dawn. He will come to understand how important this was and he will be well cared for, make no mistake!"

"Go!" Aunt Gwen cried. "I shall send for my carriage at once, and later you may return with Sheriston in his coach."

An hour later, Sophy arrived at Mrs. Keynes's home. She could not keep a blush from suffusing her cheeks as she entered the fine old house, since Sheriston was on the opposite side of the chamber and had undoubtedly fabricated a whisker as to why she was not in attendance.

"Miss Deverill," Mrs. Keynes called to her. "Have you recovered from your headache?"

"Yes." Sophy chuckled. "Quite suddenly, as it happens."

Mr. Chilmark approached her. "We were quite worried. Are you certain you are not ill?"

"Quiet certain," she said, smiling.

"Excellent. I have several friends to whom I should be enchanted to introduce you."

Since Sheriston did not immediately cross the room to her, she allowed Mr. Chilmark to escort her about the several receiving rooms and the ballroom. She met any number of congenial gentlemen who most properly begged for a flattering number of her forthcoming dances.

An hour passed before Sheriston was able to disengage himself from the ladies who had beseiged him. Because Sophy was also surrounded by admirers, he asked if she would care to take a turn about the room with him. The gentlemen near her protested, but she accepted his request happily, desiring nothing more of the moment than to explain her sudden presence at the ball.

"You changed your mind," he stated, once they had drifted into an empty antechamber. "Why? I was never more astonished when I saw you across the drawing room."

She paused in her steps and turned toward him, releasing his arm at the same time. "Your mother and my aunt spoke a little sense to me," she said, smiling. "And now I am here. Sheriston, I am sorry. I have for so long cared for Edward that it never occurred to me that anyone else would be interested in assuming the role. Can you understand that?"

His expression remained rather somber, even though he nodded. "I do understand your difficulty. However, I hope you do not think that because you have arrived here tonight, I will have changed my sentiments." His voice dropped to a whisper. "I am still of the opinion that a marriage between us would be nothing short of disaster." With that, he simply walked away.

Sophy was stunned. She realized that she had indeed believed that her presence at the ball would finally settle things between them. How silly and superficial her thinking had been.

A moment later, she was claimed for the next country dance by an enthusiastic Mr. Chilmark. This good man, once the dance was ended, insisted upon fetching her a glass of iced champagne and further introducing her to any number of fascinating individuals. He was assiduous in his attentions, which delighted her given the fact that Sheriston was proving to be so stubborn. Her only satisfaction was that more than once she found him glowering at Mr. Chilmark.

Well! If Sheriston did not wish to marry her, perhaps others might. For the first time since her London Season so many years ago, she opened her eyes to the possibilities around her. There were many eligible gentlemen present, any number of whom would make a satisfactory husband. If she was learning anything on this very strange journey from Bath to Grasmere, it was that she had always desired to have a husband and a family of her own. Now that the children were older—even Edward, at five, was certainly no longer as dependent on her as she had believed—perhaps it was time for her to begin looking about for a suitable spouse.

She therefore enjoyed herself prodigiously throughout the remainder of the evening. She danced every dance and fairly wore out her slippers. Mr. Chilmark begged to call on her the next day, and she most happily granted his request.

Later, on the drive home, seated beside Lord Sheriston, she chose not to say a word to him. So it was that they had traveled a full mile before he broke the silence between them. "You certainly made a spectacle of yourself tonight, or do you not know what an ass Chilmark is?"

She turned toward him, her chin raised haughtily, "Whatever your opinion of him might be, my lord, he never once, during the course of the entire evening, abandoned me to my own devices in an empty antechamber. Do you know how ridiculous I appeared, since though we were observed to have gone in together, you were observed leaving alone? What manner of gossip do you suppose this afforded me?"

He looked conscious, of a sudden. "I never meant—indeed, I only wished to make my position clear."

"I suppose in a way that was fortunate for me. Mr. Chilmark had undoubtedly been restraining himself out of an uncertainty as to our relationship. However, tonight he asked to call on me tomorrow, or do I mean today? Yes, I mean today, and I gave him permission."

"Does he mean to ask for your hand in marriage?" he cried, obviously shocked.

"No, of course not. But I do believe he wishes to court me a little, to see if perhaps we suit."

He merely growled his displeasure and said nothing more during the remainder of the journey home.

* * *

On the following afternoon, Sheriston stood at the drawing room windows, watching Mr. Chilmark escort Sophy and young Edward toward Mrs. Yatesbury's dock. With the sun shining and the water as smooth as glass, he was taking them out on the lake. He could not help but wonder how Edward would do after his mishap.

"Come have your tea, Sheriston," his mother urged him. "Or would you prefer a little sherry? I imagine you might with Mr. Chilmark sitting so tidily in Sophy's pocket."

He did not restrain a sigh, but crossed the room and poured himself a glass of sherry. He returned to sit near his mother, who was busily knitting a baby blanket for his youngest sister, Arabella. He glanced at his parent, wondering about her. She had been a stalwart fixture in his life for so long that he could not remember a time when she was not there. She had been a devoted mother in her day, not unlike Sophy. In his opinion, both ladies had been too devoted.

"Speak your mind," she stated, laying her knitting needles and the emerging blanket aside. "I have felt for a long time that you have held me in some disdain. I see it often in the curl of your lip, so no protestations, if you please."

"Mother, I am sorry if I have given you the impression—"

"Say it, Sheriston, then we might at least discuss the matter as adults."

Because they were alone, and he was feeling mightily frustrated that Chilmark was even now rowing the woman he loved out onto the lake, he said, "You chose your children over Father. Why did you do that? He was a very unhappy man. I do not want that for myself, for my family, for my relationship with my wife."

"I see," Lady Sheriston murmured, holding his gaze steadily. "Is that how you have perceived my rather unfortunate marriage?"

"Yes, of course. I once asked Father why he did not take you to London with him, and he said you preferred to be home with your children. I saw the anger in his face; I remember it most distinctly. I remember thinking you were at fault."

"Sheriston, because you have not been a child for some twenty years now, and because you have seen much of the world, I will tell you the truth. I trust you can bear it. Will you hear it from me?"

He felt frightened suddenly, as a child might whose candle is blown out at night. "Yes, of course."

"I was an heiress, my parents were ambitious, and Sheriston Hall was in need of a great many repairs. The marriage documents were signed without my knowledge, but I was not averse to marrying your father. He was a very handsome man, witty, congenial. I had believed in my schoolgirl way that love would grow between us, even passion perhaps. For a month, I was happy, exceedingly so.

"Your father, however, was not, though he never told me as much. As soon as I was known to be increasing, he left me alone at Sheriston Hall until well after your birth. You see, he never saw me as more than a duty he had to perform. Over the years, he had a score of mistresses. In one thing, he showed me great kindness, for he gave me the children I desired, knowing I would never have the love of a man. I would have gone to London with him in a heartbeat. I was never invited. Do you understand?"

Sheriston was shocked. The years, and all his impressions of them, were stripped away. In a few seconds, he saw his childhood, which he had adored, as the result of his father's selfishness toward his mother. "You never complained," he said.

"Of course I did—into my pillow, late at night, and even then only in the early years." She glanced out the window and began to chuckle. "Do but look. They did not get very far on the lake today."

Sheriston turned to once more glance out the window. Sophy held Edward in her arms, who in turn was sobbing hysterically.

His mother laid a hand on his knee. "Why don't you go out and relieve her of that burden. It seems to me it is time Edward learned to swim."

Sheriston looked at his mother with new eyes. "When did you become so very wise?" he murmured.

"Give me a kiss and then do as I've said."

He rose and planted a kiss on her cheek. She caught his hand before he could escape. "She is worth a dozen of our brightest London belles, but you know that, don't you?"

"Yes," he muttered, angry with himself. He then did as she had bade him and took Edward off Sophy's hands.

The boy was a little reluctant at first, but when Sheriston whispered that he had a surprise for him, Edward quieted instantly and even waved good-bye to Sophy.

Sophy was stunned as she watched Sheriston's retreating back and the smile which had so suddenly suffused Edward's face. Her first inclination was to continue comforting Edward, who had taken a fright once the boat was away from the dock, but her aunt's words had come back to her from the night before and she decided to at least try to allow others to help her care for Edward. Sheriston, so far, had been surprisingly successful.

Mr. Chilmark observed, "I suppose he will give the boy to his nanny and be done with it."

Sophy glanced at Mr. Chilmark. "Edward does not have a nanny. I have had the care of him since he was a babe."

"Indeed! This is most singular." He glanced back at the dock. "Shall we to the lake, then?"

"Yes, I should like that."

Since Mr. Chilmark said nothing more of Edward, Sophy was left to wonder just what sort of interest he would take in the boy were he to become her suitor in earnest. She suspected very little.

Over the next few days, Sophy found a dozen ways of allowing Aunt Gwen, Lady Sheriston, and even Agnes, Felicity, and George to care for Edward while she began venturing forth in the small society of Grasmere. She had eventually made peace with Sheriston, and they had begun attending soirees in the evening as they had before Mrs. Keynes's ball.

If Mr. Chilmark was a frequent visitor at Aunt Gwen's, Sheriston was polite and allowed her to enjoy a ramble now and then out of doors and quite alone with her new beau.

Felicity approached her one day, by the dock. Sophy was waiting for Mr. Chilmark to arrive and take her once more on the lake. "Do you mean to wed Mr. Chilmark?" Felicity asked, clearly concerned.

Sophy could not help but chuckle. "I do not think so. I find his society amusing, but I could not imagine spending the rest of my life with a man who has already told me that I will be fortunate to be rid of my siblings."

"He said as much?" she asked, her eyes wide.

"Indeed, his very words."

Felicity trilled her laughter. "Oh, I should like to have seen your face in that moment."

"I fear that though I frowned him down, my expression was quite lost on him."

"Well, I am glad to hear it. So when are you to wed Lord Sheriston?"

Sophy sighed. "It would seem I am not. Yes, I know it must be a great disappointment, but we have decided we shan't suit."

"That really is too bad because Edward has become quite attached to him. Did you know Sheriston has been marching him about the fells every day?"

"Yes, I did know. I only hope he does not become too attached. Ah, here is my beau now and he has brought flowers picked, if I do not mistake the matter, from my aunt's garden. How very thoughtful."

Felicity chuckled and greeted Mr. Chilmark politely. Sophy accepted the flowers and handed them to her sister. "Do put them in water for me, dearest. Mr. Chilmark and I are rowing on the lake this afternoon."

"Of course, Sophy." She then curtsied to Mr. Chilmark and disappeared inside the house.

"Ah, alone at last," Mr. Chilmark said. He smiled upon her, quite warmly.

Sophy felt uneasy suddenly. The expression in his eyes gave her pause. She could almost imagine he was tumbling in love with her except that she had come to believe he was not truly capable of such fine feelings toward anyone. He was involved almost exclusively with his own thoughts and desires and rarely asked after her opinion on any subject.

They had not been on the lake for much above a half hour when he began most shockingly to speak of his love for her.

They were rowing near the shore around a bend when he set the oars at his feet and possessed himself of her hands. "I can be silent no longer. I am in love with you, Miss Deverill. I have been from the moment I laid eyes on you. Even though I discovered you were a spinster, I could not keep from thinking about you and pondering the beauty of your face and person and how well you would appear in my drawing room, as exquisite as a princess. I wish to marry you, Miss Deverill. Please say you will be mine!"

He then pulled her toward him and placed a wet, smacking kiss on her lips.

"Mr. Chilmark!" she cried, drawing back abruptly. "I beg you will control yourself."

His ardor, however, would not be daunted, and he tried to kiss her again.

A young voice intruded. "Do not hurt my Sophy!" Edward cried out.

Mr. Chilmark immediately desisted in his unwelcome attentions. Sophy first glanced at the bank thinking that Edward and Lord Sheriston had been hiking near the lake, but he was not there. She whipped around and found, much to her astonishment, that Edward was in a boat with Lord Sheriston, and entirely unafraid.

"I am not hurting your sister," Mr. Chilmark called out haughtily. "I have been asking her to marry me."

Edward's eyes got very big, and he stood up in the boat. "You are not going to marry him, are you, Sophy? I want you to marry Lord Sherry."

"Edward, do sit down!" she called to him, extending her hand even though he was some twenty feet away.

"It's all right, Sophy. I am not afraid of the water anymore." With that, he suddenly pitched himself into the lake.

Sophy shrieked. "Sheriston, do something!" The panic she felt was terrible.

"The boy will be all right!" Sheriston returned, smiling like a madman.

She shook her head. "But he does not know how to swim!"

Sheriston said nothing, but merely continued to smile as though he had just escaped from Bedlam.

"Mr. Chilmark, will you not dive in and rescue my brother?" By now she was standing up in the small boat, which began to rock ominously.

Edward's head bobbed above the surface.

Mr. Chilmark stared at Sophy as though she had gone mad. "This is a new suit of clothes. I shan't damage them by getting them wet. Besides, it seems to me the boy can swim!"

"No, he cannot!" Sophy cried. She heard Sheriston say something to her, but she could not hear him, for by that time she herself had dived into the water and begun swimming toward Edward who . . . seemed to be smiling!

The next moment, Sheriston too, was in the water, despite his own fine suit of clothes.

By the time Sophy reached Edward, she realized he was indeed swimming. "Edward! How did this happen?" she cried, treading water even though her gown tended to tangle about her legs.

Since Sheriston was soon next to her, also treading water, Sophy did not have to make too far a leap to discover the truth. "This is what you have been doing with Edward every day!" she cried, comprehension dawning quite suddenly.

"I thought it time he learned to swim, particularly since he nearly drowned."

"Watch me, Sophy!" Edward cried happily.

He then made rather fitful lunges at the water away from the boat, imitating a true swimming form well enough to both keep him afloat and give him a little distance.

"Well done!" she cried. "Edward, you are wonderful! And so are you, Sheriston! I cannot thank you enough! You have given my heart such relief in this moment, you can have no notion! Thank you, a thousand times thank you." She slid her arm gently about his neck and kissed his cheek. With one hand he held the side of the boat, and with the other he surrounded her waist, holding her easily against him.

"I say!" Mr. Chilmark called to Sophy. "You were out on the lake with me! I . . . I was professing my love for you, my desire to make you my wife."

"I cannot allow that, Chilmark!" Sheriston called out over his shoulder. "I was reluctant to say anything to you, but Miss Deverill has been promised to me these nine years and more. You will have to find your bride elsewhere."

"I say! I say! Why was I not informed? I consider this most unhandsome of you."

Sophy turned toward him. "Mr. Chilmark, thank you for you attentions to me and for your desire to wed me, but truly I cannot marry you for I do not love you. I wish you well, and if it is any consolation, you should know that had I accepted your hand in marriage, Edward, George, Felicity, and Agnes would all have come to live in your house."

"What?" he cried, his expression altering quite suddenly. "Well, I am glad to be informed of that, at least. I could never have countenanced such a thing."

"I know, Mr. Chilmark. You may now consider yourself to have escaped a very bad bargain."

"Indeed, I do," he remarked. "I trust Sheriston will see you home?"

"I shall do that, Mr. Chilmark. Good day."

"Come, Edward," Sophy called to him as Mr. Chilmark rowed away. "Your teeth have begun to chatter and so have mine. We should return home, do you not agree?"

"Yes, and then I think you should be married right away; otherwise I know you will change your mind and I shall be very angry, with both of you!"

On the next day, Lady Sheriston stood on the gravel drive before three fully packed coaches. "Are you certain you wish to do this, Sheriston? It is most scandalous."

"Edward has commanded it," he said with a smile. "He fears we will not marry otherwise, and I have come to believe he is right."

"Very well," she said, smiling. She patted his cheek and moved to the third carriage, which was inhabited by Aunt Gwen, Agnes, and George. The forward carriage contained Edward, Felicity, and Mr. Rodbourne, the latter two of whom seemed to be striking up a most promising friendship.

Sophy settled herself comfortably against Lord Sheriston with a footstool at her feet and a small flask of brandy in her hands. "I do not wonder," she said, "if in a few years they make a match of it, for the very qualities which annoyed Agnes so dreadfully in Mr. Rodbourne seem quite suited to Felicity."

Sheriston smiled and kissed her forehead as the coach began to move forward. "You may be right."

"Would you object to such a match?" Sophy asked. "After all, Felicity is dowerless."

He chuckled. "I would only object if my ward does not mature a great deal by the time he is ready to marry. His impulsiveness and tendency to argue would not be fair at all to the infinite sweetness of your sister's disposition."

Sophy giggled. "I have had too much brandy," she said.

When the coach was moving nicely along the lane, heading toward the highway, he caught her chin in his hand and forced her to look at him. "I love you, Sophy," he whispered huskily.

"And I, you."

He slanted a kiss hard across her lips. Sophy felt the familiar magic begin to work within her soul in very much the same way the brandy was warming her veins. She returned his kiss in full, permitting him the soft entrance into her mouth which he so strongly desired.

She was lost for a very long moment as he held her tightly to him and kissed her.

"Are you certain we are doing the right thing?" he queried, sliding tender kisses across her cheek.

"Indeed, I do," she whispered in response.

He laughed. "Never in a thousand years would I have believed that I would be—how did you once explain it to Edward?"

She smiled broadly. "Marrying while traveling."

"Yes, that's it, although I daresay we shall create quite a stir in Gretna Green, for one does not always bring one's mother, one's aunt, and one's brothers and sisters on an elopement."

Sophy met his warm, affectionate gaze. "To be sure, one does not," she said.

He kissed her again, and this time the turns and twists of the road seemed to have no affect at all on Sophy as the coach headed north toward Scotland.

HAPPILY
EVER AFTER

Jeanne Savery

While waiting for her aunt, little Cornelia Dunsforth stared out the carriage window toward where an irate mother towed a small boy down the village street. She sighed. If only she and Justin had a mother. Even an angry mother! She said as much.

"We have Aunt Justina." The boy cast his sister a speaking glance. "Maybe she isn't exactly like a real mother, but she's ours."

"She isn't so very bad, I suppose, but what of next time?"

The two stared at each other. Their own mother was long dead. Justin barely remembered her and Cornelia had been too young to have any recollection at all. Their father was almost never in England. A diplomat, he was often on special missions, some of which took forever. Or perhaps it was only in childish minds that they dwelt for what seemed like forever in whatever place their father left them.

Two weeks earlier they'd been brought to their aunt.

Usually, when Felix Dunsforth was sent on a mission, he'd time to make appropriate arrangements for the boarding of his offspring. This time he was in such a rush that he was barely able to bring them himself to his sister, Justina Dunsforth, leaving immediately and laughing at her objections that she knew nothing of children.

Felix Dunsforth had stuck his head out his carriage window and called, "If you've problems, ask Theo, Lord Mowbray. You'll be seeing him. He takes an interest in Justin whenever I am out of England. His godson, you know?" He glanced at his younger child. "And in Cornelia, of course."

Then, clods flying from hooves and wheels, he was gone.

Justina cast a helpless glance at her elderly butler, who nodded and calmly suggested that the nursery party follow him. They did. Nurse panted up the stairs in the children's wake while the children, first the one and then the other, pelted Howard with questions. Nurse, thought Justina, had gained an inordinate amount of weight.

Her eyes returned to rest on the slightly bent back of her butler. Howard, bless him, had, as usual, found a satisfactory solution to her latest problem. Whatever had she done before she hired this jewel of a butler? His long experience appeared to have given him the key to any and every predicament. Justina, heaving a sigh of relief that all was settled so easily, returned to her study. She sat down to her work, sure that would be the end of it.

It was not, of course. Anyone with any knowledge of children would have known that, but Justina had already admitted she had none.

Theodore Kenwright, Earl Mowbray, bowed his head and let his wife's vituperation flow over him. He shuddered slightly when she began panting, her words more and more vicious.

Finally, looking up, he winced. No matter how many times he saw her, her appearance shocked him. Mary glared, her eyes wild and her hair untamed, matted. The long apron, worn by all the women in this place, was stained. Lord Mowbray had no desire to discover what blotched it. Too, she had torn her gown, ripping it at the shoulder and down the sleeve. Mowbray reminded himself that several copies of the simple design must be sent her.

He shook his head—although at what he did not know. Perhaps the waste of it? Mary had once been beautiful. High strung and likely to fall into moods for no reason he'd ever understood, but very beautiful.

And then had come the horrible night in which he'd awakened to see her, moonlit, approach his bed, her face an utter blank, her eyes staring at nothing at all. A knife in her hand. A blade raised to strike . . . Mowbray cut off that line of thought instantly. The memory was too painful.

"I must go now," he said, interrupting. Long ago he'd ceased wondering where she'd learned the filth which, now she had exhausted herself with ranting, merely dribbled from her mouth. "I will return next month. As always."

He turned away, knowing the attendant would control Mary if, as sometimes happened, she flew at him, her fingers clawed, some unknown motive urging her to inflict damage. The door closed, silencing the obscenities to which, each month, he forced himself to listen.

Except on those rare visits when Mary was rational. Normal.

But perhaps, in a way, those occasions were worse. During those very brief periods of sanity she would beg, desperately, to be taken home. He could never decide which he hated most, having her swear at him for some unknown crime or having to deny her desperate yearning while looking into her ravaged, tear-streaked countenance, a caricature of what she'd once been. On such occasions he'd feel the tears rise into his own eyes.

Now, for a long moment, his lordship stood outside Mary's door. His eyes closed as he sought to calm himself. Then, drawing in a breath and releasing it slowly, he moved on. Farther down the hall, just before the vestibule, he knocked at another door.

"Come in." The gentleman behind the desk rose when Mowbray opened the door. "Ah. And how did you find her ladyship, my lord?"

"Thin." Mowbray spoke with an abruptness he forced himself to soften. "Too thin, I fear. Is something wrong with her? I mean—" He bit his lip, uncertain how to finish.

"Other than her madness?" supplied the doctor gently.

"Except that she will not eat, there is nothing wrong, my lord."

Not eat? The skin thinned out over his lordship's cheekbones as he fought back conflicting emotions. He must *not* hope that he be freed from Mary. Not by such a means as that! "Perhaps," he suggested, after winning an internal battle, "if I were to send fruit from my succession houses? I remember that she liked fruit."

"We could try, my lord, but I promise nothing. When the mad take a notion into their heads, it is difficult to remove it. More often than not, we find it impossible."

"What notion has Mary taken?"

"She complains that her food is poisoned, my lord. She will drink but will not eat."

Mowbray frowned. After a moment he suggested, "Perhaps if you gave her boiled eggs which have not been removed from the shell?"

"We, too, hoped that would satisfy her. We tried, my lord. I am sorry," he added when he saw how perturbed was his wealthiest patron.

"She is, then, deliberately starving herself?"

"Deliberately?" A look of contemplation passed over the doctor's face. "How," he asked, speaking to no one in particular, "can one say that what such a one does is deliberate? Someone so irrational in every way?"

"To the death?" persisted Mowbray.

"It may be so."

"Can you not force her to eat?"

The question drew a sigh. "We have tried, my lord. She, hmm"—he looked beyond Mowbray, his eyes losing focus—"egests it."

The next day Mowbray turned into the chestnut-lined drive to his godson's current place of residence. Always, after seeing Mary, he took a few days to visit Justin and Cornelia. Either he went to their home, or if their father was gone, then wherever his friend had boarded them.

Visiting the children was like taking a bath in clean, clear water after wallowing in filth. It was necessary to Mowbray. He needed the boy's growing wonder in the world around him, the girl's happy trill of laughter, the clear logical intelligence of minds just flowering, opening to new ideas, their innocence—and their not-so-innocent pranks!

Two weeks previously, Felix Dunsforth had received his latest orders and gone off in a greater rush than usual. For the first time, he had left his children with his sister rather than in a more suitable home. Mowbray frowned, wondering just how Felix had coerced Miss Dunsforth into boarding them.

Still, Justina had given in to her brother's entreaties. And, having acquiesced, would she dare begrudge the youngsters a proper place in her thoughts, her schedule, and her household? His lordship could not approve Miss Dunsforth's attitude toward the children which, as he had observed on an occasion when she and he both visited Felix, was rather short of patience. The situation could not help but concern him.

Mowbray, after all, had known Justina Dunsforth for very nearly as long as he'd known Felix. He had always found the woman upsetting in some odd fashion, and he feared to discover that her behavior toward her niece and nephew would make his ambivalence toward her, which he tolerated when the children were not involved, still more unsettling. Mowbray knew he would find it impossible to hold his tongue if she were, in any way, ill-treating the children!

On the other hand, on those occasions when he had found himself tête-à-tête with Miss Dunsforth and forced into discourse with her, he had enjoyed her tart comments and her surprisingly incisive and logical mind. With only a touch of guilt, he reveled in the woman's sparkling conversation, enjoying it as he enjoyed no other woman's company. Not since before his disastrous marriage, at least.

Delighted in it, perhaps, to too great a degree? Given that he was not free to pursue his interest? Ah, but she was an intelligent woman, educated well beyond the average, and she read widely. It was a joy to converse with her, and he could not resist those rare opportunities that came his way. Mowbray was aware that he looked forward to this visit to his godson and the boy's sister with greater anticipation than usual. Looked forward to when the children were asleep of an evening and, dinner over, it was likely that Justina's non-entity of a chaperon would discreetly, in a self-effacing manner, settle into a corner of the cozy back parlor while he and his hostess talked.

Still, however interesting a lady he found Miss Dunsforth, in her way, Justina was every bit as selfish and self-centered as was Felix. At least it seemed to Mowbray that she was. His frown deepened. Why he liked either of the Dunsforths, he could not tell—but like them he did.

Now, as he cantered up the long drive to Chestnut Lane Manor, the small estate her father had willed to Miss Dunsforth when it became apparent she did not mean to wed, Mowbray allowed anticipation of this visit to rid his mind of the last of the horror roused by the visit to his wife. He approached the comfortably sized brick structure built in the Queen Anne style, liking its simple lines and its settled, almost complaisant, appearance.

As he neared the curve to the house, he saw a groom running up to take his horse. Before he reached the lad, he heard childish voices arguing. Vociferously. Pulling his gelding to a walk, Mowbray looked around, seeking the whereabouts of his godson and Cornelia.

He located them across the lawn and grinned at the sight of Justin shaking a finger at his sister very much in the manner of a scolding adult. The ten-year-old had tucked his mallet under his arm, and his foot rested on a ball, a second ball nestled against its far side. But then, seeing that tears raced each other down eight-year-old Nellie's cheeks, Mowbray frowned.

Uncaring that his gelding's hooves might tear up a lawn

laid in the reign before that of the first Hanoverian, he cut across it to where a croquet set was inexpertly laid out. The groom, who awaited the visitor's approach near the entrance, felt his jaw drop when Mowbray turned off the gravel. The lad sent a quick, horrified look that mirrored that on the face of the butler who just then opened the door, before he set off at a dead run across the grass toward the horse.

"Here now! What is this?" Mowbray asked sternly, swinging his leg across the back of his mount and dropping to the ground.

At the sound of Mowbray's voice, Justin whirled. "Uncle Theo!" he shouted. He dropped the mallet and ran toward his godfather.

Cornelia's voice rose with each repetition as, tears forgotten, she screeched an equally glad welcome: "Teo, Teo, Teo!"

"Teo, Teo, Teo!"
The high-pitched childish voice penetrated Justina Dunsforth's concentration. She jerked upright and her hand twitched. Ink spattered not only over the page on which she had nearly finished a clean copy in excellent copperplate handwriting, but all over the two or three sheets which, finished, she had moved to the side.

She stared. "Ruined! Those dratted children! Those blessed monsters! Those . . ."

She closed her teeth with a snap and, huffing in exasperation, she turned to glare out the window. Her brows rose. "A horse?" The scene appalled her. Her pulse raced and her lips compressed. She could not believe her eyes.

"A horse on the south lawn? Impossible!"

Forgetting the ruined work, Justina rose and stalked to the window which, after a brief struggle with a recalcitrant latch, she threw open. The horse, led by a groom, was already on its way to the stables, but the villain who rode it across her precious sod remained.

"I suppose I should have known!" she said aloud, not caring a whit how rudely she voiced her bitterness at such wanton destruction.

Mowbray, carefully dabbing at Nellie's now-smiling face, glanced up. His mouth compressed before he turned back to the child, speaking softly.

"Blast you, Mowbray!" Miss Dunsforth called more loudly. "How dare you ruin a lawn which has required the better part of a century to come to perfection? How dare you?" Then, when Justin picked up his mallet, she noticed the croquet set. "Oh, no," she groaned. "No, no, no!" She hit her own forehead with her open palm as each negative burst from her. "I cannot bear it. I cannot!"

Her butler chose that inopportune moment to open the study door and clear his throat.

Justina turned on her heel and pointed an admonitory finger at him. "You! Howard, you allowed those beloved brats to set up their stupid game on that lawn. You, who are old enough to know better! You do know better! You, Howard, are let go without a character!"

"Yes, madam. But later, if you please. Just now you must tell me which room to order prepared for Lord Mowbray, who has come a day early for his visit to the children. Mrs. Minch requires to know," he finished only a trifle apologetically.

"The green, of course," grumped Justina. It was irritation piled upon irritation that the man would importune her with such a nonsensical question when he knew it should be the suite.

"The green suite is unavailable. You have forgotten that the painters have not yet finished."

Oh yes. Those blessed painters. Would they never be done?

"Oh . . . wherever you would, Howard." She waved a hand. "It matters not a jot to me."

Dratted painters. Dilatory idiots. Mowbray's room should have been finished a week ago. But why, she suddenly wondered, *should I feel irritation that slothful workmen have overturned my plans for the man's comfort?*

She put out of her mind the idiotic notion that it had. Upset her, that is. Concern for another's comfort when nothing could be done to improve it was a waste of time and energy.

"I do not know," she grumbled, "why my brother insisted the man be allowed to visit. All nonsense, the notion that Justin and Cornelia would miss him. They are children, Howard. Mere children. A necessary nuisance, of course, but until they reach the age of reason, they are of very little use to anyone. Including themselves." She gasped slightly, realizing she had again allowed her emotions to lead her into unbecoming speech. And before a servant! "Enough of that." She glowered, almost daring her butler to make a comment. As if he would! "But Howard, if that sod was damaged . . . !"

She had no need to repeat the threat. It was the usual one and made on any and every occasion something annoyed her. The butler, knowing this, merely bowed once again, backed from the room, and gently closed the door.

Alone in the hall, Howard blotted his forehead with his handkerchief. Actually, he'd escaped far more easily than might have been expected. Miss Dunsforth was at that stage of her writing where she was very easily overset and where, if disturbed, had been known to throw things. Merely threatening to let him go without a character! Why, that was a mere nothing!

Howard continued down the hall. He recalled his alarm the first time Miss Dunsforth had "let him go without a character" and smiled gently. Eventually, when he'd come to realize she did not mean it literally, the reprimand grew no more than amusing, a habit in his eccentric mistress which was rather endearing. As was also her habit, Miss Dunsforth would, soon, give him an order which involved several days or even weeks for its accomplishment, tacitly establishing that he was not to leave her service after all.

Dear Miss Dunsforth. The lady was always at her worst when she neared the end of one of her tales. All the servants went warily at such times. Mr. Howard, treading in stately fashion toward the front door, hoped this latest manuscript might soon be finished, because, once it was, life at Chestnut Lane would, for a month or two, be calm. Normal. Very like any other household in which he'd worked before retiring to this country position.

Mr. Howard very nearly chuckled out loud. He had assumed—surely a reasonable supposition—that the rural household of a spinster lady would be a velvet-soft job for those years remaining of his working life. *How wrong,* he wondered, *could one be?* The normal peace and quiet of a small country estate prevailed for only so long as it took Miss Dunsforth to become deeply immersed in a new story!

On the other hand, thought the butler with a touch of complaisance, *we are never bored!* He entered the hall and went to the door to await their guest.

As Mowbray strolled toward the entrance, his mouth tightened. Little Cornelia's arm was so tightly clutching his neck that he feared for his cravat and knew his shirt points, too moderate to be called winkers, were already ruined. Justin, grinning up at him whenever he could catch his eye, held his hand just as tightly. His lordship forbore to speak. He was more than a trifle concerned he would be unable to control his temper and would use words one should never use before children.

And when he saw her, he feared he'd berate Miss Dunsforth in a manner that, very likely, she had never before experienced. But did she not deserve a scold? A severe scold?

Where, he wondered, *is the children's nanny? Why is there not so much as a maid watching over them? In fact, why is Master Justin not at his studies nor Mistress Cornelia learn-*

ing her letters or stitching samplers or whatever a child her age should be doing?

"Howard," he said to the butler, upon entering the hall, *"where is Nurse?"*

Howard's gaze skittered away. "In the nursery, Lord Mowbray. She can usually be found sitting—er, sewing before the fire."

"If she is there, then why were the children *there?"* Releasing Justin's hand, Mowbray pointed out the door.

"Mrs. Cornish is, well—er, I do not know," finished the butler unhelpfully and in something of a rush.

"Come, children," said Mowbray. Cornelia did not wish to let him go and twined both arms tightly around his neck. With a trifling difficulty, he set her to the floor and reached a hand to each child. "We will see what we will see. No, Justin, you must leave the mallet here. Howard, order the croquet set put away until I discuss with Miss Dunsforth where it may be put so that it will do no harm."

"Yes, my lord."

Once again Howard mopped his brow, well aware that he had been let off rather lightly for the second time in the quarter hour. Not that it was truly his fault the children had used the south lawn for their game. Nor was it at all surprising they did so. It was, after all, by far the smoothest and most level lawn for the purpose. And why should he feel guilt that Mrs. Cornish preferred dozing before the fire to watching over her charges?

Besides, wondered the butler who had not known of its existence, *just where did the little monkeys find the game?*

"Justin."

"Hmm?" asked Justin but did not look up from the history book, a chapter of which his godfather had told him, sternly, he was to read before their tea was brought up.

"Justin!"

"What do you want?"

"I don't like Aunt Justina. She isn't nice."

"She is merely old."

"Not all old people become so angry over nothing! Uncle Teo doesn't."

"Not all of them are alike."

"Is that it? I like Uncle Teo."

"Of course you do, silly," said Justin with overdone patience. "He pays us attention. We always like that."

"I wish," said Cornelia wistfully, her finger pushing against her lip, "that we might go home with Teo."

"Well, we can't. So it is nonsense to wish any such thing."

Cornelia stared at her brother for a long moment and then sighed. "Well, I can wish it if I want," she muttered. "There is nothing wrong with wishing something."

"Do be still, Nellie. Uncle Theo said I must read this before teatime, when he will test me, and it is confoundedly difficult with a great many big words."

Half an hour after climbing up to the nursery, when he had replaced his shirt and neckcloth, Lord Mowbray returned to the lower floor and tracked his reluctant hostess to her den. He had to clear his throat a second time before she heard him and looked up from her work.

"You," she said.

There was the faintest of snarls to her tone and Mowbray winced but, remaining firm in his determination that something be done, he spoke. "During my last visit, which was merely an hour or two and overly brief, I was reluctant to criticize your attitude toward your niece and nephew. But now, the children's safety demands that I do so. It is imperative that you provide proper supervision. I also find that Justin has no tutor. I tested him and he is badly behind in his studies. Then there is Cornelia. Should she not be under the care of a governess? Miss Dunsforth, something must be done. At once." When she merely frowned, he added, "The current arrangement is totally inappropriate."

"Nanny Cornish . . ."

". . . was," he interrupted without apology, "sound asleep by the fire. Asleep! The woman had not the least notion the children were gone from the nursery."

"Asleep!"

"My dear Miss Dunsforth," he said severely, "the woman must be seventy if she's a day."

Justina did a rapid calculation in her head and was astounded to realize her and Felix's old nanny must be nearer eighty than seventy.

"She is too old," continued Mowbray, "to have the care of such young and active children."

Justina could not deny it. Nor could she see what to do. "Why," she demanded, "can they not play quietly? In the nursery? Surely, at their age, that is where they belong?"

Mowbray stared. Could any woman be so utterly ignorant of childish minds and bodies? Mowbray clenched his fists to prevent himself from grasping Justina's slim shoulders and shaking her until the pins scattered and that wonderfully rich head of burnished, walnut-colored hair fell down around her and . . .

. . . and he gasped softly as he became conscious of where his thoughts were leading. He turned from her.

"My lord?"

Mowbray forced control over wandering emotions and forced aside a vision that would lead him onto primrose paths into forbidden realms. Forbidden for a number of reasons, all of which touched his honor. Not only was he married, but Miss Dunsforth's brother was his friend, and, finally and most importantly, the lady was an untouched spinster, not a married lady or a widow with whom one might, if one were the sort to do so, safely dally.

Mowbray reminded himself he must not think of her as a woman. An attractive woman.

A very attractive woman.

The children! he said silently, giving himself a mental kick and forcing his thoughts into order. *It is of the children we must speak.*

"*My lord?*" she repeated, frowning.

"Have you," he asked, his back to her, "no recollection of what it was like to be a child?" His thoughts and emotions firmly mastered, Mowbray turned.

Recognizing something in his tone that indicated his question was more than rhetorical, Justina pondered it, frowning slightly. "To be a child?" she repeated softly. She tipped her head, her eyes narrowing and her lips pursing.

He watched her, noticed the faint creases marring her smooth forehead, and his narrowed lips softened, a hint of amusement lightening his mood. Astonishment filled him. "You truly do not remember," he said softly and then, humor fading, he sobered, troubled that it could be so.

"I wonder," she mused, still thinking, "if there is anything in my history which I should recall. Perhaps I never was a child. Not as I think you mean it. Now that I look back, I remember feeling jealousy toward children who played with dolls and hoops and that sort of thing. Felix and I had no toys. They were not allowed."

Mowbray felt something akin to horror at the simply stated revelation. "Not allowed . . . ?"

"We were set to our books at an early age, my lord, and punished when we did not accomplish our lessons as directed. I was reading well before the great age of four. Felix, I believe, accomplished that feat at a still younger age."

Vaguely, Mowbray recalled his mother and grandmother discussing a form of education they had thought disgustingly rigid. Supposedly it was a method guaranteeing that the perfect child grew into the perfect adult. Could that have been the philosophy under which Felix and Miss Dunsforth were reared? If so, and even though she was the best-educated woman of his acquaintance, the system appeared to have resulted in so little understanding of human nature that, in his opinion, it was an utter failure.

Mowbray pushed aside thoughts of the past. The present was far too urgent, the children's well-being too important. He must not allow contemplation of this woman's childhood to interfere with what must be done.

"I suppose, then," he said thoughtfully, "that because you had too much discipline when young, you have decided to allow Justin and Cornelia to run wild? With no order in their lives? Have you not heard of the Golden Mean?"

At first Justina's eyes widened. Then she blinked rapidly several times. He could almost see the thoughts whirling about in her mind. Finally she nodded comprehension. He watched the process with interest, her great eyes, shadowed by long dark lashes, drawing him back toward forbidden emotions. . . .

"You suggest," she said, interrupting thoughts best interrupted, "I am allowing them the freedom I never had?"

Once again saved from potential disaster, Mowbray nodded.

"I wonder if it could possibly be so." Justina gave her head a firm shake, as if to shake the notion from her mind. "But that is not the problem. I understand what you would have me do, but surely it is my brother's place to choose Justin's tutor. Nor do I know where one would find a governess for a child so young as Cornelia. In fact, I have no notion how to go about such business." She relaxed and smiled. "Best wait for Felix," she concluded, obviously pleased by her solution.

Mowbray shook his head. "I am sorry to contradict you, Miss Dunsforth—" A lie, he thought, but properly polite. "—but it will not do. This latest appointment may keep Felix away a year or more." Her gloriously large eyes widened, and he saw her mouth the words, *a year*. He fleetingly wondered if it had ever crossed her mind to wonder how long she'd have charge of her brother's offspring. "We cannot wait so long," he continued. "Childhood is a brief moment in life and the children's needs must be met. Now."

Justina glanced at her desk, at the manuscript which was nearly finished. She had, just that morning, finally discovered how to end her tale. She needed another week, or perhaps two, to do the work. Or perhaps more if her characters refused to act exactly as she wished them to. All too often they would not, which was a terrible nuisance. She mentioned her need to finish a project in which she was involved.

"Then, once it is finished, I will have time and energy to look into what is to be done about the problem."

"No."

A combination of outrage and confusion, to say nothing of astonishment that Lord Mowbray dared reject what she believed a conciliatory and more than adequate offer, left Justina stunned and in such a muddle that she was unable to form a response.

"No, Miss Dunsforth, the situation cannot wait. Not so much as two more weeks." He frowned. "Since you are unavailable and assuming you've no objection, I shall ride into London and interview tutors and governesses and, in the meantime, you will designate a youngish maid, preferably one with the experience of younger brothers and sisters, to watch the children."

Justina felt guilty that she had thought to postpone taking action. To cover up and hide the guilt, she allowed herself to feel anger that his lordship had the audacity to tell her what must be done, to order things to suit himself. Anger turned to stubbornness. "Why should I disrupt my household in such a way?"

Mowbray closed his eyes in exquisite agony. *"Why,* the woman asks. Did I not say earlier that the children are in danger?"

"Nonsense. What is there at Chestnut Lane to harm them? How dare you demand that, for no reason, a maid's routine be interrupted, as it must be if she were forced to watch over the children? Everyone in my household knows exactly what they are to do. And when. No—" Justina brightened at a thought. "I have a better solution. I will merely forbid the children to leave the nursery."

Overly gently, he asked, "And exercise?"

Justina frowned. "Exercise?"

"You, perhaps, will take them for walks and allow them, under your supervision, to run and play outdoors for a portion of each day? You will buy a pony and oversee riding lessons? Or play tennis or croquet with them?"

"Do they actually need exercise?" Mowbray stared at her, and she flushed slightly. "Oh, well, I suppose they do," she answered her own question. "The devil!" she exclaimed inelegantly. "Why am I burdened with all this just now when I must finish—"

Justina bit off what she was about to say, casting a wary glance his lordship's way.

"—what I am doing," she finished, awkwardly.

"Your current novel," he said, nodding.

Justina's heart leapt into her throat. His words revealed that Felix, blast him, had foresworn himself. Her brother had revealed Justina's carefully guarded secret life as the author of silly little novels written for the amusement of bored tonnish ladies! Half-finished sentences formed in her mind as she planned a blistering letter which would tell Felix exactly what she thought of him!

"Can you not do **your** scribbling," continued his lordship, interrupting her rampaging thoughts, "when the children have no need of you? Perhaps when they are asleep at night?"

"My scribbling?" Outrage erased the embarrassment felt upon discovering that he knew of her writing, an occupation she never discussed. Ever. Except that once, with her brother, when her first book was published. "My scribbling!" she repeated. Anger built and she clashed her teeth together. Twice. "How dare you?" she demanded.

He blinked. "How dare I what?"

"Insult me and my work in that particularly nasty fashion. Perhaps you, my lord, would care to do your work in the dark of the night when you are tired and need your own rest? Perhaps the servants should do their work at night when the poor innocent children are in bed and no longer require that everyone fetch and carry and chase after them? Perhaps the farmer beyond the home woods should ask his cows to wait until midnight for the milking, holding himself ready to—"

She gasped back whatever nonsense she'd been about to spout. Her eyes narrowed.

"You, my lord," she finished, bitingly, "are the rudest, most inconsiderate, unthinking man I have ever met. It has often come to my attention that men are naturally rude. It is, I believe, a constitutional defect so I suppose they cannot help it, but you! You, my lord, are the worst."

It was Mowbray's turn to frown. "But what is so difficult about scratching out a silly little story for featherheaded little girls to read?"

"Silly?" Her voice rose. *"Little?"* And yet again. *"Featherheaded?"*

Justina, forgetting she held the same opinion of her work and readers, glanced around, seeking something to throw, but found nothing within reach. She recalled that she had, deliberately and with forethought, removed anything of the sort from anywhere near her desk. People, Howard had informed her, did not like having things thrown at them. Since she'd no wish to upset her servants by indulging what was, after all, a rather rude habit, she'd made the doing of it next to impossible.

Not that she cared a jot what Mowbray liked and did not like. She didn't care. Not at all.

Did she?

Yes, she did.

Justina pushed away the sudden thought that she cared and that one reason she was so very angry was that he revealed disapproval—perhaps even a trifling contempt?—when she wished for something far different from him. Although *what* she wished and *why* she wished it, she hadn't a notion. She tucked the notion away for later cogitation.

"Your writing is not relevant. It is the *children* we must discuss," he insisted, rather confused by Justina's show of temper. "I will find a tutor and governess as quickly as may be, and assuming you can tear yourself from your—"

"Silly little story?" she asked sweetly.

"Yes." Mowbray suspected he should apologize, but he was himself far too angry to do so. "If you can do that, you may see to caring for your niece and nephew until I return."

Justina used every bit of her more than adequate self-discipline to put aside a blistering tirade against his lordship's continued insults.

"My lord," she said through gritted teeth, "it has apparently escaped your notice that this is not an overly large house. Where," she asked in a sugary-sarcastic tone, "do I house two extra upper servants?"

Mowbray's frown deepened. "There must be room. You have room for me."

"You are given a guest room." Rather slyly, she asked, "I am to put staff into guest rooms?"

Mowbray's brows lowered, but he refused to admit that might cause problems among the upper servants. "Why not?" he asked. When she merely glowered, he added, "If that is all there is, then that is what you must do."

"I have only the two guest rooms," she prevaricated, halving the number available. "So, my lord, where will you sleep when you visit your godson? As I am certain you will continue to insist you must do?"

He shrugged. "If you've no room, I will put up at the village inn."

Justina gave it up. The man had an answer for everything. Blast Felix! How had he dared to disrupt her life in this manner? Her very satisfactory and well organized life. When

Felix returned, she would kill him! Cut him up into tiny pieces and feed him to the fish in the river! She would . . .

But Justina's renewed bout of temper cooled in an instant. Honesty and self-awareness made it impossible for her to lie to herself. Only a part of that last thought had been accurate. It was true that she had her life exceptionally well organized, but for some time now she had occasionally discovered in herself the smidgeon of a suspicion that it was *not* all that satisfactory.

Not that she'd the least notion what it was which dissatisfied her . . .

"I will leave tomorrow morning," said Mowbray, recalling her attention. "Early. With luck, I shall return in no more than three days, which should be no very great disruption to your schedule." He bowed. "If you will excuse me, I must discover from your excellent butler where I may set up that croquet set, after which I will supervise a game between the children. I suspect they did not know the rules and I fear that Justin was making them up as they went along. Perhaps," he added, just as Justina began to relax, "when you have finished here you will join us. We could, the four of us, have a game."

She tensed. "Me? Play croquet? But I—"

Could she admit she had never played the game? Well, why not when it was no more than the truth?

"I, along with Justin and Cordelia, haven't a notion how one goes about it," she finished, speaking in a dry tone edged with wry humor.

Mowbray stifled disbelief. "Then," he said promptly, "I may teach you, as well, may I not?" He hid his amazement that it would be necessary. Despite what she'd said about having no childhood, this seemed impossible. Did not everyone play croquet? "In half an hour, perhaps?"

She glanced at her work. Half an hour? She'd not be through the half of it since she must recopy what had been destroyed. On the other hand, the man would be gone tomorrow. And then she could stifle the idiotic excitement she always felt in his presence and hide away even more ridiculous yearnings for . . .

What? She didn't know.

For whatever it was, and get on with the life she had chosen for herself.

"Very well," she said, her voice so lifeless that it lacked the slightest trace of the emotions roiling around inside her.

He eyed her, frowning. "Half an hour, then." He left the room.

Three quarters of an hour later Mowbray returned, thinking Miss Dunsforth was deliberately defying him by not coming out to join them, only to discover her so deep in her work that he had difficulty gaining her attention. The odd notion crossed his mind that perhaps her writing was important to her. More so than it had ever occurred to him that a woman's work would be, or even could be.

Or should be?

Was not a woman merely a helpmeet to a man so that anything she did should aid and abet her mate? Or was that thought rather selfish? As selfish, perhaps, as any he had attributed to Miss Dunsforth!

Perhaps, thought Mowbray, he would buy one of Miss Dunsforth's tales while in town and read it. He would see for himself what it was she worked on with such inner intensity that she became totally unaware of the world around her, even to forgetting her visitor. Himself. Forgetting his existence!

How dare she?

Mowbray smothered the gasp elicited by that thought. And he forced fancies he should not, not under any circumstance, give the least little consideration to, back into a portion of his mind where he could ignore them. At least, he might be able to do so for *most* of each day!

* * *

Justina listened carefully as Lord Mowbray described the simple rules for the game set up out on the east lawn near the ha-ha. She asked two questions and then nodded. The children were allowed to go first and she watched, puzzled, when his lordship changed Cornelia's hands to a better hold. He also settled her at a slightly different angle, pointing out to her where she should hit her ball so that it would go in the direction wanted.

He was, decided Justina, giving instruction to the child! He was teaching her! Was Cornelia of an age where she could possibly learn such complicated physical maneuvers? It seemed she was. Justina watched the child's ball roll in exactly the proper direction although not, perhaps, quite so far as one might have wished.

Justina, recalling what Mowbray told her niece, did the same and was pleased that her ball rolled beyond the others to stop very near the first gate. For half the game, no one attempted to interfere with another's ball. But then, by accident, Justina's rolled up to Lord Mowbray's, rocking it gently. Recalling one of the rules, she glanced his lordship's way. He rolled his eyes and crossed his arms.

Justin, whooping in excitement, urged her on. "Hit it, Aunt Justina! Hard! Right into the bushes!"

Justina laughed. She actually reached out and tousled her nephew's hair as she walked by him to where the balls lay snuggled together. And then, distracted by the odd sensation of the boy's hair against her palm, she lost her concentration and gave *both* the balls a whack, sending hers after his lordship's instead of holding it steady with her foot.

Justin groaned but Cornelia clapped her hands and Lord Mowbray threw back his head and laughed. Justina felt chagrin and, when his laughter did not abate, anger. She had another stroke coming, so she stalked toward her ball. Aiming carefully, she managed to place it just within the next hoop.

A technical discussion ensued between Lord Mowbray and

his godson as to whether this was sufficient for her to continue. They concluded it was not, but the next ball knocked hers on through and Cornelia, instead of knocking her aunt's ball sideways, chose to carry on to the next gate.

Justina, who had been taught that the game, any game, was nonsense and a waste of time, could not understand why she felt relief that her ball remained in a reasonably good lie rather than beyond the boundaries of the playing field as did Lord Mowbray's. Nor did she understand why she felt a degree of satisfaction when, a little later, she managed a very difficult shot. Nor was there any logic in the sense of accomplishment and pleasure which shot through her when she and Justin, her partner, won the game.

Nor, for that matter, did she understand the depressed feeling sweeping through her when, the next morning, she and the children could no longer see Lord Mowbray. His lordship, mounted on his gelding, had ridden down the long lane between the ancient chestnuts and disappeared.

And why, she wondered, once again touching Justin's hair, did hair feel so enticing when it wound, with a life of its own, around her fingers? Then there was Cornelia's little hand, nestled trustingly into her own. Why did something so simple cause warmth to rise up inside her?

It was, she decided, exceedingly confusing.

Mowbray returned four days later. The tutor rode beside him while the governess followed after in a coach. As a surprise, two ponies followed on leads behind a groom who would care for them and teach the children to ride.

James Compton, the tutor, was a slightly plump gentleman. His nondescript hair showing gray at the temples gave him a trifling look of dignity. He was firm with Justin without being vicious, and he was willing to teach the boy beyond his books the activities a growing boy should learn, including the rolling of hoops, playing tennis, and fishing, the equipment for such pastimes traveling with Miss Gilbert in the carriage.

Justina hoped Miss Gilbert would be a pleasant addition to the household, a woman with whom she herself might have enjoyable discourse of an evening once the children slept. However, she soon discovered that Miss Gilbert had more in common with Miss Repton, the soft-spoken governess and the gray wisp of a companion effacing themselves to the point that Justina tended to forget their existence.

If Justina were to find intellectual stimulation from either of her new employees, it would be Mr. Compton who supplied the need. And he, she found, had a mind set in such conventional patterns that it would not allow him to argue with his employer.

Not, of course, that there was a need for someone with whom one might enjoy a rousing good argument so long as Lord Mowbray remained a guest.

And his lordship did remain.

Justina did not ask why, this visit, his lordship stayed on and on as he had not before. She discovered that he spent a part of each day giving each child his undivided attention. Her maid told her when he took Justin fishing, for instance, and when he taught Cornelia how to play hopscotch, and, another day, both children how to blow soap bubbles from a solution supplied by the laundry maid. There were also simple ball games, such as nine holes and castles, to learn. And he watched when they had their riding lessons, which Cornelia loved and her brother, as had his father before him, disliked.

Then one day, when taking a stroll in the shrubbery, Justina overheard Cornelia's first stuttering attempts to read. She peered through the bushes and saw that Mowbray listened patiently while reviewing Justin's arithmetic paper. She stayed out of sight and, when Nellie heaved a great sigh of relief that she'd managed her task, she heard his lordship discuss with the boy the composition he was to write the next day for Mr. Compton. Why? Had not the tutor and governess been hired to do such things?

It was all very confusing. His staying on as he did had, she found, both good and bad points. For instance, he was in the children's company for so few hours each day that, inevitably, he spent far more of his time with herself. He did not bother her in the mornings, of course, when she worked at her desk, but once Mrs. Minch had laid out a luncheon in the breakfast room, he would come to her and insist she lay down her pen.

"My dear Miss Dunsforth, it is not good for your health to spend so many hours hunched over your desk. You, as much as the children, must have exercise each day. I have had a net set up. I will teach you to play badminton."

"Even," asked Justina, mildly curious, "if I do not wish to learn to play?"

"You will enjoy it."

The most confusing point was that she did. Justina couldn't understand how wasting her time in such a comical fashion as bouncing hither and yon in order to be in position to return to the other side of the net a ball stuck about with silly little feathers could possibly be the least bit interesting. Nevertheless, it was. In fact, as one sunny day after another passed, she began to look forward to lunch so that, afterwards, she and Lord Mowbray could stroll out to the net and take up their positions on either side of it.

At first, of course, he stood to one side of her, tossing up a birdie and swatting it and then encouraging her to do the same. After she got used to having him so near and could put aside the odd feelings his closeness roused, she began, with some dexterity, to hit the thing more often than not. When she became reasonably successful at it, he moved them to a position near the net where she practiced lobbing the feathered objects over it, one after another. Finally he went to the other side and gently threw them to her until she could judge where one would arrive and, quite often, hit it back to him.

Only then did he take up his racket and begin to teach her the rules of the game.

Eventually, after analyzing the situation backward and forward, Justina decided that it was the learning of a new skill which intrigued her. Therefore she dutifully took up yet another set of lessons when Lord Mowbray, much to the disappointment of his nephew, suggested she might like to learn to cast a line after the wily trout living in the stream cutting through her land.

Justin, of course, did not wish to give up the time alone with his godfather, but Mowbray stood firm. And here again Justina found the new experience a challenge and far more enjoyable than she'd have thought possible.

Her enjoyment did not, of course, have anything to do with the fact that, this time, Lord Mowbray stood close behind her and held her arm gently until she learned the backward and forward movements which sent her line out, allowing the fly to land just so. Still, since she was pleased to have mastered the skill, she could not understand why she was unhappy that he no longer helped her.

And then, when she hooked her first trout, she grew still less happy. Justina did not find it at all pleasurable to draw the creature from the water, and she hated it when Mowbray, praising her for its size, put it with those he'd caught to be taken to Cook, who would prepare them for their dinner. In fact, for a very long moment, Justina seriously considered never again eating fish. It had been truly awful to see the poor thing gasping and miserable when held up to be admired.

Luckily Justina recalled how much she enjoyed Cook's special way of fixing trout and, sadly if silently, she acknowledged that she would continue to eat them. Still, there must be a solution to the problem as she saw it. Since she enjoyed the casting, the key, obviously, was to avoid hooking anything. Since one never knew where the silly things would be lurking, the answer was simple: In order to avoid hooking a fish, she must avoid using a hook!

She wondered if Lord Mowbray would notice if she removed the tiny barbs from the flies he'd tied for her.

He did, of course, the very next time they all went fishing. Amused by this previously hidden evidence of a tender heart, he refrained from teasing her. In fact, the proof that she had a heart that could be softened roused new warmth within his own breast. Caught up in speculation about this newly discovered facet of his hostess's character, he very nearly allowed his godson to tumble into the stream.

The boy had a particularly large fish on his line and, excited, jumped around a trifle too exuberantly as he brought it in. Despite her feelings about catching fish, Justina praised Justin for his and the boy glowed, looked at her with such happiness in his features that she felt something clutch at her heart in such a way that the sensation frightened her.

Surely such a terrible palpitation was unhealthy!

"Justin."

"Hmm?"

"Justin!"

"Fiddle, Nellie! You made me lose my place. What is it?"

"You said Aunt Justina was not so bad as we'd thought. Why?"

"Uncle Theo says, when she was our age, she wasn't allowed to learn to do the things we enjoy. He says we must be patient with her so that she, too, may have fun when we play. You were not there today when I caught my fish. The one we are to have for our tea? She was pleased for me and said so."

Cornelia thought about what her brother had said. Finally

she sighed. "Maybe it is that she isn't so very bad. Not entirely awful."

"Of course she isn't entirely awful. Wherever did you get such a notion?"

Cornelia gave him a look and Justin grinned acknowledgement before returning to the exciting, if overly moral, tale he'd been allowed to read as a special treat.

That evening Mowbray finally got around to starting the first volume of one of Miss Dunsforth's novels. He had, at the last moment before leaving London, remembered his decision to do so and sent his secretary out to purchase it. He had been irritated when it took the fellow several hours to accomplish the task.

"How can you have wasted so much time when you know we've a great deal to do? It was, after all, a very simple order, was it not?" he had demanded.

"No, it was not. Not at all simple, my lord," had retorted the overly warm young gentleman who had been forced to trot all over the city in his attempts to fulfill his errand. Crossly, forgetting his place in his just irritation, he continued in something of a ranting style. "It appears Miss Dunsforth's work is particularly popular. First I went to Hatchard's as you said to do. Then to two other bookstores and finally I was sent along to her publisher where that"—he gestured toward the elusive book—"which is Miss Dunsforth's latest, is the only one available."

Mowbray had frowned. "How strange. I never would have thought . . ." He trailed off and placed the novel with the other papers which were to be packed.

The purchase slipped his mind until he found the volumes while seeking a clean handkerchief. Howard had shoved them well to the back of one of his drawers. He took them out

and set them on the table beside his bed. Then he pushed
the lamp a trifle closer, piled his pillows so as to support
his back, and settled in to discover just what it was that Miss
Dunsforth produced at such cost to herself and those around
her.

The light dimmed. His lordship cast the lamp an irritated
glance, returning his eyes to the page before him . . . and
then back. The oil was no more than a thin smear in the
bottom of the reservoir! How could this be? Surely he would
have noticed earlier if the lamp were so nearly out of oil.
He peered across the room, but could not make out the slender hands on the mantel clock. He was forced to lay aside
the book and leave his bed in order to discover the time.

"Three in the morning?" he asked the clock. "You lie!"

Then he turned back to the bed where the lamp flickered
in an irritating fashion and, to his surprise, noticed one of
the slim volumes lying alongside the third instead of atop it.
Had he finished the first volume and gone on to the second
without noticing?

Surely not.

Mowbray frowned upon discovering he'd done more. He
had begun the third volume! But why? It was such a silly
story. Utterly nonsensical. Oh, decidedly whimsical in places,
and certainly it moved quickly from one idiotic disaster to
the next, so it was difficult to see where one might leave
off before discovering how the characters won out . . . but
still, it was nothing more than absurd drivel which could
only serve to fill a young woman's head with romantic nonsense.

So, Mowbray asked himself, a frown forming deep creases
in his forehead, *why did I continue reading until the oil ran
out? Why did I not put it aside hours ago?*

His lordship glanced at his dressing table where, on a shelf
hinged so that one could swing it out to any required position, a second lamp sat. A lamp full of oil. A lamp he could
move to his bedside table to replace the one—

"No," he said aloud, a sharp intrusion into the silence. The sound startled him. *No,* he repeated silently. *I will go to bed as would any sensible person at such an hour.*

And he did . . .

For all of half an hour, at which point he got tired of tossing and turning and not finding any position the least bit comfortable. He rose, exchanged the lamps, and settled back to finish Miss Dunsforth's silly little tale. Mowbray had found it would be impossible to sleep until he knew how the hero and heroine overcame the machinations of her evil uncle and could come together to live happily ever after, forever and ever!

Justina looked up from the paragraphs she had just finished drafting, wondering why it was so dim and dreary. To her disgust she found a rainy day had broken the long period of fine weather. Clouds scudded across the sky and rain spattered against the windowpanes. She frowned. Surely it had not been gray and drear when she awoke that morning? Surely she would have noticed.

But her curtains had been closed, had they not? And she'd not waited patiently in her bed for her maid to bring her morning chocolate, at which time the girl would also have uncovered the windows. Instead she rose and dressed herself in one of the simple sack dresses she preferred for morning wear. She'd taken herself straight to her study, where she set to work. She looked again at the pages, the words closely covering the paper and written in the oddly abridged fashion she doubted anyone but she herself could decipher. It was, she'd discovered, the only way to get her thoughts onto a page quickly enough. It was so easy to lose them!

She glanced out the window and felt her shoulders droop. Lord Mowbray had planned a picnic and that had been her reason for rising so early. They were to take the children and drive out to the crumbling remains of a monastery hidden in woods not far from Chestnut Lane.

But it would not happen. Not now.

Justina glared at the rivulets of water running down the tiny panes of the leaded windows. How dared it rain today? How dared it spoil his lordship's plans?

Justina heard her thoughts and was forced to chuckle. How foolish to suggest the weather had a mind of its own and could deliberately set out to thwart her in her expectation of experiencing still another new pleasure. At least she had been assured she would enjoy it and, previously, Lord Mowbray was correct when predicting she'd like something she was convinced she would not.

She sighed.

"What troubles you?" asked a voice from across the room.

She turned quickly and stared at the man of whom she'd been thinking. *"You!"*

"I believe so," he said with a touch of humor. "But why did you sigh?"

Her eyes narrowed. "You look tired," she said, avoiding an answer.

His smile was rather derisive. "I got very little sleep last night," he admitted. "Why did you sigh?"

"What troubles you?" she asked, again returning question for question.

"I asked first." His eyes twinkled even though they were a trifle sunken into the dark circles.

She had to think what he meant. "Oh. Well, I discovered I am disappointed we must forgo our picnic. I am surprised. Such a nonsensical thing, this taking good food out into the dirty outdoors and sitting around on rugs to eat it when, at home, one has a perfectly adequate dining room with comfortable chairs at which anyone with good sense would prefer to dine."

He chuckled. "Nonsensical, indeed. But why is it wrong, on occasion, to indulge oneself with nonsense? In fact, you, my dear Miss Dunsforth, are the very last person to say one should not!" He smiled still more widely when she frowned. "But, my dear, do you not wish your readers to do just that?"

Justina felt her cheeks heat and raised her hands to cover them. "You would once again insult my work?" she asked, unsure whether she was embarrassed or angry. Or both!

He sobered, shaking his head. "Insult work which is so utterly delightful it keeps one up all the night? How could I possibly be so contrary?"

Justina's eyes widened. *"That* is why you are tired?"

He smiled, the skin next to his eyes crinkling with humor. He nodded. "I didn't mean to do so, of course."

"But why . . . ?"

"My dear, your story is utterly nonsensical, but it is impossible to set aside a volume until one has discovered how the hero overcomes his latest difficulty. By then, however, you have already placed the heroine into a new predicament, so one is forced to read on. And on. And on." He sighed. "It is too bad of you, Miss Dunsforth. One finally finishes only to discover the sun is up and the servants stirring. One is exhausted. But also"—a frown creased his brow—"at the same time, one feels satisfied and content. It is very strange."

This time when her skin heated, Justina knew it was embarrassment. *Pleased* embarrassment, but definitely embarrassment.

"I am sorry," he continued, giving her time to recover her usual poise, "that we must postpone our picnic."

"It is also the case that we cannot play croquet or badminton or go fishing or roll hoops or just anything," she said, casting another cross look at her window. She had recently discovered she liked racing after Justin when he rolled his hoop down the newly raked drive. She had, in fact, lifted her skirts rather indelicately high—or so her outraged chaperon had whispered in her ear when she and Justin, the two of them laughing and happy, returned to the terrace on which the lady sat, inexpertly sewing still more lace to one of her gowns, while Miss Gilbert dozed beside her. And Mowbray had just stood there grinning at her in the most odious way!

Mowbray interrupted thoughts better forgotten. "We will have to play indoor games, will we not?"

His words pushed aside Justina's irritation and she stilled. "Games?" After a moment she asked, *"Inside?"*

"Certainly. Skittles or Nine Men's Morris. Or Fish perhaps, if you have the pieces." He eyed her. "Ah. You do not. Miss Dunsforth, I was exceedingly surprised to discover how true it is that you were never taught to play games. You see, it was not true for your brother."

"Was it not?" She frowned, wonderingly. "Perhaps," she added, "when he went away to school? Perhaps he learned them there?"

"Hmm. I did not meet him, of course, until we both went up to Cambridge. He is an excellent card player, you know."

"I did not know, but since he is excellent at whatever he attempts, it does not surprise me."

"Oh, not everything," contradicted Mowbray, chuckling.

"Not?" Justina sat up straighter. Her brother, it had always seemed to her, was perfect. *Too* perfect.

"He is awkward at things which require coordination. And he does not ride if he can avoid it, of course, but what I remember best is the time he tried punting on the River Cam." Mowbray laughed outright. "Poor Felix! He was left hugging the pole, his legs wound around it, and swearing in such classic style that one of the dons, hearing him, was exceedingly impressed by his fluency in ancient curses!"

Justina hid a smile. "What happened?"

"When Felix ran out of curses, the don rescued him. Before your brother ran down, the gentleman was far too busy writing out the phrases in a tiny notebook to think to do so."

"Our father thought it a great joke to teach Felix to swear in Latin after, far too young to understand what it was he said, Felix repeated something one of the stable boys said in his hearing."

"Hmm," said Mowbray thoughtfully. "That is very much in character with other things you have told me of your upbringing."

The door crashed open and Justin stood there, a huge frown creasing his young brow. Coming down the hall behind him was his tutor who, apologetic, put a hand on the boy's shoulder. He asked pardon for allowing Justin to escape him and followed that with another for the boy's bursting in on them in such a way.

"Had the two of you finished the day's lessons?" asked Mowbray before Justina could give tongue to the far less mild words hovering there.

"Yes, sir," said Mr. Compton with something other than his usual amiability. "We had just finished. The boy did not, however, put away his books. Nor did he ask to be excused," added the tutor with exasperation.

"Well Justin?" asked Mowbray. "What have you to say for yourself?"

The boy put his hands behind his back, hung his head, and dug his toe into the carpet.

"Justin, you have been asked to explain why you behaved so badly," said Justina tartly.

The boy darted his aunt a quick look, pulled a long breath into his lungs, and let it out. "It is raining," he said, scowling.

"We had noticed," said Mowbray mildly, and cast Justina a look that suggested she allow him to handle this.

For reasons beyond her comprehension, she did so. Previously, she had never allowed another to take up her burdens, so it was with decided surprise that she did so now.

"But there can be no picnic!" Justin uttered in despairing tones.

"Yes. It is a shame our pleasure must be postponed," said Mowbray.

The boy looked up, his expression hopeful. "Postponed?"

"Did you suppose we would simply forget it?"

The boy's head went down and the toe squirmed over another bit of carpet. He nodded.

"Then be easy. We will try another day. In the meantime, you will return to the schoolroom, where you will put away your books and where you will, in proper form, ask to be dismissed. You will, however, before you leave us, apologize to your aunt for your rudeness in bursting in upon her when you very well know you should knock and ask permission."

Justin cast another look toward his aunt. He sighed again. "Yes, sir." He faced his aunt squarely. "Aunt Justina, please forgive me for my rude behavior. I will not do it again."

When the lad, led away by his tutor, had disappeared, Mowbray spoke. "Very likely he will not. He is a very bright boy, and I have noticed he rarely makes the same mistake twice."

"Is he doing well with his books?"

"You do not know?"

Justina twiddled a thread which hung from a bit of lace decorating her gown. She cast Mowbray one of those speaking Dunsforth glances.

"You do not know," decided Mowbray. "Do you so much hate the thought of formal teaching that you cannot request information concerning the children's progress with their work?"

She grimaced. "How do you know so well, even before I know it myself, why I behave in a certain way?"

"I do, do I not?" He sounded surprised it should be so and then thoughtful. "I cannot explain it." He glanced toward the desk. "Have you finished with today's work?"

"I must make a clean copy of what I have written," she said, giving it a speculative look. "Occasionally, when I leave it too long, I cannot decipher it."

Mowbray stepped closer to the desk. He asked permission with a look and, when she nodded, lifted a page. He frowned. His lips moved. Finally, bewildered, he shook his head. "I read words but, on the whole, it makes no sense. Is it a secret language?" he asked.

Rather pleased than otherwise, Justina chuckled. "No, merely I do not always finish a word. And I abbreviate common words."

"Ah! I begin to see. The Greek *alpha,* for instance, in place of the word *and?"*

She nodded. "And you see the large letters standing alone? Those are characters' names."

"You have done quite a bit today, have you not?" He indicated a stack of rather messy pages on which lines were crossed out and occasional blots covered words.

"More than usual. It often happens that way. I reach a point in the book where the work goes more quickly."

"In that case, you must copy out what you have done. I will ask Howard to tell Cook to put back our luncheon." He headed for the door.

"But I do not wish to spend more time at my desk. Not just now," said Justina, surprising both him and herself. It had, in the past, been difficult to find *enough* time for her writing! She joined Mowbray and swept through the door, not wanting to think about why she'd felt deprived that he was about to leave her. She would not think of it. She would merely accept that she liked his company and that she must spend as much time as possible with him since his visit could not last much longer.

As it was, his time at Chestnut Lane had gone on and on. A reason occurred to her, and her slightly low mood dropped into an abyss. Once the thought crossed her mind, she wondered she'd not seen it instantly. He stayed on because he did not trust her to see that the children were well settled into their new routine and properly kept to their books!

But they *had* become accustomed. He knew she'd not interfere. Now he would go.

The abyss into which Justina had fallen was filled with such desolation that she felt as if a huge wet rag slapped against her, leaving her skin both damp and, at the same time, prickly. And that central organ which had been misbehaving in such strange ways felt as if something clutched it and squeezed it.

Why bands tightened around her heart, she hadn't a notion. Nor did she like it. Not as she had when she'd experienced a similar if lesser sensation when touching young Justin. This *hurt* whereas, when caused by one of the children hugging her or the feel of their soft skin or her fingers in their shining hair, it felt quite pleasant.

Once again Justina pushed aside unanswerable questions and, in a small part of her mind to which she never paid much attention, she wished her mother still lived so that she could, perhaps, ask that stern but forthcoming woman what was meant by it all.

The rain did not abate and, lunch eaten, Lord Mowbray gently escorted Justina back to her study.

"It is perhaps as well the day is so miserable," he said as he saw her settled at her desk. "You've work to do."

Once he'd seen her seated, Mowbray moved to the bookcase built into the wall. He pulled down a book before moving to the comfortable chairs arranged before an unneeded but cheering fire. He placed one chair farther from the heat. Then his lordship settled himself, opened the book, and began reading.

Justina, watching him, felt confused. She was glad he was there. His company was far more cheering then a mere fire could ever be! On the other hand, she was relieved he did not expect her to do her duty as a hostess, entertaining him when she must cope with the difficulty of deciphering her writing.

So why, she wondered, *am I irritated that he is so sympathetic, so exceedingly understanding, about it?* Expelling a very small sigh, she got down to work.

Once Justina was fully engrossed, Mowbray set aside the book he'd chosen at random. His gaze rested on her back, the spine held properly straight even when she leaned forward, one hand holding up her head as she read and reread a portion of her work, puzzling out the meaning of the scribbled prose. He heard a sigh and smiled tenderly. Then he nodded, pleased for her when, with a faint "aha," she sat up, dipped her pen, and began copying her words, the ink flowing steadily across the page with only occasional glances to the original.

Mowbray watched Justina work and thought about how much she'd changed in the last few weeks. It had been a delightful experience, seeing her open up to new ideas and new occupations, seeing her glow with accomplishment when she mastered something. Now and again, she even laughed a light, bubbling chuckle, which brought smiles to the faces of all who heard it.

Mowbray recognized a rueful ambition to hear it more often. He lay back his head and, staring at the ceiling, plotted ways of drawing it out, rousing that lighthearted woman who hid beneath the stern and duty-bound person who went through her days adhering to the rigid schedule it seemed she imbibed as she'd eaten nursery bread and milk.

After a period of delightful daydreaming, he glanced at his hostess. It occurred to his lordship that it might be dangerous to his peace of mind if he were to lighten Justina's life to too great a degree. Miss Dunsforth was, already, much too tempting a woman. That hair . . .

No! He must not wonder how she would look with that wonderful hair tumbling down her back.

Wild. Free.

There! He was doing it again.

Mowbray swore under his breadth and, forcibly drawing his eyes from Justina, stared into the fire. The days had passed so smoothly, one day fading into the next, while he enjoyed the bright-eyed wonder of the children and the equally wonderfully bright-eyed interest of their aunt. Days when he did not think—not once—of his wife.

His poor mad wife.

Silently now, Mowbray swore more bitingly. The time drew near when, once again, he would ride to the establishment in which Mary existed. He would not say lived. She no longer had a life. At least, not as one should know life. A deep sadness, one long familiar to him, settled in, pulling him down into a well of darkness that was half self-pity and half pity for the woman to whom he was wed.

And, as he'd done a million times before, he wondered what he had done wrong, how he could have caused such misery. If only he were to think clearly, surely he could discover it, could apologize, and perhaps draw her back from wherever, in her mind, she had fled to escape him. He had gone into their marriage with no great hopes, but he had certainly had no intention of wounding his new wife so deeply that she would try to kill him! If only he'd a clue to what he'd done to deserve her hate. Wild and wilder guesses, painful uncertainty, and the knowledge that he'd ruined her life, had become a painful burden years earlier. One he'd bear forever.

Again Mowbray's gaze strayed toward Justina. Wonderfully intelligent, so knowledgeable, so able to converse on interesting topics or, when roused to it, to argue in a rational and non-acrimonious fashion, which passed the time delightfully. And, with all that, so easy to look at. And so very easy to desire more than to merely look. . . .

With a not-so-silent oath Lord Mowbray rose and, remembering to be quiet, tiptoed rather than stalked from the room. He continued down the hall in less careful fashion and exited the house, heedless of the rain.

"This will not do!" he shouted to the heavens and then, shamefaced, glanced around to be certain that no one had heard his outburst. Reassured by the notion that no one with any sense would be out in such weather, he walked on. No one, unless, of course, like himself, it was necessary to be quite alone. Alone where he could lecture himself sternly and set aside, once and forever, all thoughts of Justina Dunsforth as an attractive woman.

Because even if he were the sort of man to seduce such a woman, there was always the fear of what might happen to her if he did. That constant, nearly silent murmur of fear with which he'd lived so long. *Would,* he wondered still again, *every well-bred women react to me as did my wife?*

The occasional whore with whom he eased himself did not appear to find him abhorrent, but of course one did not live with a whore. And he had never found the courage to discover how a lady, a woman from the same class as his wife, would react to his lovemaking. Assuming it was his lovemaking which was the problem. His wife, at least, had not liked his coming to her bed. She'd made excuses, avoided him. And, because of her avoidance, he feared it had been their intimacy that frightened her.

Or perhaps—a slightly more acceptable thought—it was the fear of providing him an heir, of birthing a child, which was the foundation of his wife's hatred, her madness . . . ?

In the latter case, another woman would *not* flee reality to escape him.

Mowbray's thoughts roiled and rolled along the familiar paths as he tramped toward the bridge over the stream that led to the home woods. He had almost reached it when he heard a childish scream, a splash.

The scream was followed by young Justin's panic-stricken yells for help.

Late the next morning, the doctor left Chestnut Lane to return to his own home, leaving instructions for Cornelia's care. He also left behind the impression that it did not truly matter if those instructions were or were not followed, that the child could not possibly survive the fever that had risen dramatically some hours after her dunking in the stream.

Justina, holding the paper detailing his instructions, watched him go, her gaze bitter. "The man is an idiot," she said once he was beyond hearing. "There is nothing here worth the paper on which it is written." She crumpled the instructions and tossed them toward the fire. "Come," she told her hovering abigail. "We've a distressing time ahead of us. Howard," she called over her shoulder as she started up the stairs, "send a groom to Lord Eltonstone's. Beg from him as large a chunk of ice as he feels he can spare from his icehouse. I want chilled buckets of fresh well water brought to Cornelia's room each half hour. I will get that fever down if it is the last thing I do. Tell Mrs. Minch to bring me a dose of willow bark. I have read that the bitter stuff eases fever. She must also oversee the preparation of barley water and broth. Chicken. Cornelia prefers chicken. Remind her the parboiled barley is to be soaked in rapidly boiling water and she must not stint the sugar she adds to the lemon slices. And she is to use all the lemon. . . ."

Mowbray watched Justina climb, her orders gradually becoming difficult to hear and then too faint to distinguish as she moved upward. This was a new side to the woman he had come to admire so much. This facet of the woman he loved much resembled a general on the eve of battle.

The woman he loved . . . ?

Mowbray stilled. Loved?

Oh dear God, how did I allow this? he asked silently. And sneezed. And sneezed again. He snuffled. *A head cold,* he thought. *An idiotic useless head cold.* Which, he told himself, was only what he deserved for so stupidly going out into that spring rain.

Except, had he not gone, he'd not have been on hand to rescue Cornelia from the swirling, rain-swelled waters of the stream into which she'd fallen. He stared out the open door into the sun-drenched drive, wondering what he should do. What he could do . . .

Young Justin had been sent to bed the night before without his supper as punishment for taking his sister out into such weather and then, after being so foolish as to have done such a thing, for allowing her to stand too near the rushing water. Now he inched his way downstairs. Ascertaining that the doctor was gone, the boy crept onto the landing.

"Uncle Theo," he called softly.

"Yes, Justin?" responded Mowbray a trifle absently. He swung around on his heel and saw the lad's anxiety-ridden face peering over the railing.

"Is Nellie going to die?"

Mowbray pulled himself from his own concern and, taking the stairs two at a time, lifted the boy into his arms. He stared down into the lad's frightened features. "Nellie will not die," he said, speaking firmly. "Your Aunt Justina will not allow it. But your aunt needs no more illness in the house while she deals with Cornelia. You, my lad, should be in your nice warm dayroom and not running through drafty halls without your shoes!"

"I couldn't stay there," said Justin, his hands on Mowbray's shoulders, holding himself away so he could look solemnly into his godfather's face. "Nurse shakes her head and looks gloomy and mumbles and mutters her prayers. She makes me afraid. I didn't mean to hurt Nellie. But we were sorry we couldn't have the picnic, you see, and we wanted an adventure and now she might die." His face screwed up. "It isn't *fair!*" he wailed.

"Yes, well, you see what can happen when you break rules. Rules are made for a reason, Justin." Honesty forced him to add, "Most of them anyway."

Tears leaked from the boy's eyes. Mowbray mopped them up and wondered if he had the wisdom to find the middle road which would reassure his godson but leave the boy with the knowledge that he'd acted wrongly.

They talked for a long time. Mowbray left the emotionally exhausted boy napping and peeked into Cornelia's room. Justina's maid stood behind her mistress. Justina herself washed down the child's still form. She handed back a fever-warmed rag and accepted a new one just wrung from the bucket of cool water. Mowbray watched as, again and again, Justina passed a newly wet cloth over the tiny body. A glass stood on the table by the bed in which a small amount of cloudy liquid remained. The dose of willow bark? Very likely. Or what remained of it.

Mowbray sneezed. When Justina glanced around, he asked, "Any change?"

"No. But we cannot expect one immediately. Go away. Rest if you can. You must not be sick as well." She straightened and, her hands pressing into her back, turned a glower on him. "I told you to change out of those wet clothes the instant you arrived back at the house!"

"There is nothing more irritating than someone telling one 'I told you so'—" He sneezed again. "—as you well know."

"Maybe so." Justina accepted a fresh rag and turned to her work. "But I did tell you, and see what has happened because you insisted that Cornelia must be cared for first, that you must see that she was all right."

"Except that she was not."

"I know," said Justina softly. "Do go to bed, my lord. If her fever does not come down before nightfall, I may need you to supervise this work while I rest."

Mowbray went. And sneezed still again as he closed his bedroom door.

Mowbray took over in the sickroom late that afternoon and bathed the child on into the evening while Justina slept. About midnight, she returned to working over Cornelia. The long night passed slowly and Justina, so tired her movements grew habitual, noted that her maid's mouth gaped widely as she handed over still another wet rag.

"Find someone to take your place, Mary," said Justina. "You have done far more than I should have allowed."

"I can do it, miss. I'll know it gets done if I do." Mary sniffed. "Those maids. I do not know where Mrs. Minch finds the creatures. Please don't make me go."

Justina, who had thought she might never again find humor in anything, found herself smiling. "I thought to spare you, but if you will not spare yourself, then I will not drive you away."

Silence followed the brief exchange. Another bucket of chilled water arrived and the news that there was no more ice. Justina paused in her work, her tired mind unable to cope with the necessity of making a decision. Should she send for more? She stared at her niece—and stilled.

For the first time Cornelia was restless. Her head swung from side to side on her hot pillow. Her hot, *wet* pillow! Perspiration poured off the small body. Tears streamed down Justina's face, and her heart swelled. Until this moment she had not allowed herself to hope, to feel. And now that she did, it nearly overwhelmed her.

"Miss? Do we send for more ice?" asked the footman from the doorway.

"Ice?" Tears changed to laughter. "Oh, no, James. No, we need no more ice. Cornelia's fever is broken! Mary, we did it! Wake the nursery maid who must change these sweat-soaked sheets. Mary, Mary, Cornelia will live!"

Justina bundled the small child up in a comforter and moved toward Nurse Cornish's fireside chair. She settled herself into the comfortable shape formed by the nanny's body and asked Mary to bring her a tumbler of the barley water. Cornelia, only half awake, sipped a few sips before snuggling against her aunt and falling into true sleep.

Justina touched the damp curls, gently running her fingers through them. Her hand settled around the small skull, and her other arm tightened, holding the child close. She laid her head back, feeling fulfilled and content, and then, exhausted by her labors, she too drifted into sleep.

And that was how Mowbray found them.

Mary, who had worked longer hours than any of them, lay curled on the rug before the fire, a shawl thrown over her. The young nursery maid, wide-eyed, uncertain what, if anything, she should be doing, stood as silent as a mouse in one corner. And Justina, the sleeping child held firmly in her arms, slept on. Mowbray's heart leapt at the lovely vision of woman and child. Then it settled on Justina, and the warmth of his newly recognized love filled him to overflowing.

Finally it occurred to him that Cornelia must be on the mend or Justina would be bathing her. Moving quietly, he approached. Very gently, he touched the child's curls, and Cornelia opened her eyes to smile at him.

Mowbray smiled back. He held out his hands and the child leaned toward him. Very gently, he plucked her from Justina's arms and carried her to her bed, where he offered her the glass of barley water the nursery maid rushed to pour for him. Cornelia drank the whole glass and then yawned.

She snuggled down. "I like Aunt Justina," she said. "She's soft and comfy."

"I like her too," whispered Mowbray, as he tucked the covers around her shoulders. "Go to sleep, child."

Cornelia smiled and fell almost instantly into deep, healing sleep. Mowbray watched her for a moment, smiling, then turned toward Justina, who appeared restless.

Justina tossed her head, her fingers twitching—and then opened her eyes to stare, wild-eyed, around the room. "Cornelia!"

"Hush, my dear. She sleeps the restful sleep of the innocent." Mowbray reached Miss Dunsforth's side as he spoke and, only a little less easily than he'd lifted Cornelia, he picked up Justina. She wiggled. "Now be still," he said, a laughing note in his voice, "or I might drop you." He

grinned down at her and, bemused, still half asleep, she
blinked up at him. But she also ceased her struggles. In fact,
she became utterly still. Mowbray headed for the door and
down the hall. He stopped before her room.

"I must carry you no farther, Miss Dunsforth," he said
softly, a quick glance at the footman hovering at the top of
the stairs carrying with it a trifling irritation. Reluctantly he
lowered his burden's feet to the floor.

I enjoyed having her in my arms. Where she belongs. The
illicit thought startled him. *Ah! But no! I must not think such
things,* he scolded himself.

Justina was a trifle wobbly on her feet and was glad that
Mowbray steadied her. But she did not understand why, suddenly, she felt deprived of . . . something.

"I will see you when you wake," said Mowbray softly,
unwilling to part from her, although he knew she must rest.

Justina nodded. She watched him take himself sternly in
hand and walk away. That too confused her.

Why, she wondered, *did he seem to find it difficult?*

Late that afternoon, Mowbray, frowning, watched Cornelia
chase a butterfly flitting from buttercup to buttercup. "Should
she be allowed to run about like that?" he asked, worried.
"Surely she should be in her bed!"

"She is fine, and a little mild activity won't hurt her. Children are strange that way. They can be so sick one is certain
they cannot possibly survive and a few hours later it is as
if they were never ill a moment in their life."

He glanced at her. "And how does our Miss Dunsforth
know such a thing as that?"

Justina chuckled. "How does a childless spinster, who so
reluctantly accepted responsibility for a niece and nephew
that one assumed she knew nothing, know anything about
children? Is that what you would ask?"

Mowbray felt his ears heat up. "I suppose that was in my
mind, although not in such disparaging terms."

Justina smiled. "Most likely I would know very little if I

had not been ordered to Elton Castle by Lady Eltonstone, who wished to discuss my part in a fete she planned. The funds raised were destined for the regilding of bits and pieces in the church, as the new vicar was unhappy when he found the cherubs and doves in disarray. Her, hmm—*invitation* came when I was working on the final chapter of a story, so I did not immediately run to do her bidding. To ensure that I obeyed more quickly on the next such occasion, she felt it necessary to teach me a lesson. Therefore, she left me kicking my heels for a considerable time in the lady's parlor, where, to pass the time, I perused Lady Eltonstone's late mother-in-law's day book."

"You smile. Was it full of humor?"

"Humor?" Justina cast him a startled look. "No. Not at all. For decades the dowager was the most detested lady in the region. Always poking her nose in where it was not wanted, you see. And not so much as a trace of humor in her make-up which might have greased her way." Justina's smile could be heard in her voice. "I smiled, my lord, because the primary reason her ladyship was loathed was not so much that she interfered but that she was, far more often than not, correct in her advice! I recall what you felt when I said I told you so!"

"I see the problem. A busybody may be ignored, but a busybody who is perceived to be of help must be thanked for her nosiness, which would be a terrible nuisance, would it not? But what has that to do with your knowledge of children?"

Justina shrugged, a silent way of asking "is it not obvious?" "I read her words concerning them," she explained. "Quite twenty pages, which she wrote when her own children were nearly out of the nursery."

"So it was she who claimed children recover quickly?" When Justina made no answer, he turned his head and discovered on Justina's face a look of such tenderness as he'd never thought to see there.

Unfortunately, it was directed at Cornelia rather than at himself.

Unfortunately? Still again he brought his thoughts up short. He must, he decided, leave Chestnut Lane Manor. Tomorrow he would go. . . .

"Perhaps," said Justina, interrupting his planning, "if the weather remains as bright and warm as today has been, we might indulge the children in that picnic which we were forced to postpone. Justin will adore the ruins, and there are wildflowers for Cornelia, who seems to like such things."

So, perhaps I will leave the following day. "I did not realize you'd noticed," he said.

"I am, perhaps, more conscious of what goes on about me than one would think since I am such an unsociable sort of person. I"—a tinge of red raced up her throat and into her cheeks—"like to watch people."

"For your writing."

"How did you guess?"

"Guessing was unnecessary. When I read your novel, it was as plain as a pikestaff that you are sensitive to the feelings of others." *If not of what you yourself feel,* he thought. "Such an idiotishly involved plot," he said, glancing sideways to see her reaction to that analysis. It was much as he expected, and *not* outrage. Instead she nodded agreement.

"Yes. The sillier the complications, the better it is. That is what the"—It was her turn to glance his way—"empty-headed little misses wish to read."

"But there is more involved to your work than merely the telling of a silly story," he said. "It is your *skill* in telling the tale which draws one in. However absurd one finds it, one cannot put it down until one has finished it. At least," he added, glancing her way, "I could not."

"That, my lord, is exactly as I wish it to be. For everyone!" She held out her hands. "Yes, Cornelia? Have you tired at last?"

The child came trustingly to her aunt and climbed onto her lap. She yawned, wiggled just a bit, and fell asleep.

Again Mowbray watched Justina's glowing features stare down into the little girl's face. And again, he wished she would look at him in such a way. This time, before he remembered to scold himself, his thoughts were interrupted by Justin, who came to him with a nest and the easy tears of childhood in his eyes.

"It fell from the tree, Uncle Theo," said the boy plaintively. "The poor birds have lost their home!"

Recognizing the boy's unspoken thought, or perhaps unthought emotion, that he himself had never had a true home, Mowbray took the fragile structure gently. "Look, Justin," he said, "It is very dry, is it not? Not at all like the lark's nest I showed you in the meadow. This is an abandoned nest. The storm blew it from its branch."

"No birds then?"

"Last year perhaps, but not this spring. Would you like to keep it? Perhaps we can discover what sort of bird made it by looking for similar nests which are occupied." After a glance to where Justina cuddled Cornelia, deeply engaged with the feel of the child snuggled to her breast, Mowbray rose and reached a hand to the boy. "Come, Justin. Show me where you found it. That will help us discover others like it. Birds of a feather tend to choose the same sort of place each year for their nests."

"Do they always make new nests?"

Justina, less oblivious than Mowbray thought, listened as his soft answer trailed off with distance. He was, she thought, so good with Justin. And finally, at long last, she understood why. He must feel for the boy just as she did for Cornelia. Her arms tightened ever so slightly around the little girl. The child was safe now, but what if she had not recovered from her fever? What if they had lost their curly-haired angel? What if . . .

Justina's lips thinned. She was being as silly as one of her own heroines! Cornelia was well and only needed time to fully recover her strength. It was absurd to make up what-ifs with which to frighten oneself!

Justina shut her eyes and thought of Cornelia growing older, learning new things, blossoming into beauty. It was awesome, the thought of that unfolding life, the girl's potential having only recently become evident. But now the child had revealed such bright and wonderful intelligence, it must be carefully cultivated. Justina's lips tightened. Little Cornelia was clever and curious about her world, but she must not be forced to study in the fashion her father and aunt had been made to do. No, this child must also learn the other components of being human, the joy of physical activities which had only recently been revealed to the aunt and also the peace and delight of shared friendship.

The mental stimulation of studies must be only a part of it all. *And,* thought Justina a shade grimly, *I will insist to Felix that I am allowed to see that it is done as it should be done.*

The notion, so sudden and unexpected, shocked her. When had she decided to take on the responsibility for her niece's future? And if she did, did that not mean she must also accept responsibility for Justin? What did one do with a boy? They were quite different from little girls, were they not?

Irrelevant! She would learn. She'd always been good at learning what she needed to know! Justina relaxed.

And yet, she wondered, *what will it do to my nice, orderly little world?*

Unsettle it to a very great degree. That was what it would do! Justina didn't quite know what to do with the sudden relief, very nearly overwhelming relief, which flooded through her. *Have I,* she wondered, been *so very unhappy?* It seemed she had.

Justina smiled. So what if she was? She'd be so no longer. And never again!

* * *

Cornelia played quietly with her dolls in one corner of Justina's study. She had finished dressing them all in their very best and was settling them against the bookcase when Justin quietly opened the door and peered in. He beckoned. Cornelia nodded.

Very quietly the child went out into the hall. "You finished?"

Justin grimaced. "Pretty much. He says I'm behind and that's why I must do so much. It is such a bore."

"Maybe I could help?"

"Maybe." Justin eyed her. "Maybe when I am learning my French vocabulary?"

Cornelia nodded, and then her head swung toward the front of the house. "Someone is coming."

Justin glanced toward the open door and glimpsed the crest on the carriage pulling up outside. "Lady Eltonstone. We don't want to see her. She'd find some reason to tell Aunt Justina, in that awfully sweet way she has, how badly brought up we've been!" Grinning, he grasped Cornelia's hand and raced down the hall toward the back of the house and the garden. They didn't stop running until they reached a glade in the home wood where they dropped to the ground and, the both of them, took a bit to recover their breath.

Justin lay on his back and stared up into the trees. "I wish Uncle Theo would come back."

"Hmm." Cornelia plucked a flower and counted the petals. "Do you think he likes Aunt Justina?"

"Likes her? I suppose so."

"It is great fun when we go places. All of us together," said Cornelia wistfully.

"Like a family," agreed Justin.

"Hmm."

When she said no more, Justin turned his head to look at his sister. "What are you thinking?"

"It would be nice, I think, if we were a family."

"Don't be stupid. We cannot be a family. A family has a

father and a mother and children. We have a father, true, but our mother's dead."

"And Father is not here," said Cornelia. Almost slyly, she added, "Aunt Justina and Uncle Teo are."

"Yes, but that isn't the same," objected Justin crossly.

"Almost the same."

"Stupid!" Justin shoved himself up to his feet and raced away.

Cornelia looked after him, a thoughtful expression making her appear older than her years. She made no attempt to follow him, however, since she was far too busy plotting how one might go about making oneself a family. A mother and a father and children all together. Especially, she thought dreamily, a mother.

Lord Mowbray rode slowly up to the gate of the institution in which his wife resided. He nodded to the gatekeeper who, recognizing him, came quickly to swing half the high iron bars to the side. Mowbray tossed the man a coin, his mien as somber as always when he arrived for another of his self-imposed duty visits to his wife.

He was met at the door by the matron who managed the house. Her delicately frilled cap looked outrageously out of place to Mowbray. It seemed to him that nothing should be frivolous or pretty within walls that held such misery as that suffered by his wife.

"My lord! They found you." Matron beamed.

"Found me?"

"They did not?" Her brows arched, then lowered. "Ah, well, you are here and that is what matters." She nodded. "Come along now. Peter will see to your horse."

Releasing his gelding into the care of the shambling groom, Mowbray followed the cheerful woman. She knocked at the doctor's office door and, without waiting, opened it. She nodded encouragement.

Unsettled, Mowbray hesitated. Then, squaring his shoulders, he passed her and, gently, she shut the door.

"My lord!" The doctor rose to his feet, leaning forward slightly, his fingertips on his desk supporting him. "You've come. Excellent."

"My wife?"

The doctor's expression sobered. "Not good, my lord. Not good at all."

Suddenly Mowbray remembered what he should not have allowed himself to forget. "She still refuses to eat?"

"She will drink but will not eat. It is not rational, of course, but then, the insane are not."

"She lives?"

"She is weak. Very weak. Bedridden now. But yes, she yet lives."

"I must go to her."

"Yes." The doctor rounded the desk and led the way into the hall. He frowned, casting Mowbray a worried look. "We sent messages, my lord. To your country home, your town house, and your solicitor. Please do not think we did not do our best to inform you."

"Be easy," said Mowbray, barely curbing his impatience. "It did not occur to me to notify anyone of where I could be found."

The doctor relaxed, no longer concerned that he'd be considered negligent. They reached Mary's room and entered. "Nurse?" inquired the doctor softly.

"She is the same. Just the same." The woman's features lightened. "Ah! My lord! My lady has asked for you. She will be very pleased to see you." The attendant turned to the bed. Very gently, leaning over the thin, still figure, she said, "He has come."

Mowbray stilled. *She asked for me?* he mused. *Why?*

The doctor left and the nurse came to him on silent feet, her hands folded before her. "I will leave you." She smiled and touched him briefly, gently, on the arm. "She is much changed," she whispered encouragingly, "as you will find."

"Theo?"

His name drifted from the bed on a thread of sound, and he approached.

"I knew you'd come," she whispered, looking up at him, her eyes great dark holes in her face.

She is so thin! Hesitantly, Mowbray reached for her hand, the tiny bones nearly bare of flesh. The skin around his eyes and over his cheeks felt painfully taut. "Mary?"

She smiled. It was a rather weak smile, but it was a smile. A gentle smile. "They tell me I've been . . . ill. For a long time?"

"Very ill," he said.

She squeezed his fingers, the barest hint of pressure, and he clasped the bird-like bones gently.

"We should not have wed," she said after a long moment. "You know that, do you not?"

Mowbray hesitated and then, a muscle jumping in his jaw, he decided that, if he were ever to know, he must ask now. It was obvious that, all too soon, time would run out and then he'd never know. "I have always wondered what I did to make you hate me so," he said.

A look of horror crossed her face, and she struggled to raise herself. Quickly Mowbray reached for the extra pillows set to one side and, gently lifting her, put them behind her. He laid her back and again reached for her hand.

For a long moment she lay there with her eyes closed, breathing heavily. The eyes opened, and the deep sapphire blue stared at him. The look's intensity made him wonder if she had fooled him, that she was not . . . well.

"Theo," she said, her voice urgent, "it was not your fault. You must have known . . ." She pulled free and, for a moment, her hands clenched.

"Known?" he asked when she didn't go on.

"My parents knew. They knew and still they let us wed! Encouraged us. It was very bad of them, Theo."

"Knew?"

She looked away. Her thin hand lifted again, and again he grasped it gently. "I had already shown what I . . . would become," she said. "They knew but they hoped . . ." She bit her lip, turning her gaze toward him once again. "Theo," she repeated, "it was not your fault. Believe me. I was not . . . right long before our wedding day. They hid it from everyone except my old nurse, who had very likely suspected something was wrong even when I was in the nursery."

"I knew you were—" Mowbray's lips compressed and he frowned slightly as he searched for a gentle phrase. "—volatile in your emotions."

A small, sad smile played around Mary's lips. "Oh, yes. I believe everyone must have known *that*. So giddily happy, giggling and dancing for no reason, and then, also for no reason, so sad and unhappy I wanted to do nothing, see no one . . ."

Faintly, he felt her fingers close around his. He added his second hand to the first, clasping hers between them. "It was not, then, something I did?"

"No. Of course not. Not at all. My parents . . ." Her lips compressed slightly, then relaxed. "They didn't have a notion what to do with me, you see."

"They were not so young as most parents, Mary. Perhaps they feared they would die and there would be no one to care for you."

"You are generous, Theo." She looked at him, her eyes showing just a hint of her former wildness. "Theo, when I am dead, you will remarry. Promise me. You will choose a young woman who will give you an heir. When . . . I was myself, that was the thing which worried me most, that you've no heir."

"But I do have an heir, Mary. You always liked Arthur, did you not? I do, you know. And he has three sturdy sons, so the succession has been seen to. I've not worried about that."

"But to have your own son, is that not what all men wish?"

He shrugged. "There was a time when I might have dreamed a bit of having a boy of my own. You know the sort of thing I mean? That I'd teach him to hunt and fish. To ride. That I would take him to London when the time came and teach him how to avoid the traps set for young feet taking their first steps within the *ton*. But that was long ago. And I have Justin. For that sort of thing, I mean. I will never want for a son while my godson needs me."

Mary came very close to grinning. "Felix Dunsforth still will not stay to home where he belongs?"

"Will he not or *can* he not?" asked Mowbray thoughtfully. "I have never been certain. In any case, it is true he enjoys his travels and his work."

"But his family. Surely his wife wishes it otherwise!"

Mowbray instantly sobered. "My dear! Mrs. Dunsforth died in childbirth, the baby with her, getting on for six years ago."

"Oh!" She instantly fell into intense sadness. "Those poor children."

"They are with their aunt." He watched her, fearing the sudden emotion she revealed meant she would, still again, go off into one of her . . . spells. "Do you remember Justina Dunsforth?"

"She is still a Dunsforth? But she was such a handsome woman. And so well dowered. Why has she not wed?"

It crossed Mowbray's mind that he was, for the first time in nearly a decade, having a normal conversation with his wife. "I am uncertain as to the cause, but I think it may have something to do with her unusual upbringing. She would, I suppose, be called a bluestocking by those who do not know her. Certainly her conversation takes odd paths. For a woman."

"You know her well?"

Is that jealousy? he wondered. Mowbray felt his way. "I visit the children. Since she is unwed, there is no man for Justin to turn to when he has questions a woman would find difficult to answer. And I teach him those thing his father would teach him if he was available."

"Where is Felix Dunsforth?"

"Off to try his hand at convincing a rather stubborn Eastern potentate to our way of thinking." Mowbray shook his head. "Very doubtful that he'll manage the trick, of course. Or, for that matter, that anyone could. The man is a tyrant of the worst sort!"

"Tell me about Miss Dunsforth. I seem to recall that she was rather odd."

Mowbray made a humorous tale for Mary of how he had taught Justina to play. She chuckled softly now and again and her eyes never left his face, searching it avidly for telltale clues.

"You love her," said Mary when he ran down.

Perhaps, he thought, *I have gone on a bit too long?* "Love? I cannot think it. She is nothing like you, Mary."

"I killed any affection you ever felt for me, Theo," she said quietly. "I am glad if you have found another to love."

"It would be wrong to love another when I am wed to you!"

"Would it? I cannot be said to have been a wife to you." She sighed. "You must not feel guilty, Theo. If there is guilt, it is mine."

"No, my dear. You could not help it."

"Could I not? It never seemed as if I could when I felt myself slipping away into that dark place I never quite remember when I climb out from it. I always dreaded losing myself in the maze of it. Feared it. I am told I was there, in that place, a very long time this time." She yawned. Abruptly, she added, "I am tired, Theo."

Her eyes closed. Just like that, she was asleep.

Mowbray sat beside her for the whole of that night and

the next day as well, except for brief necessary minutes away from her. Occasionally Mary roused and they talked quietly. By that afternoon, it was mostly that he talked and she listened. And, as the day passed toward evening, she weakened still more. Toward nightfall she slipped into a final sleep from which she did not wake.

Poor Mary. Such a terrible waste of a life, thought his lordship sadly when he realized she had slipped away. For the most part of another hour Mowbray sat thinking, his wife's lifeless hand within his own. He roused when the attendant tiptoed in to see to her patient.

"It is over," he said.

"The poor dear. But for the best, my lord. You'll see that in time."

"Perhaps. Is the doctor still here?"

"In his office. He said you would wish to speak to him."

Mowbray stood. For a long moment he stared at Mary. A prayer lifted from his heart and, suddenly at ease, he turned and left behind the empty husk of the woman he had not known until it was too late.

Arrangements were completed for Mary to be buried in his family's plot in the church near the home they had never really shared. That organized, Mowbray rode straight to Chestnut Lane Manor. He didn't think. He couldn't even feel. Not the things he believed he *should* feel. But he experienced an urge he could not ignore, was forced on by emotions he would not examine.

He had to go there, had to see her . . .

A groom waited to take his horse. With none of his usual friendly words, Mowbray dismounted, speaking tersely. "Hold him. I'll not be long."

He climbed the handful of steps to the door standing open to the dim coolness of the entry. Again unlike his usual self, he'd nothing to say to the elderly butler. Nor, as he should have done, did he ask Howard to announce him and see if Miss Dunsforth would see him. Instead, he turned directly into the hall leading to her study where, at this hour of the day, he knew she would be found.

As if in a dream, he entered the room.

Even the seductive image of family, of Justina at her desk with little Cornelia at the side dressing her dolls and Justin curled into the wide seat of a well-padded armchair with a book, could not breach his preoccupation, his need, to reach her side, to pull her to her feet—to embrace Justina Dunsforth.

For a very long moment he held the stunned woman close, her head cradled against his shoulder, his eyes searching her face. And then he lowered his head, his lips meeting hers in a brief, hard kiss.

And then, as suddenly as he appeared, he set her aside and left the room. And, in the moments in which it took Justina to find herself, he also left the house, remounted, and turned his roan to trot back down the lane.

Justina, one hand on her nephew's shoulder, the other holding Cornelia close, stood just outside the door and watched him go.

Very nearly a month since he'd last left it, Mowbray cantered easily along the drive up to Chestnut Lane Manor. A month in which he had had much to do and still more about which he must think.

It was not an easy month.

Arranging a proper funeral for a woman who had lived a great portion of her life under restraint was difficult. She'd no friends and few relatives. Mowbray's family, too, had little fruit hanging on the family tree and those cousins who might, for his sake, have attended, were spread far and wide. In the end, the rites were held in the family chapel, the heir presumptive, his sons, and a very few neighbors in attendance.

Legally, there was little to be done. Mary's inheritance had gone to support her years in the haven run to accommodate such as she who had enough wealth that they were not forced to end their days in a Bedlam chained to a wall and lying in their own filth. Still it was necessary for Mowbray to see his solicitor and do those things which must be done after a death in a family.

All of that had been time-consuming, but there was nothing in it to upset him. It was *emotionally* that Mowbray found himself fighting a long, hard battle.

He found it difficult, even after his talk with Mary, to rid his mind of his long-held fear that somehow he had been at fault. Too, although he had concealed it from Mary, it was difficult to accept the bitter knowledge that his father-in-law had knowingly placed responsibility for Mary onto his shoulders and did so without deigning to explain her condition to him even after their marriage. It took time to find forgiveness for the man, not young, who must have feared for Mary's future.

But, worst of all, was the soul-destroying guilt.

He had spent a lovely month falling in love with Justina Dunsforth while his wife, refusing all food, was dying and, somehow, regaining her sanity. Mowbray was forced to deal with the dread that, if he had not been so preoccupied with Justina and the children, if those searching for him had found him, and if he'd returned sooner to his wife, he might have encouraged her to eat. To live. And, sane again, to come home where she might enjoy a long life at his side.

But he had not been found and had not gone to her until far too late to do anything for her. He had stayed away, dallying, even if innocently, with another woman.

So, was it honorable to go to that woman and teach her to love him? For the two of them to find happiness together when Mary might have survived? Might have lived a long, contented life? Did he not deserve to be punished by losing the woman who lived simply *because* the other did not?

Desperate, he returned to the establishment where Mary died.

Once he had talked with the doctor, Mowbray was able to rid himself of self-recrimination and guilt. Most of it anyway. The man's assurance that Mary would not have remained sane and, as she proved, had not wished to live in that black place which plagued her, allowed Mowbray to put it behind him and accept that it was not wrong for him to enjoy the remainder of his life as would any other man.

And so, this late summer evening found him cantering up the drive between the old chestnuts and toward the house which sheltered the woman he loved just as his heart sheltered hopes for their future—and his mind the thought, the fear, it would never come to pass!

"Justin." Cornelia stared at her brother until he looked up. "Hmm?"

"Why does Uncle Teo stay away?"

Justin turned his back on his sister. "I don't know. Why?"

"Aunt Justina is unhappy."

Justin spun around. "So?"

"So if Uncle Teo would come, then she would be happy again."

"Nonsense." Justin scowled. He refused to admit how much he wanted, needed, his godfather to come for a visit. "You're just a baby. You always talk nonsense."

"Do I?"

"Yes. You do."

Cornelia stared at him. "I'm sorry." Then she dipped her head and set still another careful stitch in the hem of the new dress her governess was helping her make for her largest doll.

Justin snarled softly in frustration. He neither knew nor cared if his aunt was unhappy. He only knew he himself wanted Uncle Theo to come. There were no letters. No little gifts. There had been none of the little ways in which Mowbray reminded his godson that he was not alone.

Justin felt very much alone.

And, deep inside, somewhere he would not look, there was the fear something was wrong, that something had happened to his godfather. Justin couldn't bring himself to voice the fear, but keeping it bottled up was doing very nasty things to his temper.

It is really too bad of Nellie, thought a very cross Justin, *that she will not fight with me!*

His horse on the way to the stable, his saddle bags already disappearing abovestairs, Mowbray handed his hat and gloves to Howard.

"She is in her study, my lord," said the butler, not quite meeting his lordship's eyes. "We are very glad you have come, my lord," he added softly, as Mowbray turned toward the hall.

Mowbray paused, wondering at that heartfelt comment, but continued on without requesting an explanation. He knocked softly, knocked again when there was no response.

"Go away," he heard her say, her words muffled by the thick door. "I told you I was not to be bothered!"

Mowbray opened the door. "You did not tell me," he said. He stared across the room, watching her shoulders stiffen, her hand still. She swung around in her chair, one arm along the back and the other lying on the desk. "You."

"Yes."

She scowled. "You come. You behave in the strangest way. And then you go away. For *weeks.* It is not to be borne." Justina stared. He looked thinner. Perhaps there was a trifle more gray at his temples?

"Forgive me," he said penitently, making her forget the changes in him. "I have behaved abominably."

"Yes, you have," she agreed. Then, realizing she might be revealing too much of her emotions, Justina added, "But it is not me to whom you should apologize. It is your godson who is miserable. And, in his misery, he grows disobedient and defiant and"—she bit her lip, her eyes widening as she recalled her own grievances—"as odious as his godfather!"

Mowbray's lips relaxed slightly. "I will ask his pardon, Justina, but it is yours I ask just now. I should have explained."

Justina said nothing, just stared.

"You will not give me one inch, will you?"

"If I were so mad as to do so, you would take an ell!"

"That is more like my Justina." He smiled, but the smile faded when he saw her straighten, her shoulders tensing. She cast a wild look around the room. "Now what did I say?"

"Go away!"

As the shouted words assaulted Mowbray's ears, Justina rose to her feet. Her roving gaze rested on a book of plates to which she'd recently referred and, picking it up, she threw it. Then her pen. Then, most unforgivably, the inkwell.

Mowbray's eyebrows arched. "Justina . . . !"

"Go away!"

He did, closing the door behind him. He pulled his handkerchief from his pocket to dab at the ink but knew it was no use. The coat was ruined. He sighed. A sigh echoed his and he looked up.

"Yes, Howard?" Mowbray was still more embarrassed that the butler should know of his discomfiture at Miss Dunsforth's hands.

"Still angry, is she?" asked Howard.

The butler's fellow feeling was obvious and Mowbray glanced down, made one last useless dab at the spreading black, and looked up. "I am forced to agree that Miss Dunsforth appears to be—er, somewhat angry."

"I had hoped . . ."

"You hoped . . . what?" asked Mowbray when Howard did not finish.

Another soft sigh. "Nothing, my lord. Should I inform the nursery party you have arrived?"

"Are they angry as well?" asked Mowbray with just a touch of humor.

Howard allowed his lips to tip the slightest little bit. "Perhaps a trifle, my lord. It has been some time since your last visit, you see."

"Should I apologize to you as well?" asked his lordship, uncertain whether the question was a jest or more than a trifle serious.

"That is not necessary, my lord. I will inform Master Justin and Mistress Cornelia that you have arrived."

"Tell them that I will come to them as soon as I've—er, freshened up from my—er, travels." He glanced at his coat.

Howard's eyes twinkled with humor. "Definitely, my lord, you should refresh yourself after your—er, travels!"

Mowbray was not quite certain if Howard had said travel or travail, so he ignored what was, after all, a rather impertinent response. He was well aware what a figure of fun he was, with his coat and face spattered with ink.

It was too bad of Justina. But why, he wondered as he climbed the stairs to his room, did she do it?

Mowbray made no attempt to explain his absence to Justin and his godson's sister. He made his peace with them, discovered how they went on, and then, turning to the tutor, asked how they progressed with their studies. "Well, Compton? Has Justin caught up to where he should be?"

The tutor smiled at Justin, who cast him a worried look. "He is doing very well, my lord. Or he was. Just these last few days he has been a trifle distracted, but formerly he applied himself as he should and I feel he will again. Will you not, Justin?"

"Yes, sir," said Justin glumly, thinking of the work he would be set. Or perhaps not? Not now, when Uncle Theo had just arrived? He brightened. "Uncle Theo, will you take me fishing? Tomorrow?"

"Late in the afternoon, we will see about going out. Perhaps it will be possible to have a nursery tea picnic. I will discuss it with Cook."

"I can go too, Uncle Teo?" asked Cornelia, squeezing his hand, which she had not released since his arrival in the nursery. "Please?"

"I meant the both of you, of course. But you must pay attention to your mentors and do your work. It is only after one completes one's duty that one allows oneself treats."

"Is that why you stayed away, Uncle Teo?" asked Cornelia. "Because you had a duty you'd not finished?"

"That is it, Nellie," said Mowbray, glad the child had come up with an acceptable excuse for his long absence. "It took me a very long time to complete what I needed to do, but it is done now and I'll not stay away for so long ever again."

Unless, he thought, *Justina forbids me entrance to her home!*

His thoughts turned to Justina, he did not hear Cornelia's softly voiced plea that he not stay away at all. That he simply *stay.* Here. With them.

Mowbray went down to dinner that evening with no little trepidation. He had not seen Justina since the disastrous moments right after his arrival, and he had no way of knowing if her temper had eased or if it had grown worse. It had taken far too long for him to remove the ink from his skin, and he'd no desire to find the evening's soup thrown over him. In actual fact he had not removed all the ink. Faint splotches speckled his forehead and one cheek even now. And the coat, of course, was ruined. Soup might not be quite so permanently damaging, but he'd no wish to find out.

His lordship decided that he must approach Justina just as quickly as he could, before her mood grew utterly antagonistic. He patted his coat pocket to assure himself that the family betrothal ring was there. He'd carried it from the moment he removed it from the iron box kept in a cellar room

at his London bank which contained the Mowbray heirloom
jewelry. The pat reassured him. The ring rested there as it
had for days now. If he were lucky, it would next rest on
Justina's finger.

Perhaps.

If he were *very* lucky.

It took only one glance toward Justina to decide that he
was not only not lucky, but quite the reverse. Her lovely
mouth bore the same stern line it had worn when he arrived
for his first visit to Chestnut Lane. He was unhappy to see
it—not only for his own sake, but also for Justina's. She had
lost that severity during those days when they explored the
multitude of ways one might enjoy oneself. When, he wondered, had it returned.

"I must apologize," she said in a rather dead tone of voice.

"Must you?" he asked with forced lightness. "I had
thought it was I who must be at fault to have deserved such
dreadful punishment and I who must apologize."

"No. I should not have done it." She turned away. "I have
done my best to control what is a truly dreadful temper, but
very occasionally I forget. Please except my most sincere
regrets."

"I would be much more likely to do so," he said, still
lightly, "if I believed you meant it."

She swung back, her eyes widening and her mouth slightly
open. When she saw that his eyes were twinkling, her scowl
returned and her temper, exceedingly volatile these days,
tipped over the edge still again. "You, my lord," she said,
speaking severely, "deserve anything! You would drive a saint
to perdition!"

"Perhaps. If you say so. But you, my dear, are no saint,
so it was, in all likelihood, not at all difficult upsetting you
and nothing for which I should accept compliments."

"Compliments! *Compliments?*"

"Hmm." He cast her a mischievous smile. "No one has ever

said to me I deserve anything. But if I do—deserve anything—why, then perhaps I will gain my greatest desire and . . ."

The door opened and Justina's companion trailed in, apologies dripping from her tongue as badly sewn lace and ribbons dripped from her person. As was the custom, a maid followed picking up bits and pieces, whisking all away when the woman seated herself in an uncomfortable looking chair.

The moment was lost.

And perhaps, thought Mowbray, it was just as well. Justina would not like that he found humor in the situation. *Poor dear girl. If only she would climb down off her high horse long enough for me to explain.* He sighed softly and then said all that was proper to Miss Repton.

Mowbray was relieved that Howard arrived on the companion's heels and announced that dinner was served, since he was having great difficulty disentangling himself from the little lady's protestations and apologies. He was still more relieved to see that Justina's sense of humor had been touched by his predicament and that perhaps, if he did not continue unlucky, she would mellow before dinner ended. He might yet be able to get in a word or two in in his own defense!

In fact Justina found it exceedingly difficult to maintain the proper reserve she had concluded was the only way to deal with the man. Assuming she ever saw him again, of course! Then, from the moment he so unexpectedly arrived, she had discovered how nearly impossible was the task she'd set herself.

When he'd come before and taken her into his arms, she had experienced something so deeply moving, so utterly incomprehensible, so full of delight, to say nothing of hope, that she had awaited his return in a state of turmoil such as she'd never before experienced. Then, as days and then weeks passed and he did not return, turmoil changed to uncertainty and then to fear before settling into a deep, burning rage which would not allow her to work or to sleep properly and which left her exhausted and with little patience.

The children avoided her or, if they did approach her, did so with a caution that, even in her distraught state, she noticed. She managed to set aside the worst of her passion and had done her best to allay the children's concern. She even went so far as to admit that she was not herself, that she was not angry with them and they had done nothing for which they need fear retribution, and that they must forgive her if she forgot herself to the point that she was short with them. She had always spoken with them as she would to an adult, but Nanny Cornish, overhearing this particular discussion, took her aside and scolded her.

"You must never," the old nurse ended her diatribe, "allow children to know that the adults responsible for them might be less than perfect. However do you think you can make them obey you if they think you might be wrong?"

Justina had blinked at this. She recalled incidents in her own childhood in which she had known very well that the adults around her were in error. Children, she decided, knew far more than their preceptors liked to think. She would, she decided, go on as she had begun. After all, Justin and Cornelia had shown no signs of disobedience— or no more than might be expected of children their age. She decided it was unlikely they would change at this point.

But that was in the past and this was now, and sitting at table with Mowbray seated at her right hand, she found it necessary to fight down the satisfaction his presence elicited. She had to keep to her vow that never again would she experience those boiling emotions which made no sense to her, but which would not leave her in peace. She would not fail! She'd no desire to rigidly schedule her days as once she'd done, but she would do so if utter disruption were the alternative. Mowbray, coming for those few moments, kissing her, and then leaving without a word, leaving nothing but the memory of intense moments in his embrace, was obviously dangerous to her emotional stability. She didn't understand those feelings, but surely even rigid scheduling was better than chaos such as that!

Was it not? Yes, of course it was.

So. She'd no choice but to remain cool, distant—and out of reach of those tempting arms that sent her very soul into disorder.

Mowbray, ever polite, ever kind, was attending Miss Repton who, for reasons beyond Justina's understanding, had suddenly left off her role as self-effacing nonentity and was become a chatterbox. But at least it meant that Justina could eye her unwanted guest without his awareness.

Unwanted?

She sighed. Softly. Very softly. She could not avoid the truth that he was wanted. She had missed their discussions, which ranged far and wide, the occasional arguments when their views strongly diverged. And she had missed his gentle persuasion that turned her away from that abominable schedule to the enjoyment of a wide variety of amusing and self-enlarging pastimes.

As she listened idly to his response to one of Miss Repton's never-ending questions, Justina recalled one of his maxims. As Mowbray once pointed out, there must be a Golden Mean. If it were only possible to find it. Perhaps she could enjoy his company and still avoid that terrible pain roused by his long and unexplained absence.

She cast Mowbray a quick glance, knowing he was involved with her chaperon. Her heart raced. Just looking at the man seemed to rouse those odd sensations!

Golden Mean? Unfortunately, it seemed there was no Golden Mean where Mowbray was concerned. No, the only solution was to remain cool and distant. Especially distant. Allowing the man close enough to embrace one was the way to madness!

* * *

Justina went down to breakfast the next morning feeling nearly as tired as when she'd gone up to seek her bed the previous evening. On the other hand, she had, during those long hours in the salon, won her self-imposed battle. She had maintained that required distance and retained her sanity.

There was satisfaction in that, but how long could she manage the trick?

Justina frowned as she passed Howard in the entry hall, and the butler wondered just what he'd done to rouse her ire. Unfortunately Lord Mowbray's arrival had not provided the miracle for which Miss Dunsforth's staff had prayed. Howard sighed softly and continued on to where he must oversee the maid who was washing the delicate and, given the war, irreplaceable French porcelains displayed in the more formal front salon.

Upon discovering that she was experiencing a trifling irritation of the nerves, Justina paused and stared at the breakfast room door. Would he be there? Or would he not? And for which outcome did she wish? Then, justly irritated with her ridiculously contradictory emotions, she scolded herself, opened the door, and entered the room.

A quick glance showed it to be empty of all but the footman standing by the sideboard, stationed there to be of service. Three places showed evidence of early risers. The children's governess and tutor were always the first to break their fast, but to whom was one to attribute the third? Had Miss Repton come down early? Or did Lord Mowbray rise betimes, eating and departing before he must encounter his hostess?

Justina bit her lip.

She chose her usual breakfast of shirred eggs, toast, and a small slice of ham, and, as she did so, lectured herself. Only when she was seated, a freshly brewed pot of tea before her, did she notice the folded and sealed sheet of thick, creamy paper placed beside her napkin, her name sprawled across the starkly white missive. Justina had never seen Lord

Mowbray's abominable hand, but, since his was the only handwriting in the house she did not know, this must be from him.

Her heartbeat sped up in a strangely erratic fashion. She cast a glance at the footman, but he was more interested in something beyond her view, something seen through the window, than in her. She turned back. Surely it was not a note telling her his lordship had packed and once again gone away. Surely he knew how much the children needed him and would not disappear as he had on his last, all-too-brief visit.

Justina swallowed. Hard. And decided that whatever was in the note could—another glance toward the stolid footman—and *should* wait until she reached her study and was alone. Alone where no one would know how Mowbray's words affected her.

She forced herself to eat her breakfast.

Well. Most of it.

All right, *half.*

Unable to swallow another bite, she picked up the letter and—not running, exactly—hurried to her room. Once inside the door, she leaned back against it and, holding the thick paper between shaking hands, stared at it. Did she, she wondered, really want to know what was in it?

Really?

She glanced at her desk where normally at this hour she would be working. She recalled the ideas going around in her head while she dressed, thoughts which would send this novel in a slightly different direction than originally planned. An intriguing notion . . .

A glance at the note, another at her desk, and the decision was made. She did not want to know what message Lord Mowbray had left her. She would read it, of course, but later.

Much later.

Later arrived far sooner than she'd meant it to do. Somehow Mowbray's letter dominated not only her workspace but also her mind, and she could not concentrate on the words swirling around in her head. Justina sighed. It was too bad of him. Not only had he come and gone, upset her to the core by staying away for so long, but then, having returned, had left impertinent missives to destroy her hard-won peace.

She set aside her pen and picked up the note. Quickly, before she could change her mind, she slipped a finger beneath the seal. She unfolded the single page and discovered that her eyes were tightly closed. She opened just one, taking a quick peek.

Her other eye popped open as well. In large clear print at the top of the page were the words, *Mary died just before my last visit.* No greeting. No polite introduction. Just, in stark black, the shocking words against the pure paper. Justina read and reread them, absorbing the meaning at several different levels.

Mary dead. After all these years. Justina looked up, stared at the wall over her desk. Ever since Mowbray had first come to visit the children, knowledge of Mary's existence had been in the back of her mind, a ghostly presence which kept her from admitting the obvious, that she had fallen deeply in love with Theodore Kenwright, Earl Mowbray.

Love.

Justina's eyes widened painfully. She loved Mowbray!

Instantly her gaze dropped to the page where, farther down, more words had been scrawled.

"I mean," his communication continued, "to sit on the bench under the old oak at the far edge of the south lawn. Come to me there if you are willing to hear my apologies for my odious behavior when I last came to Chestnut Lane Manor."

The bench under the oak . . .

Justina, the note in her hand, approached the oak. She didn't think she made any noise, but Mowbray turned his head. He caught her gaze and she stopped. They stared at each other. Finally Mowbray rose to his feet and held out his hand. Hesitating only a trifle, she moved to stand before him.

"Will you sit with me?" he asked.

"Why did you kiss me?" she asked, ignoring his words.

"I had just left Mary," he said quietly, a certain sadness darkening his eyes. "I needed you, so I came to you."

"But you left."

"Yes. The instant I looked at you after I'd kissed you, I was filled with wave after wave of guilt such as I'd never before known."

Justina blinked. "Perhaps I'd better sit."

His lips twitched slightly, but he offered his hand and helped her to the bench before seating himself to her right. "Justina, can you understand? While Mary lay slowly dying, I was here. With you."

Falling in love with you, he thought.

Justina stared across the lawn. Slowly she nodded. "Yes. We *enjoyed* life even as she left it. We should not have done that, should we?"

"No."

"She was dead when you went for your last visit?"

"Very near the end. And sane, Justina. Perfectly, wonderfully sane." He sighed. "I wondered whether I might have saved her. If I had gone to her sooner, I mean. No one knew where I was. No one thought to come here to find me. I played with your brother's children and enjoyed your company and—"

Fell in love with you. The thought was a refrain in his mind.

"—and all the time she was slowly, so very slowly, dying."

"Would it be too painful," asked Justina diffidently, "to tell me how she died?"

It was Mowbray's turn to stare across the grass as he told her.

"You see," he finished the tale, "it isn't as if I did not

know something was very wrong with her." He turned and reached for Justina's hands. "Can you imagine how I felt? The guilt for staying away from her. The guilt attached to my growing feelings for you—our new and fragile friendship," he added hurriedly, still unable to broach his true reason for wishing to speak with her. "There was the fear that if I'd gone to her earlier, I could have saved her, she might have begun eating again, might have lived a long, contented life. A sane life. Justina, it was like having several enemy armies in my head marching this way and that and never knowing when one or another would attack!"

"You stayed away from Chestnut Lane until you had defeated them all," said Justina.

He nodded. "I finally did what I should have done much sooner. I spoke with the man who owns that Bedlam. He assured me that Mary drew up out of the hell in which she lived only at the last, only after it was far too late to save her." A wry smile twisted his lips for a moment. "I didn't actually defeat that last army so much as discover it was a phantom."

Justina rose to her feet, backing away. "Thank you for telling me, explaining . . ."

Mowbray too rose, the movement the automatic response of a gentleman. "Justina!" He stretched his hand toward her. "There is more . . ."

"More?" Justina interrupted. She began drifting away, shaking her head. "Not now. I've too much about which I must think to hear more."

Going round and round in her head were his words: *Growing feelings. New and fragile friendship.*

Why, she wondered, *when I have finally understood my feelings for him, did he have to tell me his for me? Friendship! When what I want is his love!*

"Which he is now free to give," she muttered.

She didn't even see Howard, who watched her climb the stairs, her skirts held very slightly higher than was proper.

Howard, listening to her footsteps so he might judge where she went, winced when he heard Justina's bedroom door slam. Then he sighed. Would the household never return to normal? Or what passed for normal at Chestnut Lane?

I am growing too old for all this worry, he thought, scowling slightly.

A shadow filled the open front door, and the butler wiped the frown from his forehead. He need not have bothered. Mowbray, his own brow creased, never looked at him, but took the stairs two at a time. He didn't slam his door, but he did close it with a decided snap.

"Now what?" muttered Howard. He shook his head. "Too old," he mumbled. "Far too old." He moved slowly and heavily toward his pantry, where the footman was polishing silver. However badly the Quality took to behaving, he would not allow it to alter his standards, and that young whippersnapper of a footman had a very bad habit of skimping on the decorated bits!

"Justin."

The boy frowned at his Latin. "Hmm?" he muttered after a moment.

"What should we do?" asked Nellie.

"I cannot play with you," said the boy impatiently. "I must finish this."

"I don't mean we should play," retorted Nellie who, staring out the schoolroom window, had seen first their aunt and then Justin's godfather come toward the house from where they'd sat beneath the oak. Both were frowning.

Justin glanced up. "Nellie," he said patiently, "I haven't a notion what you have wrapped up in the cotton wool you call your mind, but it must wait. If I do not get this translation done, I'll not be allowed to go fishing this afternoon with Uncle Theo."

Nellie pouted. Then she sighed. Finally she shrugged.

"Finish then, but maybe there will be no fishing anyway. Maybe Uncle Teo will be long gone."

Justin half rose from his chair, then dropped back. "What do you mean?"

She shrugged again. "I just saw Aunt Justina run into the house looking like a storm cloud and then Uncle Teo, maybe not quite so stormy, but not looking very happy, followed her and if you hadn't been so busy, Justin Dunsforth, you would have heard their doors slam."

Justin had heard a door slam. One. And had a blot on his paper to prove it. "Tell me what you saw."

Nellie had very little more to tell but managed to make a bit of a story out of the meeting and talking before repeating what she had already described.

Justin's lower lip thrust out and he glowered. "I will be very angry if Uncle Theo leaves as he did last time. He didn't even say hello to me that time, and we were right there in Aunt Justina's study!"

Nellie stared out the window. "If Uncle Teo married Aunt Justina, he wouldn't go away," she said and flung a sideways glance toward her brother to see how he responded. She had asked Nanny how one went about making a family, and Nanny had said that first the mommy and daddy had to get married and that was how a family began. "Then we could be a family," she added softly. "A mommy. And a daddy. And us."

Justin's eyes widened. He looked thoughtful for a long moment. "Nellie," he asked, speaking slowly, "do you suppose we *could* make them get married?"

Lord Mowbray reached for the saddlebags stored atop his armoire and laid them on the bed. He strode to the chest in which Howard always placed his bits and pieces and was in the act of opening the drawer when something made him pause. He frowned. Something was not right.

Or rather . . . it was right but very different?

He glanced around the light and airy room. Releasing the drawer pulls, he slowly turned in a complete circle. Luckily there was a chair conveniently close, because Mowbray's legs, quite suddenly, were too weak to hold him. The room, now he looked at it, was not the same as when last he'd last used it. It was fresher, more welcoming, not at all dark and drear and, on the whole, a trifle shabby. That first visit he had teased his hostess about it. It was later when he came to understand that Justina did not recognize when one jested or he'd not have done it!

In fact, at the time, Justina had responded with a sigh and the comment that she hated having painters in, the bother and the stench. She had said she could not be bothered with such nonsense.

But she had.

Bothered, that is. This room was not just repainted, but the floor was sanded and refinished, as was the other wood-work. The drapery was new, and the carpet. The furniture was polished within an inch of its life.

Mowbray rose to his feet and strolled to the center of the room, where he turned still another circle. Yes, it was thoughtfully contrived, very welcoming, and accomplished, despite the owner's avowal that she could not see the sense of putting up with the mess and time wasting effort of it all.

But . . . she had. Which meant . . . ? But what could it mean?

Surely, that she liked him. Or would she do something that made her so uncomfortable if what she felt were mere liking? Deciding that Justina Dunsforth was not the sort to put herself out in such a way for mere friendship, Mowbray grinned. *Justina Dunsforth might not yet know it, but she loved him.* He took one more look at the room and, nodding, left it, for-getting he'd been about to pack and leave.

Returning downstairs, he hunted up Howard who, done with berating the footman for sloppy work on the silver, had gone on to growl at a maid for improperly brushing out the fireplace in the breakfast room.

"Where is Miss Dunsforth?" asked Mowbray.

"I believe she retired to her room, my lord," said Howard promptly.

Mowbray's eyes narrowed slightly. *Should I demand to see her?* he asked himself. He decided in the negative. "Very well. If she asks for me"—*which she will not*—"tell her I am with the children." When Howard cleared his throat, Mowbray grinned. "You need not tell me I will disrupt their schedules, for I know it. It will hurt neither of them to have a holiday." He gave a quick series of orders as he started for the stairs.

Justin's tutor had returned to the schoolroom, chased Cornelia away, and lectured Justin on the evils of wasting time. Justin, over Nellie's strong but unexplained and, when asked, unexplainable objections, had concluded their only hope was to ask Lord Mowbray and their aunt to indulge Nellie and himself in just this little way by marrying each other. Having decided this, he was ready to return to his work. He was concentrating on a particularly difficult passage when Lord Mowbray looked in and, catching Mr. Compton's eye, beckoned him into the hall.

Compton was ambivalent about the notion of a holiday. He disliked any change of routine which interfered with his careful balancing of work and play, but he was far behind in his own work, which was a definitive history of the technical aspects of the construction of defensive structures from the earliest hill forts through moated castles to the earthwork defenses flung up in these degenerate times against the threat of modern artillery. He firmly stifled his conscience and welcomed the unexpected opportunity to get on with it.

Having collected Justin, Mowbray led the way to the day nursery, where Cornelia was attempting the satin stitch under Miss Gilbert's attentive eye. Nellie, seeing Mowbray and her brother at the door, threw aside her work and ran to hug as much as she could of his lordship, which meant she threw her arms around his legs and very nearly pulled him off balance.

Miss Gilbert tut-tutted and, with great firmness, ordered Cornelia to pick up her work and fold it away properly and admonished her to curtsy in proper form in welcome of her brother's godfather. Cornelia looked up at Mowbray with a surprisingly adult look of exasperation, but obediently she turned away. She put away her sewing and curtsied, looked at Miss Gilbert, who nodded approval, and then, crossing the room, she again threw herself against his lordship. "I am so glad you've come," she said, smiling up at him.

Mowbray smiled down at her and put his hand on her head, gently putting her away from him. Once she stood at his side, he took her hand and then greeted the governess. "I have come," he continued, "to steal Cornelia away for a little holiday. You will forgive the lack of notice, I am sure."

He was quite certain Miss Gilbert would do so because he had seen evidence in her that she was the sort of woman who would find it difficult to argue with any man and could never, not possibly, do so with a peer of the realm! He didn't like himself too well for making use of that knowledge, but neither could he bring himself to indulge in a long conversation with a woman who was pleasant enough, but not at all interesting. Not when compared to Justina.

Howard had managed miracles in the brief time available to him and, when the three truants reached the hall, a pony cart, complete with fishing equipment and a picnic basket, stood before the front door in expectation of their arrival. Justina, standing in her window and watching the trio depart, swallowed the bitter pill of the knowledge that she had, by deciding to withdraw, placed herself beyond that happy circle.

It then occurred to her that Lord Mowbray had made no attempt to draw her back into it. She sighed, turned away from the window, and looked idly about her room. Dark. Dreary.

Old and tired. Why had she never noticed how shabby everything was grown?

Because she had not noticed. Not until she saw how cheerful and lovely was the room she'd ordered freshened for Lord Mowbray. In fact, it occurred to her, the whole house was in need of attention and she had not noticed. The wry thought crossed her mind that, if she were to set in motion more of such work, perhaps Lord Mowbray would become so uncomfortable he could not bear it and would go away.

And then, perhaps, out of sight, out of mind . . . ? Or would the other adage come true, the notion that absence made the heart grow fonder? Justina knew she could not bear it if her heart was so disobedient as to fall still more deeply in love with Lord Mowbray. So, no redecorating. Far better that he stay around!

Mowbray, lounging with his back against a tree some distance upstream from where Justin inexpertly taught his sister to cast a line, smiled at the intensity of the children's discussion. He wondered what meant so much to them. Did Justin scold Cornelia for her miscasts and the tangles occasionally caused by them?

Or perhaps had it had nothing to do with the fishing lesson?

Mowbray recalled that something was between the two while they were in the pony cart. There had been two low-voiced squabbles during their drive to this particular stretch of the stream flowing through Justina's property. In fact, several times when Justin would have asked him something, Cornelia had, with obvious intent, interrupted her brother, raising her voice to override Justin's.

Mowbray frowned. Was there, perhaps, a problem the child was reluctant to bring to an adult's attention? A problem Justin believed should be discussed? Several possibilities, frightening possibilities, passed through his lordship's mind and, unsettled, he sat up.

"Children," he called. They turned to look his way. "Pull in your line, Cornelia, and the two of you come here."

Cornelia turned a glare on her brother. "It won't work," she said in a penetrating whisper. "You'll see."

"Uncle Theo says it is always best to talk things over," retorted Justin, his lowered voice barely carrying to his lordship's ear.

"You'll be sorry," said Cornelia, and Mowbray could discern a certain sadness crossing her young and expressive features.

"Nonsense. There. The line is straight now. Come along."

Justin took the rod from her hands and walked briskly to where Mowbray waited. Cornelia, much more slowly, her feet dragging, came along behind. Mowbray waited until both stood before him. "Something has upset you," he said gently.

"Not upset, exactly," said Justin. Cornelia had convinced her brother he must be tactful, and the faint lines of a frown creased a brow unused to such effort.

"We like it here with Aunt Justina," said Cornelia, hurriedly interposing herself between Mowbray and her brother. "Everything is just fine. Really."

She spoke in a rush, her eyes wide in her effort to convince him even as Justin growled something into her ear. She cast a despairing glance at Mowbray and reluctantly moved aside. She turned her back, disassociating herself from the others.

Mowbray glanced at her, then back at Justin. "What is it, boy? Something must be very wrong for the two of you to be at such odds as this!"

"No, no. Nothing is wrong exactly. Truly," the boy added when Mowbray's expression questioned the assertion. "It is simply . . ." And then he stopped, biting his lip. He glanced at his sister as if seeking help. "Well, you see, sir, we thought . . ." And again he seemed unable to find the proper words. Cornelia turned farther away. "It is like this, sir," Justin began and, for the third time, hesitated. Then he clenched his fists. "Sir! We think it would be the very best thing if you were to marry Aunt Justina and then we could all be together. Be a family." He gasped, heaved a sigh of obvious relief that the words were said, and then shrugged. "That's all. Sir."

Mowbray blinked. "Be a family?"

Cornelia came close, knelt beside him, and put her hand on his fist where it rested on his bent knee. "You see, Uncle Teo, I asked Nurse, and she said the way to begin a family is for a man and woman to wed, so we think you and Aunt Justina should be wedded and then we could be a real family. You see?"

"And you want a family?"

"Oh, yes." She nodded firmly. "Very much. A real family with a mama and a papa and us." She brightened at a sudden thought. "And maybe babies?"

Mowbray swallowed. He had been aware the children were not exactly happy with their life of living here and then there and sometimes, but rarely, with their father who, even then, paid them less attention than Theo thought right. But were they this unhappy?

"So," said Justin, quite willing to talk now the worst was out, "if you married Aunt Justina, then we could always live with you and her and everything would be as it should be. Do you see?"

Mowbray thought that perhaps he saw more than the children had ever thought. What was more, the notion had already crossed his mind that if he and Justina were wed, the children could have a home with them and Felix, on those occasions when he was in England, could live with them as well rather than hiring new servants and opening up his townhouse for the few months it would be required.

It had not occurred to him, however, that the children would be strongly in favor of the notion. More, it would never have crossed his mind that they might come up with the idea all on their own!

Would *this* argument convince Justina that they should

wed? Mowbray stared across the stream to where a flock of sheep grazed. When he looked back, he discovered the children staring at him, their eyes opened in a painfully widened manner. Too, Cornelia had pulled her lower lip between her little white teeth and was biting it, and her body seemed to tremble slightly with the tension of waiting for his decision.

He smiled and instantly the two relaxed. "I like the notion," he said and pulled Cornelia into the crook of his arm. "But there is a problem. Your aunt may not like it. I haven't a notion what more Nurse told you about the making of a family—." His brows arched. When both children looked faintly bemused, he concluded it had been nothing of a specific nature. "But it involves far more than simply getting married. The two who wed must spend the whole of their lives together, even after their children, you in this case, have grown up and married and made families of your own. One must think very carefully about the notion of putting the whole of one's existence in the hands of another. Do you see?" He did not wait for their response, but hurried on. "Now, for myself, I had already decided, before you spoke of it, that it would be a very good thing indeed. The thing is, it might not be for your aunt. It is not something which can or should be decided quickly or easily." When he continued, it was in a stern voice. "Justin. Cornelia. Will you promise to wait patiently while I do what I can to convince Miss Dunsforth that she would like it as much as I would like it?"

The children looked at each other. The long stare they exchanged appeared to be a form of silent communication, ending in agreement.

"We promise," said Justin.

"But could you make it just as soon as you possibly can?" asked Cornelia, a wistful note plain to Mowbray's sensitive ear. "I do so want us all to be a family," she finished a trifle plaintively.

* * *

Justina spent the long, lonely afternoon contemplating the last few months and thinking ahead to the years to come. They were an enlightening few hours in several ways. For one thing, she realized how lonely her life was before the children arrived. And how lacking in stimulation. Mowbray's company showed her how the right person made everything seem brighter. Livelier and happier.

Contemplation led to decisions. She easily concluded that, in future, the children would remain with her. Felix, assuming he wished to do so, could visit them here at Chestnut Lane on those rare occasions when he was in England.

But that was only one result of her afternoon-long efforts to know her own mind, her heart, and what she desired for her future. The one was an easy decision. The other was far more frightening. She was forced to admit she would never again find joy in life if Mowbray were to leave it, leave her, forget her. It had been still more difficult to reach the decision that she must, herself, do something to see that sad possibility did not occur.

The tinkling bell, rung to announce dinner, would send out its cheery message in only a few moments now. Justina stared at herself in the cheval mirror which she had had brought from the sewing room to her own. The reflected image did not entirely please her, but there was nothing more she could do to improve on it. The dress, although not new, nevertheless flattered her, the short train and open skirt of brown silk over the blond underdress fitting her to perfection. Her hair, done in a slightly more elaborate fashion than usual, was, however, already softening, wisps escaping to curl at her forehead and neck. Even if she were to fix that dishevelment, she knew it would take no time at all to reappear. Her hair had always been the most rebellious thing about her! The toe of a black sandal showed and she lifted her skirt, frowning. Should she change to the red pair? Ah, but they were not quite so comfortable, and she needed no more discomfort than she must, inevitably, feel when she confronted Mowbray with her plan. The black would do.

Justina straightened her shoulders, firmed her spine, and turned toward the door. At the last moment, her hand on the knob, she hesitated. Dared she? Dared she attempt it? Could she actually find the courage to carry through her plan?

A wry sound, half chuckle, half sob, escaped her. Find the courage? That was the least of her worries. After all, if she did not, she would be no worse off. And if she did—

Justina bit her lip.

—she might very well induce the very thing she most wished to avert! He might depart in panic!

But he had kissed her.

She must not forget that he'd kissed her.

Justina opened the door and went down to the salon where the party would assemble for dinner. Mowbray was ahead of her.

Now? she wondered, a panicky feeling all her own rising up to choke her. Relief followed when she realized the others would come far too soon for anything to be settled. She was reprieved, allowed to postpone all until after dinner.

At dinner she found she could not force more than a bite or two down her throat. Mowbray, surreptitiously watching his hostess, had to use all his control to remain silent. He did his best to cover her silence by encouraging a string of anecdotes from the children's mentors about students they had formerly served. It was not a perfect solution but, once the two began attempting to out-do each other in their tales, making something of a competition of it, it answered the problem. No one else, he thought, had observed Justina's lack of animation. When the meal ended, he rose when she did and caught her arm, constraining her to stay when the others, still talking, filed out of the room.

"My dear? Is something wrong?" he asked softly.

She cast him a startled glance and looked back to where his hand seemed to burn into her glove-covered arm.

"Wrong? Why, no, nothing is wrong." She drew in a deep breath and forced herself to look back into his face. "I have reached a few decisions, that is all. I would like to discuss them with you. Perhaps, when you finish your cigar, you will be good enough to go to my study rather than join us in the drawing room. I will excuse myself early and join you there."

It was agreed and Justina, who had intended using just that as an excuse, was soon able, quite truthfully, to tell the others that she suffered from the headache and meant to retire. She endured her companion's twittering concern, refused offers of headache powders and a tisane, and finally escaped.

"You look worn to the bone, Justina," were Mowbray's first words when she entered the study.

Not the words one wishes to hear when one has done all one knows how to do in order to look one's best! She compressed her lips, relaxed them, and sighed. "I have been thinking, and I am not one to look closely into my emotions. It is not easy."

"As I discovered after Mary died."

She nodded. "I understand better now. Not that my poor cogitations can have been anything like what you suffered." She drew in a deep breath. "However that may be, I have done it and have come to some conclusions. I would like to tell you."

He nodded, a rising tension, the fear she was going to ask him to leave and not return, coming into his mind.

"First," she continued, "I have decided that I do not want to lose the children. I mean to inform Felix they are to live, in future, with me and he may visit them here when and if he pleases."

Mowbray started to relax but then realized this was only one of her decisions. The tension returned. "I believe it is the right thing," he said. "Felix will know they have a stable home and, when Justin goes off to school, a place to come to during the holidays. He has, you know, rather put off sending the boy to school because he has not liked to make him a permanent boarder, which would be necessary whenever he is out of England."

"I am surprised he took so much thought to Justin! He will," she said tartly, "feel relief at the notion that I have charge of them and he need no longer suffer the occasional pang of guilt that he sees so little of his offspring. The *very* occasional pang, I am sure!"

The faintest of smiles tipped Mowbray's lips, and a glint appeared in his eye. "I too have wondered how often Felix feels concern for his children. He need not, however, if you will take them and raise them, give them the home they want and need."

"I mean to." Justina fell silent. After a moment, rising agitation led her to shift restlessly. *Why,* she wondered, *have I never before noticed how uncomfortable are these chairs?*

Mowbray, experiencing the distasteful sensation of a bead of sweat running down his temple, leaned forward. He had to know. Now. He cleared his throat. "I believe you intimated that you had come to further conclusions?"

Justina rose abruptly to her feet. "Yes."

Mowbray rose as well. "Well?"

She turned her back. "I think it would be best if we were married," she blurted out.

Startled and relieved, Mowbray burst into a shout of laughter.

Justina, horrified, cast him one brief glare and raced from the room. Mowbray, realizing he had done just the wrong thing, ran after her but not quickly enough to see which way she had gone. Then he heard the faint slam of a door and guessed she'd taken the exit to the south lawn. He followed.

Justina, her skirts hiked up in an unladylike fashion, ran across the sod. Mowbray raced after her, catching her, swinging her around—at which point he tripped over a grass tuft missed in the last scything, taking them both to the ground. Pulling Justina onto his chest, he put one hand behind her head and put his other arm firmly around her waist and then kissed her.

Thoroughly.

Justina's hands beat at the grass on either side of his head. Gradually they stilled. Soon she relaxed, her untutored lips learning from his and partaking fully of this new lesson, perhaps the most interesting of those he had yet taught her.

Very gradually the kiss ended. A few quick, tender meetings of lips. The pressure of his hand on her back. And then he rolled them so she lay beside him. "This time will you let me explain? *Before* becoming angry with me?"

She swallowed, nodded, never took her eyes from him, and was glad the long dusk allowed her to watch his features, made it possible to judge his words by how he looked, not merely by the sense or the sound.

"But before I begin . . ." Mowbray sat up, unbuttoned his coat, and dug into a tiny pocket set low in his vest. He scrabbled with one finger, said, "Ah!" and pulled something out. There, circling the end of his finger, rested a ring. A lady's ring. "It was the surprise, Justina, that made me laugh. When I have been racking my brain to find just the proper way that I could convince you we should wed, you neatly turned the tables on me." He smiled, a smile begging her to smile with him. "It was the shock, you see. The laugh a happy reaction, but you took it wrongly, as any idiot could have predicted, of course. You thought I laughed at you, but it was not that. Never that." He sobered. "Justina, why have you never given me a hint you loved me?"

She closed her eyes, then peeked at him with one only partly opened. "Did I say I loved you?"

"Not in so many *words,* of course." He smiled tenderly.

Justina felt embarrassment. He knew she loved him, but . . . did he love her? Again she chanced a quick look into his face. And then, seeing his expression, she stared. "My lord?"

"Can you bring yourself to call me Theo?" he asked gently.

"Theo," she said obediently.

"I love you, my dear. I think I have loved you ever since you knocked my croquet ball into the rough and your own with it."

Her eyes widened. "For so long, my lord?"

"Theo."

"Theo," she repeated after him.

"For at least so long. Sometimes I've wondered if perhaps I began to love you when you were only Felix's odd little sister with the big eyes and so full of impertinent questions."

She nodded. "When you visited during school holidays." She drew in a deep breath. "Perhaps, even then, something drew me to you. I do not recall bothering any of Felix's other friends in a similar manner."

"We will have years to delve into such matters, my love. Right now I wish something far more important settled. Will you wear this ring? Will you wed me? Soon?"

Justina sat up. "I asked first."

"Ah! So you did. Are you suggesting I wear the betrothal ring?"

She reached for his hand. "Would you?"

"If you asked it of me."

"I believe you would," she said, awed. "I'll not ask that, my lord—"

"Theo," he said, his hand tightening around her fingers.

"Theo. But you've not said you'll wed me."

"I will wed you, but will you wed me?"

Solemnly, Justina nodded. "I will."

Very carefully, Mowbray removed her glove and placed the ring on her finger. Then he lifted her hand to his mouth and, holding her gaze, kissed her fingers all around the ring.

It was much later when, back in the study, Mowbray revealed that the children would be happy.

"That we are to wed? Why should such a thing have crossed their minds?"

He smiled. "Luckily I had already decided to ask you to be my wife, or I might have been shocked out of my mind this afternoon when Justin told me he and Nellie had decided you and I should wed. They want a family, you see, and Nurse told Nellie that the start of a family was for the man and woman to wed. To achieve *their* goal"—his brows arched—"*we* must wed."

Justina chuckled. She snuggled against her love's shoulder and turned her head up to look at him. "Perhaps we should not tell them."

"That we will wed?" he asked, playing with a long tress of the hair he'd managed, gradually, to release from its pins.

"No. Not that. That we didn't *need* their encouragement?"

Mowbray's brows arched. "We are to allow them to believe it their idea?"

"Exactly. They will feel as if they made our little family and feel more as if it is their own. Does that make sense?"

"And feel more responsible for it because it is of their making? As one feels about one's accomplishments? Yes, I see." He set her from her. "I must leave early tomorrow."

"Leave!" Panic entered Justina's heart, and she pushed herself from his arms. "Leave?"

"I have done it again, have I not? Shall I explain?"

"You had better do so immediately, my lord."

"Theo." He waited, but this time she didn't oblige him, merely firming her lips and narrowing her eyes. He grimaced. Then he smiled. "I've had another notion," he said. "Once we are wed, you must call me my lord only when you are angry with me. It will be a cue, you see, for me to examine my behavior and discover what I've done to upset you."

"I am still upset, *my lord.*"

But he could tell his jocularity had helped her relax. "Ah! Yes. My leaving. My darling Justina, if we are to wed quickly, then it is imperative I leave for London as soon as may be. It is, you see, the nearest location where I may purchase a Special License!"

The children stood nearby, hand in hand, while a beaming minister married the two most important people in their young lives. They were very happy children. Nevertheless, happy as they were, they were not half so happy as Auntie-Mama and Teo-Papa—as Nellie called them.

Thrilling Romance from
Meryl Sawyer

The Queen of
Romance
Cassie Edwards